THE TRADE

L.M. SUTTON

To Amanda and Steven,
my life would not be complete without you two.

THE TRADE

PRELUDE

The heat is oppressive, suffocating, the air thick and humid. Sweat drips down her body, drenching what remains of her clothes. The dress clings to her body like a second skin. No distinction where one ends and the other begins. Coming to, awareness starts to envelop her. Grasping her head, the pain is excruciating. She tries to open her eyes, but everything is black. Rubbing her eyes, she tries again. Black, it is all black. Then she sees it, a small sliver of light, high, up to the right. Her body starts to come to life. Pain, all she feels is pain radiating throughout her body. What happened? Where am I? Suddenly everything comes rushing back like a tsunami. She was taken, another victim. The operation failed. Will he find me? Will I ever be free again?

1

Taking long slow breaths of the slightly cool morning air, Lila turned into the entrance of the building complex. Once again looking at her note with the address, the only confirmation she was at the correct location were the numbers displayed on the small sign on the approaching gate. No name, no business sign. The place looked like a fortress. A very large building stood back some distance from the gated entrance, surrounded by high security fencing. While it was a large industrial building, it was sleek in appearance, with some sort of gray brick or stone exterior and very few windows. Lila would have thought the place was vacant, a newly built commercial property, if it wasn't for the few cars in the parking lot. No other buildings bordered the property. She suspected it was a new commercial development just getting started.

Pulling up to the gate, Lila noticed several cameras pointing toward her car at different angles and what appeared to be an intercom panel. Since the gate did not open with her arrival, she pushed the button on the intercom panel.

"Hello, may I help you?"

"Yes, good morning. This is Lila Norris. I am scheduled for a 10 o'clock interview."

Hearing a buzzing sound, the gate started to open. The nameless voice instructed Lila to proceed to the front of the building and to buzz again at the front door. Pulling into one of the empty parking spots, Lila took one last look at herself in the mirror. Exiting her new silver Toyota Camry, she slightly adjusted her clothing and proceeded to the door.

Touching the button beside the door, another buzz and a click, Lila cautiously opened the door and entered the waiting area. Walking toward her was a very tall, thin, extraordinarily beautiful woman. Her raven black hair and striking features radiated a very exotic allure to her appearance. Lila was immediately a little intimidated. This woman was perfectly polished and dressed exquisitely, exuding sophistication in her cream-colored pant suit, cheetah print shell, and black stilettos.

Lila felt underwhelming in her basic black skirt and blazer. Insecurities immediately bubbled to the surface. Lila had always been insecure. A late bloomer, she was tall and lanky most of her youth. It took a while to catch up to her peers. The teasing she endured in her middle and early high school years gave her a false sense of inadequacy, something she still struggled with at times. Those who know her never understood this struggle. Lila was not lacking in the looks department. She was tall, not as tall as the Grecian Goddess approaching her; but at 5'8" Lila was fit and firm, even if not overly endowed. Her naturally curly long blonde hair, deep blue eyes, and perfectly proportioned oval face frequently attracted the opposite sex.

Extending a hand, a bright smile lit up the face of the approaching woman.

"Hey there. I'm Shayla. It's so great to meet you, Lila. I have been looking forward to chattin' with you. Why don't you follow me and we can get started."

"It is a pleasure meeting you as well. Thank you for taking

the time out of your day to see me," Lila said as she shook Shayla's hand.

"No problem. We've been eager to speak with you about the position," Shayla said as she escorted Lila through the lobby.

The inside of the building was modern. Not in an unusual way, with clean, sleek lines. Not industrial in appearance; professional and functional. They walked through an opening into a wide hallway. To the left was a short hallway with a few doors. To the right, the area opened up to a large space. Doors surrounded the space with another long hallway extending to the far right. In the center was a very spacious workstation which appeared to be for the potential assistant. It was very quiet, no other sounds or movement other than the click of their heels on the floor.

"Let's go into the conference room," Shayla said as she opened a door to the left of the open space. "Have a seat. Can I get you anything? Water, tea, coffee?"

"No thank you," Lila said as she nervously settled into the chair.

Opening her satchel, Lila pulled out a folder containing extra copies of her resume, a note pad, and a pen. To her surprise, Shayla sat in the seat directly to her side, not across from her like most interviews.

"So, why don't I start by explaining a little bit about our company and what your roles and responsibilities will be as the new Executive Assistant? I know I was a little vague during our telephone call, but we don't disclose a lot of information until we conduct a background check and get a non-disclosure signed.

"Donovan Security represents high-end clients in various types of security, investigative, and retrieval services. Our clients include high profile individuals such as politicians, wealthy businessmen and women and businesses, those in the entertainment industry, as well as the government. We handle various types of security needs including designing and setting up security and surveillance equipment, providing security at events, one-on-one security in questionable locations, investigate various matters, and retrieval services. Any questions so far?"

"What are retrieval services? You also mentioned the government is a client."

"Well, as for retrieval services, that can include kidnappings, going in and retrieving the individual. We also handle high-level, high-risk operations for the government. 'Plausible deniability' so to speak. Where a low profile is needed."

"Oh wow, that sounds very interesting. I was already intrigued about the position. It sounds like you all handle some very fascinating but important and complex matters," Lila replied.

"That we do," Shayla said. "Now let me tell you more about the job. Basically we are looking for a very well-rounded Executive Assistant who can help me and the guys in all kinds of matters. You'd be working directly for me and Drew, even though you'll support everyone. I am the CFO and oversee a large volume of the administrative, non-operative functions. Drew is the CEO, and Drake is the COO. They are brothers and opened the business together. I'm also Drew's wife, if you did not already realize that.

"All of the guys on the team have some sort of military or enhanced law enforcement backgrounds. Both Drew and Drake were Navy Seals. As you get to know everyone, I will give you more details on their backgrounds.

"Back to the job, we'll need you to handle various types of administrative responsibilities including bookkeeping, proposal preparation, and calendar management. Basically you will be our 'Jill of all trades.' We need someone with a lot of experience to handle a wide variety of administrative functions. Is there any area I mentioned that you don't feel you have sufficient experience or will need training?"

"I have never had to write proposals, but I am sure I can learn. Once I understand your protocol, I believe my legal writing skills will help me adapt easily. Also, while I have managed billable hours to clients and expense accounts, I did not personally handle the billing and bookkeeping for the firm, thus I would need training and guidance. Like the proposal writing, I am sure I will be able to learn your system and do a great job. I take pride in my work an always strive to excel."

"I'm sure you will as well. Do you have any questions about your responsibilities?" inquired Shayla.

There she goes again, speaking like I already have the job, Lila said to herself, asking instead, "How many people overall does the position support?"

"In addition to me, Drew, and Drake, we currently have seven agents. It may sound like a lot, but I'm confident you can handle the workload. I believe your prior experience will fit in perfectly."

"I believe so also. While my background was not in security, I handled a multitude of matters for my prior firm including many of the tasks you mentioned."

"Exactly. This is why you stood out from other applicants. I believe your legal research and writing skills will really help the guys. Do you have any other questions about the work responsibilities?"

"No. I believe you went over what the position entails and an overall description of the requirements."

"Well, I think we're done this part of the interview. I'll go get Drew so he can speak with you on his portion of the position. Would you like to use the restroom, or do you need something to drink?"

"The restroom, please."

"Follow me and I'll show you. If you'd like something to drink, the refrigerator is in those cabinets."

Lila and Shayla rose from their chairs and headed out the door. Shayla pointed to a door slightly diagonal from the conference room.

"The restroom is right there. Please take your time, and feel free to head back into the conference room. We should be back in shortly."

Walking into the restroom, Lila placed both hands on the counter, dropping her head. Taking a deep breath, she lifted her head and took a look at herself in the mirror. Grabbing some paper towels, Lila wetted them and dabbed them on her face. Her nerves settled a bit, but she was still a little anxious. This job sounded fantastic, and she really liked Shayla. While the intimidation she felt when she first saw Shayla dissipated as soon as she smiled and greeted her, all the changes in her life over the last six months continued to keep her on edge. She just wanted a sense of normalcy again, and if she gets this job, hopefully she would feel settled.

Relax, you are strong. You are smart. If this position does not work out, another one will. You can take care of yourself, Lila tried to convince herself. Taking one last look in the mirror, Lila headed back to the conference room.

"SHE'S PHENOMENAL DREW. I think she's perfect, as long as we can keep the guys hands to themselves. She is quite pretty, so much prettier in person," Shayla shared.

"Hmm . . . well, we shall see. What makes you like her so much?" Drew asked.

"Besides her experience, she answered the questions well, and she was genuine. I really like her, liked her personality. She still seems a little reserved, but that's understandable. It's just . . . I don't know. I immediately felt a connection with her as soon as we started talking. I can't describe it. It felt like my long-lost best friend just appeared. It was a strange feeling, but comforting actually."

"Well, let's go in and see if she continues to be 'honest and genuine' as you say she is."

The door creaked and in walked Shayla. Lila thought Shayla looked like the perfect Greek Goddess, but directly following her was a very tall, very handsome man. He exuded military. His face was expressionless and intimidating, until he smiled and reached out his hand. Just like Shayla, the intimidation ceased with his smile.

"Hello Lila, I'm Drew. Shayla filled me in on the initial part of the interview. I just have a few questions as it relates more to our operations and working with the other staff. I am aware Shayla gave you more information on some of the operations we handle."

"Yes, sir. She did."

"As you were made aware, our work involves very confidential information, some which may not be easy to swallow."

"Can you provide me with some examples?"

Pausing for a moment, Drew explained, "We deal with kidnappings and contract out for the government. Sometimes we have pictures of people who have been tortured or killed."

"In my prior position I had to view pictures of murder scenes and graphic information in the investigative file. I believe I will be able to handle this type of content."

"Another issue may be your conscience. Some of our operations are unorthodox and we have to take measures that may bother some people."

"If the ultimate goal is to right a wrong, you will not have to worry about my conscience. Sometimes there are casualties to get the job done. Hopefully the casualties are only the bad guys."

Nodding at Lila's response, Drew continued. "As Shayla

explained, you will be working mostly with men. Men who are not politically correct, may curse, and be . . . let's just say inappropriate at times. Never in a harmful way, but in their banter."

"That will not be an issue. Have you ever worked with lawyers?"

"Enough said," Drew chuckled. "They can get rowdy, but they will always have your back. Now can you explain to me why you decided to relocate to Texas?"

Lila's expression dropped. Nerves settled into her core. "How can I answer this," she contemplated. "I was looking for a change, and since I am still young and unattached, it was the perfect time."

Silence overcame the room, and Drew stared at Lila. Tension permeated throughout her body. After what seemed like forever, Drew finally spoke. "Lila, as you know, we do an extensive background check, including interviews with friends, family, acquaintances, and colleagues on all candidates. Why don't you tell me again why you relocated?"

Closing her eyes just for a moment to gain the strength she needed, the past flashing through her memory, Lila responded. "While what I said was true, I am looking for a change, and I am young and unattached, what pushed me toward this decision was multi-faceted. I was lucky enough to win a rather substantial lottery enabling me to have a better head start than others. Unfortunately, the person I was seeing at the time thought he was entitled to my winnings. I disagreed, and it was ugly. The winnings, while not enough to live on for a lifetime, are enough to afford me the opportunity to travel and live in new places."

"Was it hard to leave your family and your job?"

"Yes. I am close to my family, but they understood and encouraged me. I also loved my job. But if I was ever going to have the guts to try new experiences, I needed to leave my firm. They told me I always had a job if I ever decided to move home. I could have chosen not to work for a while, but I am someone who needs to stay busy and was getting bored not working. When I saw your job posting, it sparked my interest and sounded like a position I would enjoy."

"Thank you for answering my question and honestly. Would you mind waiting here for a few minutes while Shayla and I take a moment to speak?" Drew asked.

"Not at all. I appreciate you taking the time to meet with me today."

Drew and Shayla left the room and went to Drew's office, Shayla sitting across from Drew on the edge of her chair.

"So what did you think about Lila?"

"Well, obviously I already knew she did not tell us everything on the reason why she moved, but she did answer very professionally based on the circumstances."

"I thought so, too. Gosh, she has been through a lot. I thought she held her own in the interview."

"I agree. We already knew about the incident, and she is clearly skilled. Her former employer was devastated she was not returning. They loved her and said she was a shining star."

"So, can I go ahead and make the offer?" Shayla asked.

"Sure. Go for it. I think she will work out great."

"Me too!"

SHAYLA RETURNED to the conference room and once again sat down next to Lila. "Thank you for waiting."

"No problem."

"Drew had some calls to make, but we'd like to offer you the Executive Assistant position with Donovan Security."

Lila's jaw dropped open slightly. Stunned, she asked, "Are you sure?" You just interviewed me. I am sure you still have other candidates to interview."

"Lila, we know almost everything we need to about a candidate before they are interviewed. In fact, very few people make it to an interview. Today was to see if your personality was the right fit and if everything we learned in the background investigation matched the real life person."

"Wow, I am just stunned. I have never been offered a position during my interview before."

"Yes, I know we are a little unconventional, but it works for us. So, do you accept the position?"

Lila did not respond immediately, then it struck Shayla. She hadn't even gone over the pay and benefits.

"Geez, how can you accept when I've not even gone over the details? We offer full medical coverage, including dental and vision, at absolutely no cost to the employee. You will get four weeks' vacation to start, and paid sick leave. We're flexible with the working hours, but are usually here from 8 to 4 Monday through Friday. Overtime is sometimes necessary, or altering your hours based on an active operation." Shayla continued on to tell her the proposed salary and other perks of the position. "So now that I have gone over our offer, what do you think?"

"Thank you so much. That is such a wonderful, generous offer which I am happy to accept. I look forward to working with you. When would you like me to start?" asked Lila.

"How about now? You're here. We can start the paperwork, I can show you around, and Monday we can hit the ball running."

"Sure. The rest of my day is clear, so I can stay. Umm . . . the only issue we may have with the paperwork is that I am currently staying in an extended-stay hotel. I did not want to look for a permanent place until I knew where I would be working."

"That's no problem. When you get settled you can just

update your file. If you need some assistance finding a place, we will be glad to help," stated Shayla.

"Thank you, that is very kind."

"No worries. We're one big family here. Like Drew said, we take care of our own. Let me show you around."

"That would be great."

2

P icking up her purse, Lila followed Shayla out of the conference room. "This area is obviously your new work-station. You should have everything you need, but if you don't, you can check the supply room or just place an order. If you would like to put your purse in here, please feel free to so you don't have to carry it around."

Lila scanned her new workstation. The large U-shaped workstation took up much of the open space. There was a lot of desk space, cabinets, shelving on the wall side, a laptop, and three monitors; plenty of room to work comfortably. Putting her purse in one of the large drawers, Lila turned toward Shayla, ready for her tour.

"To your left at the end of the hall is Drew's office. My office is on the right and Drake's is on the left. Obviously you know where our conference room is."

Walking to the right, Lila noticed several other doors.

"Here is the supply room. Like I said, take whatever you need. I would like you to help ensure it is kept fully stocked. We will go over our normal supply list and how we process our orders next week. The next two doors on the right are office space for all of our guys."

Lila took a peek in one of the rooms. It was very spacious and had four generously-sized desks strategically placed at each of the four corners of the room.

"The next room is basically identical. This last room on the left is our tech room."

Shayla opened the door, and Lila followed her inside. The lighting was low and had a gentle bluish tint. Lila was in awe. Computers and monitors filled the place. A multitude of large television screens lined the walls; a variety of information broadcasting from news reports, weather, and maps. An assortment of additional equipment filled the space. In the center, a large conference table and chairs was the focal point. It reminded Lila of what a war room would look like. As they proceed into the room, Lila noticed a man in the back left corner with headphones on his head.

Tapping the man on the shoulder, Shayla introduced him to Lila.

"Lila this is Dallas. Dallas, this is Lila, our new Executive Assistant."

"Well hello there darlin'. Aren't you just a ray of sunshine?"

Is everyone in this place gorgeous? Lila speculated. Another tall, handsome man. He was a little more slender than Drew, but just as tall and clearly very fit based on his physique. His dirty blonde hair was a little long and brushed against his shirt collar. His name was quite fitting as he looked like a cowboy. Tanned skin, a sexy crooked smile, and of course he was wearing Wranglers and cowboy boots.

"Now Dallas, don't be flirting with Lila already. You can't scare her off her first day."

"Aw, Shayla, but doesn't she look like a ray of sunshine?"

Shayla rolled her eyes at him while Lila extended her hand.

"It is nice to meet you. If you need a little sunshine, it is quite nice outside. Maybe you should take a step outside and soak it up for a minute. A little extra Vitamin D never hurt anyone."

Dallas and Shayla started laughing.

"I think I'm in love. She's gonna to fit in great here," Dallas said.

"Yes she is. That was perfect Lila. Love it. So this is our Ops Room where we handle all the technical work, ops planning, etc. You working on the Sanderson event, Dallas?"

"Yep. Just trying to get some baseline background info so we can start planning."

"Dallas here is one of our technical whizzes. He handles a lot of our complicated technical needs."

"Those are not all my skills now darlin'," he said winking at Lila and Shayla.

"You are too much, Dallas. Where's the rest of the crew?" Shayla asked.

"They're in the Dome working with Rocco."

"The Dome? What is that?" Lila inquired.

"It's where we are heading next," replied Shayla.

"It was nice meetin' ya darlin'. We'll chat soon."

"Nice meeting you too, Dallas."

Lila and Shayla went back in the direction of her workstation then down the long hall. There was a double door at the end. Lila was just thinking the place looked so much larger from the outside until Shayla opened the door. They walked into a large space, the size of a warehouse, a set of double doors on each side of the entryway. The center opened up to a very large area with high ceilings, within the space appeared to be two pseudo or fake rooms. Lila heard a lot of muffled sounds from the others in the room. Trying not to get distracted by the grunts, groans, and laughter tickling her ears, she focused on Shayla.

Moving to the right doors, Shayla opened them and explained that the room contained all of their security equipment. The room was very impressive. It was full of equipment, very neatly organized, and appeared to have bar codes on the shelving. Exiting the room, Shayla directed Lila to the room on the left.

"This room holds all of our tactical equipment."

Peaking in, Lila observed another well-stocked, well-organized room. All kinds of equipment, including bullet proof vests, Tasers, and many items she did not recognize, filled the space. Lila noticed the bar codes again and decided to inquire.

"I noticed both rooms have bar codes on the shelving. What do they represent?"

"Good observation and good question. Equipment is scanned in and out and each recipient is identified. Most is op-specific. Helps us track who has what, what items are used, and also helps track when something needs to be replaced for end of life. Some equipment we only use so many times to help ensure its functionality."

"You all are a very well-oiled machine. It is very impressive."

"Thank you. The safety of our guys is first and foremost since they deal with dangerous situations often. It helps us track inventory and to make sure they return what they take. I'll teach you how we manage the system."

"Sounds interesting. I'm very eager to learn and help in any way I can."

"Let's show you the rest of the Dome and meet some of the guys."

Lila followed Shayla into the center of the Dome and toward a group of very large men who appeared to be fighting . . . all except one. They were on what appeared to be a large wrestling mat. Lila noticed a large workout area with a lot of weights, equipment, punching bags and cardio equipment just off to the side of where the group was training.

"You will meet Drake and Matt in a few weeks. They are out on an operation," Shayla commented.

Approaching the group of men, Shayla addressed them, "Hey y'all. Can you stop for a minute so I can introduce y'all to our new Executive Assistant?"

Immediately everyone stopped, turned, and stared at Lila. Again, Lila was facing a group of very large, well-built, good looking men.

"Guys, this is Lila. She is our new Executive Assistant. Please welcome her to our family."

The first man approached, extending his hand.

"Hi there. I am Trent. It is nice to meet you."

"Nice to meet you too, Trent," Lila said shaking his hand.

Trent had light brown hair, close cut and very polished looking, even though he was in workout gear.

"Trent came to us from the FBI, or should I say we stole him. This is Jax, Jace, and Garrett. Jax and Jace are brothers and former Army Rangers, and Garrett was in the infantry."

"Nice to meet you all," Lila said, shaking hands with Jax and Jace. You could clearly tell they were brothers as they looked almost identical. Lila wondered if they were actually twins. A question for another day. Garrett just nodded his head, a little standoffish. Lila noticed a long scar on his left cheek, making him look like someone you do not want to meet in a dark alley.

"And last but not least, this is Rocco. He's in charge of our training."

Lila turned to greet Rocco. He was slightly shorter than everyone else, but he was huge. Built like a brick wall. Not fat, just solid. Rocco was older than the others, probably in his mid-forties, but not any less intimidating. Maintaining her courage, Lila once again extended her hand.

"It's such a pleasure meeting you Rocco. Maybe one day you can give me some training pointers. I have always been active, but I am confident you could teach me so much."

Immediately Rocco's face softened and he took Lila's hand. Instead of shaking her hand, he turned it over and placed a soft kiss.

"The pleasure is all mine. It is nice to meet you Miss Lila. I am at your service. You just name the day and time."

Lila took an instant liking to Rocco. A gentle giant in her eyes. She didn't doubt he was not someone to mess with, but something about Rocco immediately put her at ease.

"You also come to me if one of these buffoons gives you any trouble."

Lila laughed as the guys bantered back and forth with Rocco.

"Alright guys, we won't hold up your training any longer."

"We appreciate the break. Rocco has been kicking our butts," Trent said.

"Speak for yourself, light weight," Jax or Jace said. Lila couldn't tell which one was which yet.

"What is that area over there?" Lila asked. "It looks like a building within a building with rooms. Do you use it for training?"

"That is exactly right," Rocco said. "You guys get back to your training. I am going to show this little lady the rest of the Dome."

Rocco put out his elbow for Lila to take and led her and Shayla into the building inside the building.

"We use these rooms to simulate real-life scenarios. The walls are movable so we can get it as close as possible to our target, including furniture, etc. to help during an op or a security event. It helps everyone prepare for any possible situation that may arise," Rocco explained.

Lila took it all in and went through the rooms currently set up. "This is impressive. What kind of operation was this set up for?"

"It was a security detail for a foreign dignitary who was visiting the U.S. We simulated his hotel suite."

Moving through the final room, Lila noticed a glass wall that took up most of the right side of the Dome. "What is over there? The glass wall."

"That is the shooting range. Let's take a look," Rocco said as he walked over and opened a door for Lila and Shayla. Inside were four long shooting stalls with targets and an observation area. "This room allows us to practice using various calibers of weapons. Through here are rooms set up similar to the room configuration you just saw in order to keep up with our shooting skills. Over here is our weapons room."

Putting in a code, Rocco opened up the door to a vault-like storage room. It was filled with weapons, many different kinds; handguns, rifles, shotguns. The back wall contained shelves full of ammunition. Just like the tactical and security equipment rooms, the weapons room was very organized and bar coded. Very impressive.

Rocco noticed how wide Lila's eyes were and spoke up. "I am sorry if you're uncomfortable in here. I did not even think to ask you how you felt about weapons. I'm sorry. I know some people do not like them," he said as he tried to move them out of the room.

"Oh, I am not uncomfortable. I am impressed. I was just thinking how my Dad would love to try out some of these guns. I was raised around guns and would go hunting with my Dad."

A big smile spread across Rocco's face. "A girl after my own heart. I knew I liked you. We will get you in here one day and see what you got."

"Game on. You name the day and time," Lila said beaming.

Exiting the shooting range, Shayla thanked Rocco for helping out with the tour. Rocco kissed Lila's hand again, and they said their goodbyes to the guys. Walking back to Lila's new workstation, Shayla said, "Why don't you make yourself comfortable and get acquainted with your desk. See what supplies you need and go grab them. I'll be back in ten with your computer access, and you can get started filling out the rest of your paperwork."

"That sounds great. Thank you so much again for offering me this position. I think I am really going to enjoy working here."

Lila settled in, went through her desk, and filled up on supplies as Shayla suggested. When Shayla returned, she showed Lila how to access the system, the folder with the required paperwork, and one with various company policies and procedures. Lila completed the new-hire paperwork, insurance information, and reviewed the policies and procedures. Just as she started some online training for a few of their systems, Shayla and Drew were at her desk.

"It's four o'clock. Time to go for the day," Shayla said.

Looking at her watch, Lila was amazed time flew so fast, and she signed off of her laptop.

Shayla held out her hand and gave Lila a set of keys. "Here are keys to the front door just in case the system goes down. To get into the complex and doors, just use the last four digits of your social security number to gain entrance. I've already entered you into the system. Also, here is a work cell. Everyone's numbers are already programmed in. It's secure, thus we want you to use the phone when you need to reach one of us when not in the office."

Lila took the phone and thanked them, amazed at the level of trust they had, even though they just met her. Gathering her purse, the three of them exited the building. Lila tested the door to make sure it worked. Walking toward their vehicles,

Shayla mentioned they are a very casual office. She does not need to dress up and that she only dresses up for client meetings and, of course, interviews.

"Have a good weekend," Shayla and Drew said to Lila.

"The same to you, too. See you Monday." Lila got into her car and headed back to the hotel.

SEVERAL WEEKS PASSED since Lila started with Donovan Security. She settled in quite easily and loves her job. Everyone treated her like family and she quickly acclimated. Shayla and Drew were impressed with her work and couldn't believe how much Lila had been able to contribute in such a short period of time. Lila and Shayla also have developed a budding friendship. They got along so well, Lila worried it would be an issue since she is an employee. Shayla ensured her it wouldn't and that it was fate she walked into their lives. They needed a reliable Executive Assistant, and they were meant to be best friends.

As Lila was finalizing a client report for Drew, the intercom on the phone buzzed. "Lila, can you let me know when the report for the Sanderson event will be ready?" Drew asked.

"Actually, I just finished making the changes for Trent and can bring it right in. Be there in a sec."

Hanging up, Lila quickly printed two copies, emailed an electronic copy to Drew, and headed to his office to go over the changes she'd made. She handed Drew a copy for his review. As Lila pointed out and discussed her changes, the door to Drew's office flew open, banging the wall behind it. In walked in a huge form of a man, and he was angry.

"Who the fuck is parked in my spot? I am going to kick his ass when I find out," the giant bellowed. Just as the words escaped his mouth, Drake noticed Lila, her eyes wide.

"Sorry. Did not know you were with someone. Just tell me

who the asshole is and I'll leave you two alone," Drake commanded.

"Drake, this is Lila our new Executive Assistant and *she* is the person who parked in your space. I told her to because I did not expect you back yet," Drew replied.

Getting up, Lila grabbed her papers. "I'll go move my car. I'm sorry."

"Don't you dare move your car! Drake can deal with it for today. It is not like he has to walk more than ten extra feet from a different parking spot."

Drake was getting ready to argue with Drew until he locked eyes with Lila. He just stared at her, looked her up and down.

"Fine. We will catch up later on the op," he said before storming out.

"I'm sorry, Lila. I do not know what put him in such a bad mood. I promise you this is not normal. He is a hard ass, but usually has some semblance of manners. Back to the report, it was perfect, as usual."

"Thank you. I sent you the electronic copy so you can send to the client. Let me know if you would like me to do so on your behalf."

Leaving Drew's office, Lila headed back to her workstation. She could not help looking at Drake's office door as she passed. A rush of heat swept over her just thinking about him. Surrounded by alpha males, she thought she just met King Alpha. Drake clearly resembled Drew, but he appeared to be just a little taller and a little larger. His eyes were so intense, hard expressions like someone who has seen a lot in his lifetime, not for the better. He had a masculine face with a strong jaw. Drake was very handsome, too handsome. His eyes were a striking green compared to Drew's hazel eyes. Just thinking about him got Lila flustered. He was very intimidating, but something about him made Lila's body tingle. Something that had not happened for a long, long time.

"No, get it out of your head. It is totally wrong."

"What's totally wrong sugar?" Dallas asked, approaching Lila's desk.

"Jesus. You scared me, Dallas. Nothing is wrong. I was just talking out loud."

"Hey, most of us are going to go to *McGarvey's* in a bit for happy hour. We want you to come."

"I don't know. It's been a long week, and I am supposed to go apartment hunting with Shayla in the morning."

"Drew and Shayla are going too. We won't keep you out too long. Promise," Dallas said as he wiggled his eyebrows.

Laughing, Lila shook her head at Dallas and agreed to come to happy hour.

PACING his office Drake did not know why he was so amped up. The op went well. Maybe he needed to get laid. A trip to *The Manor* may be in order. Suddenly his thoughts went directly to the new Executive Assistant. What was her name . . . Lila, Drake recalled.

His mind reminisced on his first view of her. Long, beautiful legs. Legs that should be wrapped around his waist. Luscious, long, curly blonde hair he imagined getting his hands into and grabbing tight. And those lips. Let's talk about those lips; full, kissable, fuckable. She was beautiful, perfect.

"Stop. You do not need to go there. She is an employee and looks like a 'nice girl.' She would never be the kind of woman you need. Submissive, available only for a fuck, nothing more. She is probably one of those white picket fence, planned her wedding when she was ten kind of girls. I do not need another distraction. Just be professional, but distant, That will work," Drake said to himself.

Unfortunately it was not working. Every time he tried to settle down, his mind kept wandering to Lila. Maybe he could focus if he went and briefed Drew about the op. Gathering his file, Drake headed to Drew's office. This time he knocked.

"Come in."

Entering Drew's office, Drake raised his hands, "Before you say anything, I know I was out of line and I will apologize later, when I know I can do it properly."

"Yep, you were a real asshole. What's up? Did something happen on the op? I haven't seen you this worked up in some time."

"No. The op went as planned. In and out. Quiet as a mouse. We planted the devices. If they find them, I will be surprised. The General will be happy."

"Did anyone see you two?"

"What do you think?" Drake said laughing.

"Sorry I asked. Just make sure you get the report done and to Lila next week."

"So tell me about Lila. When did she start?"

"She has been here for a few weeks now, and she is great. Super smart and learns fast. Rocco has taken a liking to her. He has her right under his wing. Protective, too, like she is his daughter," Drew said smiling. "I will give you her file so you can get the 411. She has been through a few things, but got through the process with flying colors."

"Fine. I'll take a look at it soon."

"Why don't you come to *McGarvey's* tonight? Most of us are going. Shayla and I are also having a barbeque tomorrow evening, steaks. I'm sure you could use one after the op."

"Sure. I'll bring the beer."

FILING the last of the paperwork on her desk, Lila went over her checklist to ensure everything had been completed. It was Friday and she did not want to leave anything unattended.

"What are you still doing here?"

Lila peaked up to see Drew and Shayla approaching her desk.

"I'm just finishing up."

"Alright. I think everyone else is gone. See you at *McGarvey's*."

Logging off her laptop and gathering her purse, Lila saw Rocco striding toward her.

"Come on Miss Lila. It's time to go. I can't let those buffoons get too much of a head start on me. You're still coming aren't you?"

"Yes, but just for a little while."

Rocco walked her to her car and Lila followed him to the pub since this was her first time. While Lila and Shayla had lunch a few times and had gone shopping, this would be the first after-hour's event with her colleagues. Lila did not know why she was nervous. Everyone had been so nice and welcoming, well everyone except Drake. What was up with that guy? Dismissing the thought, Lila exited her vehicle and met Rocco at the door.

Entering *McGarvey's* they spotted the crew and headed over to the table. Looking up Lila locked eyes with Drake, her body immediately reacting. She did not understand this strange response to him. Drake did not come across as a nice person, a little too alpha male for her. She told herself she would do her best to stay clear of him tonight, if possible, but Lila wondered why her eyes always reverted back to him.

Their gaze never wavered, like a staring contest each daring the other to break away first. Drake would not break eye contact with Lila, his stare intense. Was this his way to intimidate people? Did he not like her or was this just the way he looked, she wondered. Too bad his attractiveness did not match his personality. Oh well, he was one of her bosses anyway, she thought. She would find a way to act professionally when around him and just do her job.

"Hey everyone."

Multiple hellos rang out in response.

"Sorry we are a bit behind. Had to finish up a few things."

"Not only are you my little ray of sunshine, you're also such a hard worker. You deserve to kick back, relax, and enjoy tonight, darlin'," Dallas said as he put his arm around Lila.

"Do you ever stop flirting?" Lila said lightheartedly, slapping him lightly on the shoulder.

The group made room for Lila and Rocco at the table. Lila sat in between Dallas and Shayla as the waitress approached to get their drink orders.

"What can I get you, Ma'am?"

"I'll have a Bud Light bottle please."

"Can I get you anything to eat?" the waitress asked.

"Not at this moment. I'll take a look and order during the next round. Thanks."

After the waitress left, Dallas, his ever flirtatious self oohed at Lila. "Bud Light? My little darlin' drinking beer? Never would have guessed. I figured you to be a wine or fruity drink kind of gal."

"Oh Dallas, there is so much you still don't know about me *darlin'*," Lila teased, wiggling her eyebrows. The group erupted into laughter and carried on with several conversations at once.

HE SAW her as soon as the door opened. Who could miss her? Beautiful. Those legs . . . peeking out from her white and yellow sundress. A lot of male heads turned in her direction, and she was oblivious. Either she was a snob or had no clue how attractive she was. As Lila approached the group, she looked up, their eyes meeting. There it was again, a pull toward this woman, the wrong kind of woman. Why was his first thought about bending her over a table, pulling up that good-girl dress, and fucking her to oblivion?

Drake just starred at her, drinking her in, the forbidden fruit. Wonder what she is thinking? Probably that you are a dick based on the way your first interaction went down. As she approached the table, Dallas started flirting, as usual, then put his arm around her. Out of nowhere, a sudden rush of anger overtook Drake. Mine, he thought and was pissed someone had his arms around Lila. Disturbed by this reaction, Drake tried to control his anger. It was not like him and Dallas had not shared a woman before, so why did he feel so protective.

Shaking the thought out of his head, he reminds himself "she is not yours." Drake kicked back, drank his beer, and just observed. Maybe later he could apologize for how he acted this morning. Make amends since he clearly started off on the wrong foot.

When the waitress came around and Lila ordered a beer, he was surprised. Impressive. "The little princess likes beer," Dallas put his thoughts to words. Drake just watched her that evening. Soaked up all her mannerisms, how she interacted with the group. They all seemed to really like her. Even Garrett, 'Mister Standoffish and Lack of Words' smiled, laughed, and seemed to generally like her.

When they ordered food, she surprised him again ordering a burger and fries. How could she put down all that food and still be that thin? Maybe Lila was not what he initially thought.

Drake saw Lila get up and head to the restroom. This may be the perfect opportunity to apologize, away from everyone else. A minute after she left the table, Drake casually made his way across the pub in the direction of the restroom, waiting by the bar for Lila to exit. A few moments later she appeared.

"Lila," he said.

She stopped momentarily and looked at him before responding.

"Hey, Drake."

"Can I talk to you for a minute?"

"Sure. What's up?"

"I just want to apologize for this morning. I was rude and inappropriate, and for that I'm sorry."

"It's okay."

"No, it's not. I was out of line."

"Okay. Apology accepted. It didn't bother me. I am used to it."

"Thanks," Drake responded as they headed back to the table. He wondered what she meant by she is used to it.

A few hours after arriving at *McGarvey's*, Lila rose from the table, pulled some cash out of her purse, and placed it on the table.

"Well, I'm outta here. Please use this to pay my portion."

"You can't leave yet," Trent said. "We are just getting started."

"Well, I have an early day tomorrow, and I want to review the listings for the apartments I will be seeing and note any questions I want to ask."

"You okay to drive?" Rocco asked protectively.

"Yes, Rocco Taco. I only had two beers."

Everyone laughed at her name for Rocco, but he loved it.

"We are out of here soon, also. I'll pick you up at eight," Shayla said.

"See ya then. Bye everyone."

As farewells were exchanged, Lila made her way out of *McGarvey's* and into her car. Smiling, she reflected on the evening. They were all a great bunch of people. She was blessed to be working with this group.

3

Lila and Shayla set out on the apartment search early Saturday morning. They looked at seven different apartments, Lila filled out her checklist for each one, asking all her pertinent questions. Ever meticulous, she prepared a checklist in order to make notes, evaluate each one in order to help her make a decision. Shayla teased her about the checklists, telling Lila when she saw the right one it would hit her and the checklists would be out the window, just like when she found the right man. Lila just snickered and continued with her process. They saw the last apartment and headed back to Shayla's SUV to go back to her house for a barbeque, making a quick stop to pick up a few items on the way.

"My head is spinning. I liked several of the places and don't want to make the wrong decision."

"You have time. The agent said to call him back mid-week with your decision. That gives you about five days to do your analysis," Shayla twinkled.

"Ha ha, you are such a comedian. I can't help it. It's the way I am."

"I know. You want me to drop you off at the hotel or just head over to our place?"

"Well, I will need my car to get home."

"Don't worry about that. One of us will get you home. We are closer to the house now."

"I can always get an Uber. Go ahead to your house. We can work out my ride situation later."

Shayla headed to a gated community with very nice, stately homes. Lila's eye's bulged. Even though they had become friends over the past few weeks, Lila had not yet been to her house.

"You live in here? Wow. These homes are gorgeous."

"I'm very blessed. I love my home. Just hope one day to fill it up with a couple kids."

Pulling up in front of a large two story house with a three car garage, a few vehicles were already in the driveway. Shayla approached and parked her car in the garage, thankful the guys remembered to leave her space. The home was large, like all the others in the community, with a gray stone façade on the front. It graced a nice-sized front porch with a beautiful wooden double front door. It was very elegant, very Shayla. Lila was positive the inside would be just as grand.

"Did I make you late by having you come with me today?"

"Of course not. I already prepared a few side dishes, we just picked up that last few things, and Drew took care of the rest. He's a big boy, and he's in his element. He thinks he's the grill master."

Giggling, Lila replied, "I can't wait to see him in action."

Entering the house through the door from the garage, they went through a mud room and then directly into a spacious kitchen. The cabinets were a light gray with what appeared to be quartz counter tops, top of the line appliances, and a long center island which finished out the kitchen. It was magnificent and beautiful.

Setting the bags on the counter, the ladies started to unload as Drew entered from French doors which connected to a back deck. The doors were in between the eating area and the large two-story great room which opened to the kitchen.

"Hey there, ladies. We got the grill going and some appetizers started. If you can take care of what you just brought in, then come out and relax. We got everything else handled."

Kissing Drew, Shayla said, "Thanks, honey. We will be out shortly."

"Oh by the way, how did it go today Lila?"

"It went well. I found several good prospects."

"Now you know she will have to 'analyze' them to death before deciding," Shayla teased.

Sticking out her tongue at Shayla, Lila thanked Drew for asking and proceeded to help her boss/friend with the rest of the food.

Carrying trays with the remaining food out to the deck, Lila practically tripped when she spotted him. Standing next to Drew at the grill was the most masculine shirtless body she had ever seen. The others who were already there also appeared to be in swim trunks, but only one person immediately caught her attention. Of course she knew exactly who it was, Drake. God, couldn't she at least have the weekend to come to grips with the affect this man had on her. She had known him all of one day, but the attraction was strong, strange.

"You okay?" Shayla asked.

"I'm fine," Lila said just as Drew and Drake turned around.

"Let me get that," Drake said as he took the tray from her.

"Thanks."

Drew did the same for Shayla.

"Wow this deck and backyard is outstanding. And that pool—"

"Oh shoot. I forgot to tell you to bring your suit as we would be swimming. If you want to, of course."

"It's okay."

"I have several. You can borrow one of mine later. We are about the same size anyway."

"Sure, thanks."

Jax and Jace were already lounging in the hot tub connected to the pool, Trent and Garrett appeared to be deep in conversation, and Drew and Drake went back to the grill. Just as she was recovering from her reaction to seeing Drake's shirtless body, she heard commotion behind her.

"Howdy, everyone," Dallas said as he appeared on the deck, Rocco following on his heels. "It's time to get this party started."

Typical Dallas, always fun and games.

"About time you showed up with the ice," Drew said, tossing a towel in Dallas's face. "The beer was going to get hot."

Rocco headed over to the table where Lila and Shayla were arranging the food. He set down a dish and kissed Lila on the cheek.

"How is my sweet girl today? Did you find a place?"

"I'm good," Lila said returning the kiss to Rocco's cheek. "I have a few I liked that I need to pick from."

"That's good. You let me know if you need anything. I am at your beck and call."

"Thanks Rocco. What's in the dish?" Lila asked, as she tried to see inside the opaque container.

"Oh, just some cupcakes."

"Rocco makes the best desserts. I always ask him to bring dessert when we get together," Shayla added.

"I love to bake, also. You will need to share some of your secrets with me."

"For you, anything little lady."

Everyone started to gather around the table. Trent and Garrett filled plates with appetizers as Jax and Jace dried off, heading in their direction.

"Hello there," a voice from behind echoed.

"Hey Matt," they all said in unison.

Matt, the final piece of the team Lila had yet to meet. He was tall, fit, like she did not expect that, with dark brown hair still with the military buzz. Shayla introduced Matt to Lila, then everyone settled at the tables and feasted on the wonderful spread in front of them. The food was delicious. Shayla was not kidding when she said Rocco was a great baker. His cupcakes were phenomenal, and there was no doubt Lila would be requesting the recipe.

Observing the group, Lila admired the comradery amongst them. They would banter back and forth, but all in good fun. Garrett was still quiet, but was more talkative than normal. Everyone talked with each other and also teased Lila a bit, being the newbie. Everyone except Drake. Drake barely spoke to Lila even though he was involved in other conversations. She caught him staring at her a few times since she arrived.

Why does he keep staring at me, but won't talk to me, she wondered. Lila tried to ignore his behavior so she could enjoy everyone else's company.

"Who's up for some competition?" Dallas asked.

Multiple "hell yeses" and "I'm ins" echoed through the group.

"You up to play Lila?" Dallas asked while doing his signature eyebrow wiggle.

"What kind of competition are we talking about?"

"Just some fun in the pool. Marco Polo, Volleyball, you know, the typical pool games."

"I can't. Did not realize they had a pool, and I do not have my suit."

"Remember, I told you I have one you can borrow," Shayla hollered.

This was just wonderful. Now she was going to be barely dressed in front of all her colleagues. Not something she had to endure in the past. The intimidation factor set in. These men were the hottest, most handsome group of men she had ever encountered with their perfectly sculpted bodies. Then there was Shayla, the Grecian Goddess, tall, lean, beautiful. Lila felt like the ugly duckling among the group. Not wanting to be the only man out, she gained her courage to participate.

"Only if you are. I'm not going to be the only girl in the mix with all these goofballs."

"Of course. I like to give these guys a run for their money."

Shayla led Lila back through the house and upstairs to the master bedroom. Entering the large walk in closet, the size of a Hollywood starlet, Shayla opened a drawer and started pulling out some very little bikinis.

"I think I am going to wear this one, but you can take your pick from the rest. I think this one would look perfect on you," Shayla said as she held up a very tiny aqua string bikini. "It matches your eyes. Once they see you in this little thing, you will probably win all the games. Their tongues will be hanging out of their mouths, and we need any advantage we can get."

Lila took the bathing suit and silently groaned. While the bikini was cute, it left little to the imagination. It was clearly not a full bottom, and the top was a cute triangle with a very small ruffle outlining the upper edge.

"The guest bathroom is just down the hall to the right if you want to get changed. Just let me know when you're done, and we can head back down."

Lila headed to the restroom and started to change. Once the suit was on, she took a peek in the mirror. The bikini fit and looked better than she thought. Taking a deep breath, something she seemed to do a lot lately, Lila met Shayla in the hall, and they both headed back down and out onto the deck.

DRAKE HEARD WHISTLING and turned around just in time to see the epitome of sexy walking toward the group. He knew she was gorgeous, but seeing her in that barely there bikini set his libido on fire. He could kill Shayla for loaning Lila that particular bikini. She was perfect. Her long legs led up to nicely rounded hips, a completely flat stomach and beautiful, natural breasts. Not too big, not too small. Perfect. She turned around briefly and he got a peak at her backside. Drake hardened instantly. Groaning internally, he had to get control of himself. He did not need the guys seeing him react like a teenager.

"Time to pick teams. Shayla and Lila, sorry but you cannot be on the same team. Need to make it even," Trent said.

"My girl is on my team," Rocco said as he approached Lila and put his arm around her.

"Well my girl is going to be on my team," Drew said.

"No way! I want to play against you dear. Come on Drake, you are on my team," Shayla said as she was dragging Drake over to her side.

Drew came over to her and Rocco and the rest of the guys split up to balance out the teams. The teams were set. Lila, Rocco, Drew, Jax and Dallas were on one team. Drake, Shayla, Jace, Garrett and Matt on the other. Trent was the referee this round.

"Pool volleyball first?" Jax inquired as he went to a large but stylish bench, opening it and pulling out equipment.

Rocco led Lila over to the deep end. "How is this going to be fair if we are in the deep end and they are on the low end?" she asked.

"We switch sides to keep it fair. Don't worry. We got this."

They started playing, and Lila surprised the guys. She was pretty good and was holding her own.

"That's my girl. I knew you were an athlete. I thought these guys were competitive, but they don't hold a candle to you," Rocco smiled.

"Got to make sure they realize we are not the weaker sex."

Drake could not keep his eyes off Lila. He was glad she was not on his team, but thought this may be worse. He had to watch her the entire time. It was very distracting. The water glistening over her body did not help his focus, making his thoughts wander to having Lila tied up to his bed, under his command to do whatever he wanted to her. Suddenly the ball hit Drake right in his face, his distraction now apparent to everyone.

"Drake, get your head out of your ass and stop drooling over Lila," Trent said.

"I'm not drooling over Lila. I was thinking about something I forgot to do," he grumbled.

"Sure," a few of the guys said.

Drake focused, and now he added a little aggression to his play, especially toward Lila. But she kept pace and her team won.

"Now it's time to play chicken. Ladies first. Drew lift up your bride. Drake, you lift up Lila," Dallas instructed.

"I'm tired. One of you can do it."

"Yeah, right. Stop being a pansy and lift her up."

"I don't want to go against my boss. She may hold it against me," Lila said.

"Bring it on girlie. We'll still be friends no matter who wins," Shayla laughed.

Grudgingly, Drake went under water to lift Lila onto his shoulders. This is just great. Her legs are now wrapped around my neck, even if in the wrong direction, he thought. Holding onto her legs, all Drake wanted to do was rub his hands up and down, caressing her body. Trying to focus, he moved forward to start the game.

Lila wrestled with Shayla and won. Next she had to wrestle Dallas. She won again, but was sly in her approach. Stretching with her arms up before starting, pressing out her breasts, Dallas got distracted. Of course, Lila went in for the kill and took him out before he even knew what hit him.

"Game on girlie. I won't get distracted like Dallas, and I'm not afraid to take a lady down," Trent said teasingly.

Lila lost that round, but when they went over, Drake tried to grab her and his hands went straight for her ass. Coming up for air, they just stared at each other, Lila still in his arms.

Coming back to reality, Drake released Lila and asked if she was okay. Nodding her head in acknowledgement, Lila moved to the side of the pool next to Shayla just as Jax got on top of Drake's shoulders.

"He likes you. You know that," Shayla said.

"Who likes me?"

"Drake."

"No way. I do not even think he even remotely likes me. He barely has acknowledged me."

"You're wrong. He can't keep his eyes off you."

"Well, I do not see it. Anyway, he is not my type."

"Why not? Drake's wonderful. He's just had a crazy month. Why is he not your type?"

"He just seems like he is too controlling, too extreme alpha male for me. I did not have a good experience with a wannabe alpha male."

Shayla grimaced. "I know you went through a bad situation before, but that guy was evil. Just because someone is an alpha, dominant type of guy does not mean he will hurt you, Lila. If you have not yet figured it out, Drew is an alpha male, and he is my Dom."

"All these guys are alpha types, but what do you mean he is your Dom?"

"He is the dominant in our relationship, and I am his submissive. In all aspects of our life."

Shock etched in her face, Lila finally responded.

"No way. You are such a strong, professional woman. Sure he has an alpha male personality, but he treats you like a queen." Pausing, Lila braced herself for the next question. "Are you really a Dom/Sub if you know what I mean?"

"Yep. Sure are," Shayla said cheerfully. "Look, not all Dom/Sub relationships are what the average person thinks. There are all types of relationships. It's not all about tying someone up and spanking them, and having their way with you. Which is totally fine by the way. It's also not all master/slave scenarios. Of course, some go the full, stereotypical route in their relationships. For me and Drew, he is the head of our family, and he does make a lot of the final decisions, but he treats me like I am a precious stone. He takes care of me, but also values my opinion. It's very refreshing, actually."

"Okay. Please stop me if I am crossing the line by asking, but do you do all the extreme things I have read about, go to dungeons, etc.?"

"Ask me whatever you want Lila. We do partake in bondage and spanking from time to time, but not anything like a punishment or what is called extreme play. Drew is not a sadist. We do go to a place. I guess you can technically liken it to a dungeon, but it is exclusive, high class, and very tasteful."

"Really, you do? I have never been to a place like that. Shoot, I would not even know where one was or have thought about it."

"I might as well get it out there, but don't tell them I told you. Almost all of the guys are Doms and members of *The Manor*. All except Trent and Rocco."

"So those guys just pick up a random woman at *The Manor* for a night. None of them have girlfriends as far as I know."

"There are always willing Subs, or they may join in on the fun with another Dom/Sub."

"Wow. I am just a little flabbergasted. Wouldn't a different woman all the time get old? I just can't wrap my head around it."

"In actuality, most Doms are always seeking their perfect Sub or you could just say partner. I would suspect it would get lonely at times. I hope I haven't scared you off or you now think we're weird by telling you. Your friendship is important to me. You would have found out eventually. I'd rather you hear about our lifestyle choice directly from me."

"Hey, to each their own. I am by no means sexually repressed or not open to new things. Just don't know about someone controlling me, though."

"After what happened to you, I understand. But like I said, not all Dom/Sub relationships fall into the stereotypical box."

"True, I suppose."

The rest of the party went well. Lila really enjoyed herself, even though Drake clearly was avoiding her like the plague. As it closed in on 11pm, Lila started to say her goodbyes.

"Okay everyone. I think I'm outta here. It's been a long day, and I am tired. Gotta call an Uber."

"I'm leaving too. I'll just drop you off," Drake said, surprising Lila.

"Thanks Drake. I was going to have Drew take her since I was the reason she didn't have a car," Shayla said.

"See you," Lila said, hesitant to leave with Drake.

Everyone said their goodbyes, even though she was called a light-weight by Dallas and Trent.

Drake and Lila made their way toward his F250. Lila was nervous. Why didn't she insist on an Uber? He did not even like her. Why was he taking her home? Surprisingly, Drake opened the door for her. Hmm, he has some manners, I see.

"You did not have to take me home, but thanks. I appreciate it."

"Well, I wanted to talk to you anyway and was getting ready to leave, so I can kill two birds with one stone. Where to?"

"I am staying at the Extended Stay out on Jefferson."

Drake put the truck in reverse and headed out of the development. The hotel was only 15 minutes away, but those were the longest 15 minutes Lila has experienced. Long, silent minutes. Pulling into the hotel parking lot, Drake parked the truck. Turning to face Lila, Drake just looked at her.

"I want to apologize again for how I acted during our first encounter. It was rude of me to burst in like that, but there are a few things I am particular about and one is my parking spot. Everyone knows not to park there. Drew knows, so I blame him, not you. So again, I'm sorry."

"No problem. You do not have to worry. I will never do that again. Being particular and all about your parking spot, I would not want to upset you," Lila responded, perturbed with his so called apology.

"I was apologizing here. Why are you getting an attitude?"

"I don't have an attitude. I guess I just do not understand how someone can be so anally retentive over a parking space. It is not like anyone has to walk far at the office."

Fuming now and not recognizing how childlike and arrogant he sounded, Drake reacted to Lila's last comment.

"That's not the point, little girl. I'm the boss. It's my spot. There are rules, and people should follow them."

Pissed now, Lila was not going to take his crap.

"First, I am a woman not a little girl. Since we are not in the office, I will let that slide. Second, yes you are one of my bosses, and I will respect and follow your rules about the parking space and will follow all 'rules' of the office, but I will also expect to be treated professionally as I will treat you. If you have an issue, please speak to me as a professional and not like a child. So, I accept your apology. Thank you for the ride. See you Monday."

Lila started to exit his truck before Drake could make another comment out of his arrogant mouth. "What a fucking asshole," she spurted out loud. Shit, I hope I did not just screw up and end up getting fired. He is one of the owners. I think Drew and Shayla would have my back, maybe not. He is family and family is first with them, thought Lila. Lila hoped she did not step over the line. She would call Shayla tomorrow and tell her what happened. At least she could get her side of the story out to avoid being fired. This was going to be a long, long night and weekend.

"WHO DOES she think she is talking to me like that? I am her boss. I should have taken her over my knee and spanked that beautiful little—"

Putting his head into his hands, he couldn't believe he went there, again. Now all he could think about was her firm little ass up in the air, begging him to spank it. "I cannot believe she spoke to me that way. She has some balls. Well, I'll show her who's boss."

4

Monday morning rolled around, and Lila was a bit nervous when pulling up to the office. She called Shayla on Sunday and told her what happened. Shayla laughed, got Drew and told him. They both told her 'good for you putting him in his place' and for her not to worry, her job was safe. They both said Drake sometimes needed someone to bring him down a notch or two, and they thought it was hilarious a woman did so. Shayla insisted again she believed Drake had eyes for her and thought Lila just makes him flustered. Lila thought Shayla is insane. Drake did not like her personally or professionally from what she could tell by his behavior.

As usual, Lila was one of the first to arrive in the office. Rocco was already there and approached her desk, food in hand.

"How's my sweet girl? I brought you some tea and some homemade croissants." Rocco was the only one who could refer to her as a "girl" as he said it in a nice, loving, fatherly way.

"Why thank you, Rocco Taco. You spoil me. Love you."

Just as the words were out of her mouth, Drake walked in the office and glared at them.

"Good morning, Mr. Donovan," Lila said.

Drake just grunted.

"Hey D. There are some croissants in the break room. Go get some before the knuckle heads get in."

"Thanks, Rocco," Drake said, leaving the area.

"Mr. Donavan?" Rocco asked, raising his eyebrows.

"Let's just say we have not gotten off to a good start, thus I will keep everything professional with him."

"Really, and here I thought on Saturday Drake kept looking like he wanted to peel your clothes off and take you right there. Then when he drove you home . . ."

"Ha. Yeah right. Sure, he drove me home and wanted to apologize for his 'outburst' at our first meeting, only to make it clear he is not my fan."

"Could've fooled me. So we still on this afternoon?"

"You betcha. Looking forward to you toughening me up."

"See you later, sweet girl."

"Later, Rocco."

The rest of the day went by fast. Lila barely saw Drake. Clearly he was avoiding her. As 4pm approached and everyone else was leaving, Lila changed and headed to the Dome. Seeing her enter the Dome, Rocco asked if she was ready to start training. He was as eager to train Lila as she was to learn.

"Yes, sir. Teach me everything. I want to be able to do what you guys can do. I know it will take a long time, but I am a hard worker, learn quickly, and will practice. I promise."

"I know you will. That's why I said I would train you."

Rocco also knew the details of the incident Lila went through. She'd confided in him, and he had also talked with Drew. Rocco would never tell anyone else, but he also wanted to make sure his girl could take care of herself. He knew there was something deep inside Lila she feared, and he wanted her to be able to erase those fears her ex caused. Rocco truly loved her like a daughter and would do anything to help Lila.

A FEW WEEKS PASSED, and Lila and Drake's interactions were limited. Lila kept herself professional and addressed him formally when she must speak. She did catch him staring at her again at a staff meeting when they were going over some upcoming jobs, but she ignored him.

Her training continued with Rocco, and Lila caught on quick. Rocco was impressed. He never expected her to be doing so well so fast and felt more confident Lila could handle herself if she ever encountered trouble again. He was even more impressed at her shooting skills. Sure, she said she grew up around guns, hunting and shooting, but in testing mode, she scored even higher than a few of the guys. Rocco knew she was smart, but Lila thought quickly on her feet. He even believed in time she would make a good agent based on how well she excelled in her training.

Later that afternoon, Drake quickly strode toward Lila's desk. "What the hell is this? I already gave you the signed report to send. Why am I getting a different version on my desk to sign?" Drake yelled, heads starting to peek out of offices due to his raised voice.

"Mr. Donovan. I made appropriate changes per my job expectations so a finalized, professional report would be sent. If you would sign it, I will be glad to put it in the mail."

"I did not ask you to make changes. Now send out what I prepared."

"Okay, sir. If you would like a report that is grammatically incorrect to go out, I still have your copy."

Snickers and laughter rang out from the guys who were watching this scene play out from their offices.

"My office. Now!" Drake demanded.

Taking her time, Lila rose, straightened out her skirt, and proceeded to Drake's office.

"Close the door," Drake barked.

"Yes, sir. How can I help you?" Lila said smugly. She was not going to react or tolerate him being an asshole.

"When I ask you to do something, I expect you to do it. I did not ask you to change my report. I asked you to mail it," he yelled.

"Mr. Donovan, Drew and Shayla instructed me at the start of my employment to make corrections and rewrite portions of reports as necessary. Can we please go speak with them so we all can be on the same page? I want to clearly understand the expectations and be consistent with the work product," she replied calmly, not reacting to his outburst.

He felt like steam was coming out of his ears. This woman drove him to the brink of madness. Rounding his desk, he approached Lila, "I do NOT need to ask Drew or Shayla. I am an owner, and you are my employee. I gave you a document and you, you—"

Drake stopped talking, clearly mad. Lila was getting a little nervous and starting to once again feel that scared, insecure feeling build as Drake moved closer into her personal space, backing her up against the door. Until he grabbed her face and kissed her.

Instantly, Lila forgot everything else, her surroundings or the fact that he was just yelling at her, and she melted into his kiss. What a kiss it was. Hot, aggressive, but seductive. Oh God, what he could do with his mouth. Dampness instantly presented itself between her legs, her libido on fire. She could stay right here kissing him for hours. It was such a mind melting kiss.

Three knocks and someone trying to open the door against Lila's back was the only thing that broke the trance.

"Is everything okay in there?" Drew asked.

They separated and moved to let Drew in, Shayla at his heels.

"Everything is fine," Drake said, quickly recovering.

"We heard yelling, and Dallas said you were mad about a report."

"Just a misunderstanding. We have it settled."

Drew and Shayla kept looking back and forth between Lila and Drake. They weren't stupid. They knew something happened. Trying to also help diffuse the situation, even though she was still trying to wrap her mind around what just happened, Lila reassured them.

"Everything is fine. Drake and I had a small mishap in communication, but it has been resolved."

"Not buying it," Drew deduced. "Good because we have a meeting in one hour with Senator Henderson," he said.

"No problem. We will be ready. Thanks for the heads up," Lila said.

Drew and Shayla left Drake's office. Before Lila could say anything, Drake spoke first.

"Sorry about that. I don't know what came over me. I was unprofessional and inappropriate. It won't happen again."

Lila internally sank as she wanted it to happen again, but made sure he did not see her disappointment.

"It was good. I mean it's all good. No worries. No apologies needed," Lila said, trying to find the right words. "I'll send out your version of the report," she said trying to make a smooth exit.

"No. Send your version," he said while signing the report. "The changes were good."

On that note, Lila exited Drake's office, still tingling, still aroused, still trying to figure out where that hot, steaming kiss came from.

Drake doesn't even like me, but that kiss. She had never been kissed like that before. So pure, so raw, so intoxicating.

It would not happen again. Drake even said so. Lila was so confused. She couldn't allow herself to a desire a man like Drake. He was rude, controlling, and seemed like the kind of guy who would get what he wanted from you and when he was done, would just push you to the side. He is handsome, no, not handsome. Hot, sexy, a body you wanted to run your hands all over, someone who would bend you over and bring you such pleasure . . . Stop! Enough thinking about Drake. He was a no go. Focus, a senator is coming in less than an hour. You need to talk to Shayla and prepare, she instructed herself.

JESUS, what were you thinking? You're one of her bosses. To grab her like that and kiss her, idiot, Drake scolded himself as he paced his office.

Remembering her obstinate little face when she would not take the bait to his rant just made him want to show her who was boss, in a different manner than most would think. She looked so sexy in that shirt, tight black skirt, and strappy sandals. Her face turned up at him, he could not help himself.

Kissing Lila was better than he would have imagined. She instantly let him take control. God, he was growing hard just thinking about it. She let him take what he wanted. Her tongue danced step for step with his. She tasted so sweet, better than he imagined, and he didn't want to stop. If Drew did not knock, who knows how far it would have gone. Time to get her out of his head. The senator was coming. It had to be serious for an impromptu, but urgent, meeting to be requested.

LILA FINISHED PREPPING the conference room just in time. The intercom at the gate buzzed indicating the senator had arrived. All hands were on deck for this meeting. Lila quickly went to the lobby to greet the senator along with Shayla.

In addition to the senator, there were three other men. They showed their badges, one FBI agent and the senator's personal security detail.

"Good afternoon Senator Henderson. I'm Shayla Donovan, this is Lila Norris. If you would please follow me, the team is in the conference room."

The group followed Shayla to the conference room, and greetings were exchanged. Lila offered the guests something to drink and everyone settled into a seat.

"So senator, you advised it was urgent you meet with us. Seeing you have brought along the FBI, I take it the government has a situation they need our assistance with," Drew said.

"Actually, Mr. Donovan—"

"Drew, please."

"Drew. In actuality, it is a personal matter in which the FBI needed to get involved, and they suggested your firm may have some expertise which could assist in the investigation and recovery of my daughter."

"Your daughter? Please explain."

"My daughter has been missing. While trying to locate her, we revealed the disappearance of several other young ladies, thus the FBI's involvement."

"I have not heard any news reports on her disappearance."

"That was a strategic decision. You see . . . everything that has been and will be said is confidential."

All heads shook in agreement.

"Caroline went missing from an alternative lifestyle club. Due to my current position and platform, I do not want that fact revealed."

"I presume you are referring to a BDSM club," Drew clarified.

"Correct. Caroline apparently liked to partake in that lifestyle, much to her mother's and my disapproval. When we could not reach her for a few days, we were able to track down her friend and she also had not seen her in two days, ever since she went to the club. I called in some contacts, and Agent Harris and his team have been discretely working the case. Unfortunately they are reaching dead ends. Since we are running into these dead ends and cannot broadcast the fact that she was at this type of club, we cannot ask around the bureau for someone familiar with this lifestyle to assist. Agent Harris knows your agent Trent Roberts, here, and said you all may have some inside knowledge to this lifestyle that may help in the investigation. I am going to ask Agent Harris to bring you up to speed."

Agent Harris filled them in on the investigation. "As you can see, we are at a roadblock. We know she left with a regular, but do not know who he is. We do not have anyone we can trust to secretly imbed them into this type of club scene and look like they fit in. You do, and with your company's track record, confidentiality is not an issue. Basically, we would like to have some of your agents blend in and see if you can locate the man Caroline left with. Also, we found out several other women have not been seen in some time, and they all had been seen with the same man. The witness unfortunately did not give a great description. It is vague, and she said she is done talking. It has now been a week with no leads. We will leave you a copy of the investigative file and would like you to review it and get back to us by tomorrow with what you think you can do."

"You help find my daughter. Money is no object. Just find her," the senator added, distress in his voice.

"Thanks again for meeting with us on short notice," Agent Harris said.

"No problem. We will be in touch first thing tomorrow," Drew replied.

The senator and his posse left, and the group got down to business. Lila was amazed to see the transformation in the team and the focus in the room when a job needed to be done. She was thankful they let her be a part of the discussion. A few options were floating around the group as they went over the details.

"So it is clear we need a few of us to start visiting the club —what's its name—*Pleasure Palace*. How clever," Jax said.

"Well, I won't be a good one for that part," Trent replied. "It would need to be a few of you seven, for sure," referring to Drew, Drake, Dallas, Jax, Jace, Garrett, and Matt. "Y'all would fit best for obvious reasons; the rest of us will handle the surveillance part."

"For sure some of us need to get into that club and blend in, but if any of us starts asking around about missing girls, anyone with information may clam up," Drake said.

"There has to be another way," Jace reiterated.

"I have a suggestion," Lila chimed in. All eyes turned to Lila in surprise, and the room suddenly went quiet.

"Lila, please do share your thoughts," Drew instructed.

"Well, listening to all your ideas, I agree you need to imbed yourselves in the club. The fact that you know if you all start snooping around will only call attention, I suggest a woman be a part of this, in addition to some of you. If they are targeting women, you need to give him a target."

"Smart and beautiful," Dallas said. "She's on to something."

"No way. The only woman we trust that knows that lifestyle is Shayla. She is my wife. I will not allow her to be a part of this. It's a hard no!"

"I don't think I would be able to pull it off anyway. I would cling to Drew, and no one would get close enough. Also I don't think I could keep my facial expressions or reactions at bay."

"Well, guess we're back to square one if the FBI can't provide someone. We need to come up with another plan," Matt said.

"What about me?" Lila asked.

For a second time in a few minutes, silence filled the room as shocked eyes zeroed in on Lila.

"Lila, you are not trained. I can't put you in harm's way, and you know there are other reasons," Drew said.

"Drew I can do it. I have been training every day with Rocco since, what . . . my third week or so here. I am strong, smart, and what other alternative do you have?"

"She's telling the truth. This girl can kick ass, thinks fast on her feet, and shoots better than some of you," Rocco added. Several jaws dropped in disbelief. "It's true. While I don't want my sweet girl in harm's way, she does make a point and I think she can do it."

"Have you ever been to a BDSM club or taken part of this type of lifestyle?" Jace asked.

"No."

"Exactly. You cannot do it," Drake commanded.

"Yes, I can," Lila said firmly. "Look, what if I go with one of you as a trainee or something. Someone acts as my Dom, but people are told I am only in training, learning about the lifestyle. This exposes me to others since they know I am new to the scene. If it is another Dom that has been taking the girls, I may appeal to him."

"No. You can't do this," Drake replied firmly. "You are not a sub."

"Yes, I can, and you are not the only decision-maker in this room. Sure, I'm not a sub, but . . . ," Lila heard "yes you are" murmured low by someone. Focusing back on Drake and the group, "I can learn. See, being a sub in training is ideal. If I am nervous or a little unsure, it would make sense and not be surprising to others."

"Lila, do you realize what you would be getting yourself into? You would most likely be naked, in public, in front of colleagues. When under cover, there are sometimes sacrifices we have to make. We talked about this when you first started. You will need to actually submit, be intimate," Drew said. "Are you sure you are really ready for that?"

"Yes. I am, and I understand what I may have to do." Looking hard into Drew's eyes, she said, "I cannot just sit by when women are being taken and most likely harmed when I can do something about it. I can handle it. As long as you all don't treat me differently after seeing me naked, or you know, doing other things, I'll be fine. All we need now is a volunteer to be my trainer Dom."

"I'll do it. I'm your man," Dallas said as a few other hands flew up.

The word "no" echoed loudly throughout the room, everyone turned toward Drake.

"If we go forward with this plan, I will be her Dom. Period," Drake said as his eyes bored into Lila like they were burning the clothes off her body.

"First we need to see what you got," Trent said.

"Excuse me?" Lila said in surprise. "I'm not stripping here. You have seen me in a bathing suit. Use your imagination until I have no choice."

Laughing, "No silly. I meant your fighting, defense, and shooting skills."

"Oh."

"I agree. Lila head to the Dome," Drew said.

"Give me a minute to change. I'll meet you all there."

Lila went to grab her workout clothes, Shayla followed.

"Lila, are you sure this is a good idea with what happened with your ex? Are you sure you are ready for this?"

"I know you are worried Shayla, but since I have been here and working with Rocco the past few months I really think I am at peace with what happened. I will never forget, but I will never be a victim again, ever. If I am able to help someone else, I can handle whatever comes at me."

"But can you handle Drake? You can say what you want, but I can see the fire burning between you two. Why do you think he shut everyone else down back in the conference room?"

Lila sighed, "Yes Drake. I don't know. Seems like we have a complicated relationship. He is brusque and demanding one minute, then staring at me the next like he wants me. And after that kiss—"

"I knew it!" Shayla exclaimed. "We interrupted something earlier when he was yelling."

Blushing, Lila closed her eyes for a moment. "I'm confused about Drake. Why in the hell would he kiss me if he acts like he does not like me."

"Honestly, I think you have thrown him for a loop and he does not know how to handle these new feelings. Personally I think you are perfect for him."

"Why do you say that? He is a Dom. A real Dom. I am not a sub."

Smiling, "Yes, you are. Like I told you before, don't stereotype what a sub is. You put Drake in his place when needed, but I see you melt into a submissive mode around him at other times. The question is, do you think you can do things with Drake for this op?"

"I hope so. Part of me feels he is the only one I could or would want to touch me. Another part of me wonders if someone else would be better in order to separate personal and professional feelings."

"You don't have a choice if you move forward with this. Drake is not going to allow one of the other guys to play your Dom."

"I think you are right."

"I know I'm right."

Lila changed, and she and Shayla headed to the Dome. Rocco had already set up some equipment. Everyone was there ready to observe. Lila's eyes immediately found Drake's. His expression hard, skeptical.

Grabbing Lila's hand, Rocco started to wrap them in preparation.

Speaking low for only Lila's ears, Rocco said, "Let's go through the drills like usual. I am going to get someone else involved to show them what you are made of. Just focus. If you can't do this in front of the crew, you will not be able to handle the field. I know you are ready."

"Hey, darlin'. How come I did not know that my ray of sunshine was training?" Dallas questioned.

"You never asked *darlin'*," Lila teased.

On the mat, Rocco put her through the normal warm up, then through her fighting skills. She got a few hoots and hollers from the guys.

"Looks good, but can she handle hands on?" Drew asked.

"Well, let's find out," Rocco replied. "Jace, come up here. I want you to come at Lila like you are going to attack her."

"Game on," Jace said, rubbing his hands together.

"Listen to me," Rocco whispered. "Jace will come at you high and usually moves to the right. You know what to do. Take him down."

"Yes, sir."

"Oh this is going to be fun sweetheart. You know I do not mind taking on a girl," Jace said with a wink.

"Stop mouthing off Jace, and don't give her any slack. We need to see what she is made of," Drake said.

Lila waited for Jace to move. As Rocco expected, he went high and to her right. She was able to spin out of his reach then take him down with a swipe of her legs, putting him in a choke hold. Jace did not know what hit him.

"Time," Rocco called. Laughter ensued along with some teasing, especially by Jax.

"You think it's funny. You get in here Jax."

"Fine, brother. I'll show you how it's done."

"Now listen, Jax is going to come at you straight on. Don't back down. Come in fast and punch him in the face, and before he can do anything, follow through with an upper cut, and move. Kick behind his knees and take him down and go for the gonads. He will give up as he won't want to be racked or actually hurt you."

Once again, Lila did what Rocco said and landed her punches. Jax was stunned. The next thing he knew he was down and Lila was positioned to strike his manhood. She stopped and backed off.

"Anyone else?" Rocco asked as everyone looked at Lila in astonishment.

"Well done, well done, Lila. Very impressive," Drew said. "Let's go to the range. Show us what you got."

Rocco retrieved a shotgun and handed it to Lila. She shot one. Bull's eye. Shot two, three and four, all center hits. Changing out the paper, Rocco handed her the Glock. "There are ten rounds, five head shots, five chest shots. Make sure they can see each shot."

Lila took the gun, checked it, and took off the safety. She let off ten quick rounds. Pulling up the paper target, everyone was speechless. One in each eye area, three making a smile, followed with five in the chest.

"Did she really just do that?" the usually quiet Garrett said. "You are a goddess."

"Good skills, but shooting a target is not the same as a real scenario," Drake said.

"Oh come on, Drake. You just saw what we all saw," Garrett added.

"Let's see how she does in the pit first."

"Fine by me," Lila retorted.

Stepping up to the challenge, Lila grabbed the special weapon used in the Pit from Rocco and headed inside.

"Okay Drake. I've been practicing. Let's see if I can meet your minimum standards," Lila said with a little sass. "Rocco, any scenario you want."

"Alright, sweet girl. You know the drill."

Lila entered the Pit, their high-tech shooting simulator. Large screens outside lit up, the cameras showing Lila and the other rooms of the simulator. This enabled the team to be able to evaluate each other and adjust training as needed.

"Don't make the simulation too easy, Rocco. We need to make sure she can handle herself before she is put in any possible danger," Drew said.

"Okay, sweet girl. The scenario is you are trying to save a young woman who has been kidnapped. This is the house she is being held hostage in. You do not know how many people are inside but are aware there are at least three suspects. Do what you have to do to save the victim. Ready?"

Lila nodded and the blue light came on indicating it was go time. Slowly she moved down the makeshift hall. A figure popped out from an opening and raised a weapon. Lila shot first, hitting her target. Slowly she moved down the hall to the doorway the suspect exited. Entering, gun raised, Lila determined the room was secure and no other suspects were present. She carefully headed back into the hallway and entered an open area, the living spaces, and was met by two men in different locations in the room. She immediately shot one, dropped and rolled and took out the other mark as she adjusted from the roll.

Back on her feet, Lila proceeded through the simulated house. Kicking open the closed door off the living space, Lila saw a man with a gun to the head of the victim. A simulated demand came from the man for her to drop her gun. She slowly entered, not dropping her weapon, pointing it directly at his head. All of a sudden, Lila shot and the simulated kidnapper dropped to the ground. The lights then came on and Lila headed back out to the group.

"That was a ballsy move. You could have had the victim killed," Drake scolded.

"I saw him flinch, and I took my shot. Had to make a decision, and if I did not take the shot, he would have either shot me, the victim, or both of us. Wasn't that the goal? Save the victim?"

"What flinch? He didn't flinch."

"Yes, he did."

Thankfully the system automatically recorded all simulations. Rocco backed up the recording and found the part where Lila entered the room where the victim was being held. He slowed the play back down. There it was. A split second flinch when the kidnapper looked away and Lila took her shot.

"So, did I pass?"

"You're hired," Drew said.

"We have one little problem," Drake remarked.

"What?" Lila and Drew said in unison.

"You do not have the first clue about the BDSM lifestyle."

"Teach me what I need to know."

"It is not that easy."

"Like I said in my proposal, I would be posing as a trainee, thus others would expect I am learning. If I am taught the basics, we should be good to go."

"We don't have enough time."

"I'm a quick learner. Just ask Rocco."

"She is," Rocco confirmed.

"This is different."

"Hold up," Drew interjected. "Call Edward at *The Manor.* I am sure Julie has a trainee class going on or starting. They could put Lila in for a few days, to acclimate her."

"I'll take care of it," Shayla said.

"Maybe she could do a one-on-one training for us. Julie

and Edward are very discreet. They will understand our urgency without asking a lot of questions."

"I should probably brief Edward anyway without giving him too much information, at least he can step up security and make sure his club does not get hit by the perpetrator," Drake added

"Who's Edward?" Lila asked.

"Edward is the owner of *The Manor*. It is an exclusive, high-end clientele BDSM/alternative lifestyle club. People are carefully vetted prior to acceptance of a membership. We are members."

"Okay. Let's get moving then. Caroline and who knows else cannot keep waiting for help."

Shayla called Edward and explained the urgency. They were able to get Lila in tomorrow morning with a class in progress. Drew and Drake would meet with Edward and explain the situation in more detail in order to protect his clients.

5

Lila was nervous. She was unsure what Julie would have in store for her. Shayla had gone over some basics last night, but that did not quite put her at ease. She was a mix of excitement, anticipation, and trepidation. Drew drove her and Drake to *The Manor*. It was about twenty minutes from the office in a very serene, scenic, slightly rural looking area.

"We're here," Drew said as he pulled up to a gate. After speaking into the intercom, the gate started opening. They proceeded up a long drive lined with trees which then opened up to a stately looking mansion.

"This is *The Manor*?" Lila asked. "It looks like someone's estate."

"It was in the past. Like I said yesterday, *The Manor* caters to a very high end clientele. Very confidential. You may see politicians, sports players, those in entertainment, high profile businessmen. *The Manor* allows those who partake in this lifestyle to be around like-minded people, without the worries of being exposed; very discreet."

Parking the car, they all exited and proceeded to the front door where they were greeted by a very polished, attractive, well-dressed man. Reaching out his hand first to Drew, then Drake, they exchanged greetings.

"Edward, this is Lila. Lila, Edward," Drew said.

Edward grabbed her hand, raised it to his lips, and pressed a kiss to the back of her hand, all while maintaining eye contact.

"It is lovely to meet you, Miss Lila."

"It's nice to meet you, sir."

"Ah, and you said she was not a submissive, Drake. Clearly she knows who is a master. Please, come with me. Let's talk for a bit, and then I can introduce you to Mistress Julie," Edward said as he lightly led Lila by her elbow.

They proceeded inside and through a few halls and open rooms toward what must be Edward's office. The inside was just as beautiful as the exterior. Rich dark wood, well adorned rooms that exuded elegance. Edward's office followed suit, except for a wall of monitors by his desk. He motioned Lila, Drew, and Drake to the seating area. Edward sat on the coach next to Lila.

"If you do not mind, I would like to speak with Miss Lila first so we can get her in with Mistress Julie. You two can then fill me in afterward. If Miss Lila is still with Mistress Julie when we are done, I can have my driver bring her back."

"Sounds good. You agree, Drake?"

"Fine."

"So Miss Lila, the guys here tell me you need a quick tutorial on being a submissive."

"Yes, sir."

"And you have not previously participated in this type of lifestyle?"

"Not really."

"Ah, not really. So that means you have done something in the past. Can you elaborate?"

Lila glanced around the room, then back to Edward.

"Lila, you cannot be shy with me. Clearly the reason you are here is very important. What you tell me will help Mistress Julie. Do you trust me?"

Interestingly, she did. "Yes, sir."

"Now, why don't you tell me what you have done and what pleases you."

"I have been tied up to a bed before, spanked a few times, and I do tend to like the outdoors."

"How are you with a demanding partner taking what he wants?"

Lila hesitated momentarily before she continued, "Uhm . . . while I like initiating sometimes and pleasing my partner, I used to like my boyfriend to take control, call the shots."

"Used to?" Edward quickly asked.

"Unfortunately, the last person I was seeing did not turn out very well," Lila said, dropping her eyes.

Edward quickly picked up on the reference. "Sweet Miss Lila, please know you can submit to your partner and have the confidence that they will never bring harm to you, but only seek to bring you pleasure. A true Dom will be demanding, but will only want to please you, never harm or scare you, and will understand your limits and needs. I think it is time to take you to Mistress Julie. Gentlemen, if you will excuse us for a moment. I will be back, and we can continue our conversation."

Edward led Lila to the other side of the mansion to a door on the left. Inside were four people, two men and two women, kneeling on pillows, and a petite, lusciously shaped woman dressed in skin-tight black leather standing over them.

"Mistress Julie, may I interrupt for a moment?"

"Don't move. Hello Edward, who do we have here?"

"This is Lila. The new trainee I told you about. Lila this is Mistress Julie."

"Hello, Mistress Julie."

"Lila will be joining your group for a few sessions. May I speak to you privately for a moment?"

"Yes. Grab a pillow, kneel and look down like the others. Everyone, don't talk, don't move."

Lila did as she was told, but did quickly glance at the others in the room. One lady was middle aged, a little on the plump side, a man about her age or a little older, a petite brunette, and a big, very built guy that looked familiar. Lila did not look long enough to get a good look and went and kneeled down next to the older lady.

Edward filled Julie in as quietly as possible to give her some insight on how to handle Lila. He returned to the room to join Drew and Drake. "She is lovely. A true submissive."

"You've got to be kidding," Drake barked.

"I see it too," Drew responded. "Drake does not want to see it because he likes her, and you know Drake never gets attached."

"Yes, that is quite accurate," Edward said.

"Hey. I'm sitting right here and you're wrong."

Edward and Drew just exchanged looks. "Back to Lila, I think she is a true submissive. She seems smart, strong willed, but wants someone to take care of her. Clearly something went wrong in the past to make her uneasy, but if the trust can be restored, she would be a well-rounded sub/partner. Maybe I will need to mold her."

"Like hell you will. Only I will touch her," Drake yelled.

"And there it is. Just as I thought. You finally met your sub," Edward said. "So do you know what happened to her?"

"Yes," Drew said.

"You do? Why haven't you shared this information?" Drake asked.

"Because you have had your head in your ass. Like we don't fully vet our staff. I told you that you needed to read her file, but you have done so much to avoid her because she makes your dick hard."

Drake knew Drew was right.

"You both need to know what happened to Lila. Mistress Julie can help her so Drake can handle her appropriately during this op."

Drew started to fill them in. "Lila was dating this guy, someone who liked to drink a little too much. I cannot figure out what she even saw in him based on how she is. He was part of her social circle, so I guess maybe things just fell in place. Anyway, almost a year ago Lila won the lottery. Not the big jackpot, but several million."

"No shit," Drake said.

"Oh, that is what started all her problems. This guy, Seth I believe is his name, thought he was entitled to her money. They had not even been dating that long, around four months, and were not in a fully-committed relationship. One afternoon, Seth came to Lila's house; he had been drinking, and demanded she share her new-found wealth with him. He had this false sense that he was the reason she was lucky and won, thus she owed him. When she refused and told him she no longer wanted to see him, he went ballistic. He beat the shit out of her, to the point she was hospitalized for approximately a month."

"You've got to be kidding me," Drake said, stunned at what Drew was telling him.

"Go on. Clearly there is more," Edward uttered.

"She was in a coma for about a week, had a collapsed lung, broken ribs and arm, her face was beaten to a pulp, she was unrecognizable. She could not see out of her one eye for a month. Thankfully her vision was not damaged. It took her a long time to recover. I saw the police file. It was not pretty.

"This Seth guy was a douche. Controlling, telling her what she could and couldn't do even though they had just started dating. After Lila got out of the hospital, she still had another month of recovery. She moved back in with her parents. Once she fully recovered, she decided to just move. She wanted to be away from any reminders of the incident. Start over in a new place, new surroundings, new people, new life. Since she had the winnings, it allowed her to do so. Her parents understood, and her employer was sad to see her leave. They loved her. She traveled a bit to see where she would like to move and ended up here in Texas. She liked the area, and the rest is history."

"Poor girl. I could see some hesitancy in her even though she is, deep down, a submissive," Edward said.

Drake was fuming. He wanted to kill the bastard who hurt her. He couldn't believe Lila went through all of that. She seemed so strong, so together. If she was his, she would be treasured.

"This is unbelievable. I cannot believe she is going forward with this op after all that has happened."

"Rocco has a lot to do with it," Drew said.

"Rocco?"

"You know those two are close. He loves her like a daughter and knows everything. She told him herself. I think it is another reason he has trained her so well. It is healing her. You saw how strong she is. You know as much as I do, Drake, that someone can be submissive by nature, but strong."

Those words were so true. For a guy like Drake, if he ever had a life partner, she would need to be strong, be able to put up with his shit, give it back to him, but also let him take care of her.

That's what scared him about Lila. She checked all the boxes, and to top it off, was so beautiful and sexy. For a night he could be with a sub who gave in to everything he demanded, but did not have the backbone to stand on. But if he ever wanted to build a life with someone, they needed to have the qualities just like Lila.

"So Drake, you know what you need to do. Build trust, cherish her and make it about her. Then you will have the perfect person to handle this op and also the perfect sub," Edward said. "I'm envious, actually. She has the qualities I have been looking for, but unfortunately has already been claimed. So gentlemen, why don't you fill me in on the rest. What is going on, and what do I need to do to protect my club?"

THE DOOR OPENED. "Eyes down, Samuel. Do not make me tell you again."

"Sorry, Mistress."

"Everyone, please sit up and welcome Lila. She will be with us today and tomorrow."

"Welcome, Lila," a multitude of voices rang out.

"Thank you."

"As I was saying prior to Lila's arrival, a good sub will follow the instructions of their Master, no hesitation, no questions. Your Master will learn your limits and, you should have already discussed your hard limits, thus do what your Master says. Only use your safe word when you are very, very sure your Master has overstepped or is about to go past your limit. Do not use it loosely."

For the next few hours, Mistress Julie put the group in all kinds of scenarios, gave many commands, but also explained and taught them what everything meant. She was firm, but Lila did not mind following her directions.

"Okay my little slaves. We are done for today. Tomorrow, be prepared to be exposed, both physically and mentally. I will push you all. It will help prepare you for the open room. We will be going to the open room tomorrow to observe after your training. Therefore, our training starts at 6pm promptly. Feel free to wear whatever you feel comfortable wearing in the open room. Good night all."

Everyone started gathering their belongings. The really big guy approached Lila. "Hi, I'm Sam."

"Nice to meet you, Sam. Have we met before?"

"Nope, but you may have seen me on television."

"That's it. You're Sam Wilkins the tight end for the Cowboys. Wow. Never would expect to see you here, or should I say in this capacity."

"Most would be. I have to be in control for many parts of my life. It's nice to have one aspect where I can let it go and let someone else be in control for a while. I like this place because of its confidentiality."

"That's what I am told. Well, nice to meet you. See you tomorrow."

Sam left and Lila sought out Julie. "Mistress Julie, do you know where I can find Edward? I am sure my ride is gone by now, and Edward said he would get his driver to take me."

"Sure, and it's just Julie now as your session is over. You did great by the way. You are a true submissive, unlike Sam."

"Sam? He told me he needed this as he always has to be in control."

"Sammy likes to switch. I think he truly is a Dom, but learning the sub side will help him understand what he truly is and find the right sub for him."

"Interesting."

"Yep. We get all kinds in here. Oh, wear something sexy tomorrow. Make sure your undergarments follow suit. You're too pretty not to show off that body. Come on, follow me. We'll go find Edward."

Lila thanked both Edward and Julie and said her goodbyes.

As Lila left, Edward said, "You need to call Drake."

"I know." Picking up her cell, she dialed.

"Donovan."

"Hey Drake, it's Julie."

"Hi Julie. So what do you think about Lila? Will she be able to pick up enough in a few days?"

"She is a delight, but I think you need to join us tomorrow. She did good, a natural, but tomorrow it should be you guiding her. She won't know it's you at first, of course. You in?"

"Yes."

"Okay. Be here before 6pm."

"Roger."

Lila left with Edward's driver. He took her back to the office. As soon as she walked through the door, Shayla pounced.

"How did it go? You okay? Was it good or overwhelming?"

"Slow down, ladybug. Give me a sec and I will come to your office and fill you in."

"Okay, but don't take long. I want the details."

Lila went to her desk to put her stuff down and to take a moment before Shayla started with the twenty questions. Heading to Shayla's office, she saw Drake standing in his doorway looking at her.

Lila was hoping she would not see Drake tonight since it was already late. Throughout the entire session, all she could think about was him. Pretending it was him giving her the commands. Guess he will be soon enough. Keeping her composure, she approached and asked, "Is there something you need Drake? I need to talk with Shayla, then I am going home. I could take care of whatever you need first."

You can get on your knees and put my cock in your mouth, Drake thought. "No. Just want to make sure things went well."

"Everything went fine. Mistress Julie is a good teacher and was very informative."

"Good," he said turning and heading back into his office.

Shaking him off, Lila went into Shayla's office.

"Okay girl. Give me the scoop. How did you feel after today?"

"It was fine. Easier to acclimate than I thought. Mistress Julie does a good job."

"I'm sure you did a good job as well. I told you I thought you were sub material. So when you were going through the training, did it turn you on?"

"Not really. It was more about following commands, kneeling, body positions, use of safe words. That kind of stuff."

"Did you think of Drake when you were there?"

"No!" How did she know? Lila wondered.

"Sorry," Shayla said laughing. "I was hoping. I would have been thinking of Drew."

"Of course you would. He's your husband."

"Maybe I would be adventurous and fanaticize about, oh, George Clooney."

"You are too much," Lila said, shaking her head.

"So do you go back tomorrow?"

"Yep. At 6pm. I was told to wear something sexy, including my undergarments. I have a feeling I will be removing some of those said garments."

"I think you are right."

6

The next evening rolled around. Some of the guys already left for the night, including Drake. Thank God. Lila was hoping he would be gone before she changed and headed to *The Manor*. Shayla hung around as she wanted to approve the outfit. Lila brought two just in case.

"You know you need to leave in a half hour. Better start the fashion show," Shayla said, leaning on Lila's desk.

"I was just heading into the restroom to change."

Lila slung her bag over her shoulder and went to change. She chose a black lace thong and matching bra and paired it with a short, tight black dress and high, strappy heels. Lila let her hair down, tousled her curls, and touched up her makeup, adding a scarlet lip. Grabbing her bag, Lila exited the restroom to be greeted by a squeal from Shayla.

"You look hot. Perfect. I do not even need to see what else you brought. Wish I was going to be there to see some tongues wag. Well of course if Julie does not put you through the ringer first."

"Thanks. I guess. You sure this is good?"

"It's perfect."

Whistling came from behind. "Watch out. Here comes a hottie. Is that appropriate coming from your married boss?" Drew said.

"In these circumstances, I think we have surpassed being politically correct."

"You're too funny. By the way I arranged for car service for you. I did not want you to have to drive."

"That was not necessary. I will be fine plus, I will need my car for tomorrow."

"Covered it for tomorrow morning also. It's all arranged, Lila. I am sure Mistress Julie is not going to be that easy on you tonight. She knows you need a crash course. Then you will get your first taste of the open room. It can be overwhelming at first. I do not want you driving home distracted. No argument. Now, the car is ready and you look great."

"Yes, you do. Now get going," Shayla added, giving Lila a hug before she left with the driver.

Lila arrived at *The Manor* and entered the lobby. The others from the group were waiting.

"Yowsa! You are hot, hot, hot." Sam said. "Too bad I am not a Dom."

"Thanks, Sam. You don't look too shabby yourself."

Next thing they knew, a loud snap rang through the air. Turning around, they saw Mistress Julie with a whip in her hand.

"Mouths shut, eyes on me. Follow me, single file, to the training room." Everyone complied with her directive.

"Grab a pillow, stand side by side, and put the pillow on the floor in front of you. Tonight is going to be much different than yesterday. It may be too much for some of you, or at least identify where you need work. We will be working on your senses, first, with a little bit of touch. We will also have a guest Master with us. Before we get started, take off your clothes only leaving on your undergarments. Place your clothes in the cubbies."

Lila and the others did what they were told and went back to stand in front of their pillow. Mistress Julie walked the room, looking each of them up and down. Circling behind them, she took out a leather crop and ran it across each one of them.

"Lovely. You all look so lovely. The best way to test you is to remove one of your senses," she said as she walked over to a drawer and retrieved something.

"Kneel." Everyone quickly followed her instruction. "Take a blindfold and secure it firmly. Do not move, do not peak. Anyone who does not follow my commands will be punished. Five lashings."

Lila quickly secured the blindfold. She heard a door open then soft whispers by Mistress Julie she could not make out. It amazed her how instantly her other senses enhanced by taking away her sight. She heard another set of footsteps enter the room. This must be her guest Master.

"Sam, palms up," Mistress Julie reprimanded as a slap of flesh rang through the room. Sam must have been hit by the Mistress.

"My guest is now among us. I will still be your Mistress. You will follow my commands. Our guest Master will help in the process. Do not speak to him. Do not touch him. Understood?"

"Yes, Mistress," the group said.

Lila could hear the guest Master walking around her. She got a sudden chill by his presence. A strange sensation, one she has only felt with Drake. It must be the anticipation of not knowing what will happen next. Lila jumped when she felt something run across her shoulder blades. The guest Master lightly tapped her on her shoulder. Lila took that to mean 'be still.' Next the crop, or whatever it was, ran up and down her spine. Lila's body tingled wherever he touched.

"Ladies," Lila jumped when she heard Mistress Julie speak, "remove your bras. You should experience the same sensations as your fellow male slaves."

Reaching behind her, Lila unfastened her bra and gently placed it to her side. She heard a slight intake of breath. It must have been the guest Master. Did he find her attractive, or, worse, lacking? Lila quickly got her answer as she felt the cold of leather run across her collar bone, then circle over her right breast. He repeated the process on the left breast. Lila's breathing started to quicken. It was so seductive, turning her on. Like she was when Drake kissed her.

She did not want to be turned on by a stranger, only Drake. To help ease her mind, Lila imagined it was Drake touching her, controlling her. Suddenly a little smack on her nipple brought her back into focus. Ouch, she thought then suddenly a hot sensation engulfed her body. She felt the wetness build between her legs. God, how she wished it was Drake and that he had his hands on her body. She got her wish. Hands went in her hair, running through, grabbing snugly, then around her neck and shoulders. The touch felt so right, felt so perfect, Lila let out a little groan.

"You like that, little girl, don't you," Drake whispered in her ear.

Shocked by the sound of his voice, Lila yelled his name.

Suddenly a hard slap hit her thigh. "I told you not to speak to our guest," Mistress Julie reprimanded firmly.

"Sorry, Mistress Julie."

It was Drake. He was doing this to her. Touching her, making her wet, wanting more.

"I told you no one else would touch you except me, and I meant it," Drake said.

Lila relaxed and let herself embrace the process. It was Drake. For how much he frustrated her, Lila desired him even more. She would take what she could get out of this situation as she knew they would never work. Heck, he did not even like her that much, and he is a love-them-and-leave-them type of man. Not something she needed.

Drake continued to torment Lila. A tickle here, slap there. Touching her was torture. All he wanted to do was pick her up, take her to a private room, and fuck her to oblivion. Seeing her sitting there blindfolded, her golden curls flowing over her shoulders. When she removed her bra, Drake thought he would lose it. Those perfect breasts. He wanted to put them in his mouth and suck until she came. He had to get control of his thoughts.

Drake could not believe how responsive Lila was, especially when he would take the crop to her nipples. With each tap of the crop, more and more color surfaced throughout her entire body. Her breaths quickened, she was reaching for more. His little angel had a wild side. A perfect combination. So much was going through his head. He did not want to get attached to her. She wanted the white picket fence he could not, and would not, give her. For now, he would just enjoy these moments.

"Very good, my little slaves. You all are going to get a short break, and then we will be going into the open room. Most of you will be with me under my command. Lila you will be with our guest Master. I believe you have previously met," Mistress Julie said with a snicker. "Go ahead and remove your blindfolds. Ladies, put your bras back on. Be ready in 20."

Lila removed her blindfold; Drake was towering over her. She locked gazes with him, desire in his expression. Quickly she grabbed her bra and put in back on. Standing, she addresses Drake. "How long did you know you were going to be here?"

"Since yesterday. Julie called and said I should handle your training."

"Really? Did you enjoy yourself?" Lila snapped.

"Oh yes, I did. Remember, little girl, you are under my command when we go into the open room."

"Mistress Julie said we are only observing."

"You will be, but you will do what I say. Lila, you need to be able to convince people you are my sub."

"Do I have to call you Master?"

"You can call me Sir or Drake. I have never been into the Master/Slave persona."

"Fine, *Sir*."

Mistress Julie gathered everyone together. "My sweet little salves. We are now going to go into the open room. There are a few patrons inside, but I anticipate over the next hour the room will fill. You will be exposed to all types of people, and all types of fetishes and activity. It can be overwhelming. Your job is to observe and do as I say. You will not be a participant in any activity, unless I see fit."

The group started to follow Mistress Julie, but Drake grabbed Lila's arm.

"Hold on for a minute," he said as he pulled something out of his pocket. It looked like a choker. "Turn around."

Lila complied, and Drake placed the choker around Lila's neck. Drake guided her shoulders until she was facing him again.

"I want you to wear this until we have finished this op."

"All the time? Work, grocery shopping?"

"Yes. All the time. You need to live the role in order to help embrace being a sub. It will be more convincing. Now let's go."

Gently grabbing her elbow, Drake led her out of the training room, up the grand staircase, and into the open room. It was completely different than she expected. There was a bar in the back left corner. The dark, elegant wood theme continued. Leather couches and chairs were spread throughout the room. There was a main play area in the back center with all kinds of apparatus and some smaller areas to the sides. Drake guided her a little bit away from the group over to a couch with a direct view of the main play area. Drake sat and told Lila to sit on his lap. She started to say something, but Drake cut her off.

"Sit, Lila."

She sat on Drake's lap, and he positioned her legs over his, put his left arm around her and settled her close against him.

"Relax."

Letting out a big exhale, Lila just melted against Drake. She was surprised how good it felt to be in his arms. She felt secure, protected, a feeling that had escaped her in previous relationships. But this was not a relationship. Drake was her boss and they were doing an operation.

A few minutes later, a woman approached and asked if they would like a drink. Before Lila could respond, Drake ordered a beer and a water.

"I will decide what you drink tonight. I do not want any impairment. You need to see what really goes on."

"Yes Sir," Lila said with a little annoyance in her voice. "Am I allowed to ask you any questions tonight?"

"Of course, but if we are approached by others, do not speak unless I tell you that you can."

"Fine." Drake raised his eyebrows in question. "I mean, yes Sir."

The waitress brought back the drinks, and Lila noticed two men and a woman approach the main play area. She was a petite blonde. Probably around thirty years old. The men were slightly older. They leaned the little blonde against something that almost looked like a horse used in gymnastics and started kissing her while their hands started to explore her body.

Drake, watching Lila's reactions, saw surprise, only to be followed by interest, in her expression.

"Those are the Johnson-Pratt's. They are a throple."

"What?"

"All three of them are in a relationship together."

"Wow, really?"

"Yes, really."

"Do, do . . . the men . . . ?"

"No. The guys are not gay. They just share Kimberly."

"How does that work? Wouldn't someone get jealous?"

"I am sure that could happen, but it works for them. They have been together for several years."

"I do not think I could ever do that. Are you into that sort of thing?"

"I would be lying if I said I have not participated in three-somes, but no, I could not share the woman I claimed. You seem to like what you see. Do you want to try a threesome?"

"The idea is kind of exciting, but if I was in a relationship, I could not imagine someone else having sex with me. I know I could not share my man with another woman."

Lila watched as they started taking the blonde's clothes off, next they put her on the bench, face down. One of the guys bound her hands underneath. Her head rested on the bench, but she was close enough to the front. Her hips were bent over the other end, with her private parts exposed for all to see. The taller man took off his belt, bends it in half, and struck the blonde on her ass, the noise echoing throughout the room. What mesmerized Lila the most was the look on the blonde's face. Pleasure entranced her. The lashes continued over different parts of her ass and thighs. The other man went to her and pulled out his fully erect cock and put it in her mouth. Holding onto her head, he controlled how fast and how deep he went. Next thing Lila knew, the other man stopped the lashes, stripped, and was riding the blonde hard from behind. He was relentless, not letting up.

Focusing back on the other guy who was overtaking her mouth, Lila looked just in time to see him pull out and ejaculate all over her upper back. The man pounding her from behind yelled, "Don't you come," as his relentless pursuit continued. The other man walked around and started fondling the blonde's bud as the onslaught continued. "Now," he yelled, and pure utter ecstasy spread across the blonde's face as she screamed out in orgasm. The man then pulled out and ejaculated on her backside. The little blonde was quivering, still reeling in the aftermath of her orgasm. Gently, the men simultaneously cleaned her off, started kissing and caressing her body. The bindings were removed, and the dark-haired man picked her up and carried her to a couch as the other followed behind with her clothes.

Lila could not take her eyes off them. The love in their eyes toward the little blonde was unmistakable. Lila realized she was staring as well as how turned on she was. Lila turned and looked at Drake, their eyes holding. She knew he was aware of her arousal. Breaking eye contact, Lila just looked around the room. Anything to not look at Drake. If she did, she would probably jump him then and there.

Edward was moving about the room and approached Drake and Lila. "So how is our lovely sub's training going?"

Lila went to speak, but Drake lightly pinched her arm reminding her of his instruction.

"She is doing well. Better than I expected."

"Wonderful. I knew she was a natural."

"That she seems to be."

"Well, I will leave you two. Keep in touch and keep me informed of any new information."

"Will do, Edward."

Edward moved on, greeting others in the open room. Drake and Lila stayed for another hour when Drake finally spoke.

"Time to go," he said as he patted her hip.

"I need to check with Edward about my ride. Drew said it was taken care of."

"I'm your ride, Lila. Let's go."

Lila was hoping to get away from Drake. Now she would have to spend another half hour with him, alone. She needed to separate herself from him as her emotions were all over the place, along with her libido. Lila retrieved her items from the training room and followed Drake to his truck. He helped her up, given her attire and the height of the door. They were silent for a while.

"You did well tonight."

"Thank you."

"Do you have any questions or was there anything that made you uncomfortable?"

Only you touching me, stroking my desire, she thought. "No. No to both questions. I am sure something will pop up as we move forward."

"Understood. That is one reason I gave you the collar and told you to act as my sub to ensure you are living the part until this op gets started and is over."

"Makes sense."

Drake was turning onto the road of Lila's extended-stay hotel. She was glad to be able to be alone and clear her head. Parking the truck, he exited and came around to get Lila.

"You don't have to walk me in."

"Yes, I do. At least to the door."

They walked inside. Drake followed her to her room, stopping outside her door.

"Well, good night."

Lila started to open her door when realization struck her. "Oh, do you know when the driver will pick me up in the morning?"

"I will be here at 7:30am sharp."

Swallowing the lump that formed, Lila replied, "Okay. Usually I am already in the office by 7:30."

"Not tomorrow. Be ready. I will come up to get you."

Turning to go into her room, Drake tapped Lila on her shoulder. "One more thing," he said as he grabbed her and kissed her. Just like the first time Drake kissed her, Lila immediately melted into the kiss. God he was a good kisser. She imagined him using that tongue on her special spot. Breaking the kiss, Drake looked deep into her now glazed-over eyes.

"Goodnight." Turning on his heels, he walked away. No other words, nothing.

Lila went into her room and decided she needed a cool shower and to somehow get some sleep, which now seemed impossible. She was sure Drake was going to fill her dreams.

7

A s promised, there was a knock on her door at exactly 7:30. Lila had already been up and dressed for an hour. She figured, since sleep was intermittent as she kept waking up aroused dreaming of Drake, she might as well get up and get ready. She needed something to do to clear her mind.

Lila was wearing the collar as directed. Drake's eyes directly zoned in on her neck when she opened the door. A smile flashed across his face, quickly replaced with his normal, unreadable expression.

Drake and Lila rode in silence to the office. Thankfully, the ride was short. Lila's body was already responding just being in his presence. She hurried to her desk as Drake went to his office. Lila busied herself, getting logged in and checking incoming emails.

"Good morning, Lila," Shayla said as she walked toward Lila's desk. "How did it go last night?"

"It was fine."

"Just fine?"

"Yep. Just fine."

Drew approached them before Shayla could say anything

else. "Meeting in 15. Another woman has disappeared. We need to fast forward our plan."

"We'll talk later."

Everyone gathered in the conference room. Lila and Shayla were the last to arrive as they were copying the reports from the FBI on the latest disappearance. All eyes immediately went to Lila, zeroing in on the collar on her neck. Drew and Shayla exchanged looks and smiled.

"So you all know by now another woman has allegedly disappeared. Once again, the last place she was seen was *Pleasure Palace*. We need to re-evaluate our strategy and start this op by the weekend. Edward called and said the training went well. Do you agree?"

Lila looked at Drake and knew to let him answer. "Yes, affirmative."

"And I see you collared Lila."

"She needs to be living the part in order for this op to be successful."

"You know, that is a great idea."

"Thanks."

"I feel in order to have the best cover, Lila needs to fully live the part of your sub."

"I agree. That's why I put the collar on her for the time being."

"I'm thinking more in depth. Lila, you need to move in with Drake."

"What?" they both said in unison.

"It would be the best way for you to really be able to come across as Drake's sub. You need to be able to portray this role well. All of these guys have had a lot of training in covert operations. You have not. I think from this moment on until this op is done, you need to live fully as Drake's sub. It will only enhance your ability to blend in."

"I don't think this cutie could ever blend in. Just look at her," Dallas said winking at Lila.

"Dallas, you know that is not what I mean. Lila, from right now you will only take direction from Drake. You also need—"

"But, I am only supposed to be his sub in training."

"Correct. That's my point."

"I think it's a brilliant idea," Shayla said. Lila immediately began pleading to Shayla with her eyes. Others chimed in, agreeing.

"If she fully assumes the role, I think we can start the op in the next few days. It gives you two days to get in sync. You're going to be in a new place soon anyway, so why not just stay with Drake. By the time the op is over, you will be ready to get your own place."

"But . . ."

"No buts. It's done," Drake said.

"Wait. Don't I get a say?"

"No. You actually don't," Drew said. "Look Lila, I am not trying to sound harsh, but you knew going into this you would be challenged in order to get the job done. This is one of them. It is the best solution for you to pull this off."

"Lila," Drake said firmly.

Hesitantly, Lila looked up and nodded her head yes. "You're right. I agreed."

"Actually, darlin', you came up with the plan," Dallas added.

"True. I will do what you suggest," she said, feeling slightly defeated.

For the next few minutes, Lila sat down in her seat and just listened. The group continued discussing their plans. On Thursday they would go to *Pleasure Palace* to make their faces known.

"Drake and I went over the op plans. Dallas, Jax and Jace, you three will need to be inside the club, but separate. Except

Dallas. You can interact with Drake and Lila. We need someone else she is comfortable around and other patrons can see you two know each other. Jax and Jace will not interact. Lila, make sure you do not let on you know them. Just listen to Drake. Anything else?" Drew asked.

"I will need to check out of the hotel."

"I'm aware," Drake said.

"Good, so now that this obstacle is over, I think we have a good plan in place. Drake will go over any fine details tomorrow before we start surveillance. Have a good evening."

"Wait," Drake barked. "Lila, will you please stand up and come to me."

Lila complied and went and stood in front of Drake.

"Now, please remove your blouse."

"What? Here in front of everyone?"

"Yes, do what I say. Remember it all starts now."

Lila hesitated and Drake added, "Lila, you will be exposed to these guys and a whole bunch of other people during this op. You need to get over any insecurities now. So take off your blouse and give it to me."

Nervously, Lila started unbuttoning her blouse, took it off, folded it and handed it to Drake.

"Now your skirt."

Lila never broke eye contact with Drake the entire time she was undressing. It was weird. Like she was in a trance, no one else was there but her and Drake.

"Good girl. Now kneel."

Immediately Lila went to her knees. Drake grew hard instantly. She was beautiful, compliant. Wearing a pretty little white lace bra and tiny panties. Everyone was silent, observing the interaction between Lila and Drake.

"Your bra please. Take it off and hand it to me."

Lila reached around and released her bra and handed it to Drake. She dropped her eyes, arms resting on her thighs, palms facing up. Drake started caressing her hair. Still silent, the others in the room just looked at each other. Finally, the silence was broken by Dallas.

"Drake, you are a lucky man."

"Yes, I'm aware. You all can go now. See you tomorrow."

Everyone left the room except Drake and Lila. She held her kneeling position. Drake lifted her chin so she would look at him.

"Thank you, Lila. You did good. Stand up please."

She did without hesitation or words. Drake slowly started dressing her. Once he was done, he gave her a slow, soft kiss on her lips.

"Beautiful. Now can you gather your things? I need to speak with Drew before we leave."

"I need to talk to Shayla. Is that okay?" she asked quietly.

"Yes. Get your things. Talk to Shayla. I will get you from Shayla's office, and then we can get you checked out of the hotel."

Lila went and retrieved her things from behind her desk and walked into Shayla's office, collapsed in a chair, putting her hands over her face. Shayla immediately came around and hugged Lila.

"Are you okay?"

"Yes."

"You sure? What are you feeling? I bet all that was a lot to take in."

"Yes it was, but not what you think."

"What do you mean?"

"I had a lot of emotions, but it was about my feelings for Drake. It felt like no one else was there but us. I could not see anyone, hear anything, but him. This sudden need to please him . . . it was overwhelming."

"It was beautiful," Shayla said softly.

"What?"

"You two looked so connected. Such a beautiful Dom and Sub moment."

"But we aren't, that is the problem. How can I allow myself to let go and get personal with him, while still staying focused on the op. Then it will all stop when it is over. I do not know if I could return to normal."

"Just focus on the op and on the moment. Take one day at a time."

"You're right. One day, one moment at a time," Lila said just as a knock sounded and Drake peaked his head into Shayla's office.

DRAKE HELPED Lila pack and check out of her hotel. Few words were spoken throughout the process. Drake recognized Lila's need for quiet. Leaving the hotel, Lila noticed they were heading in the direction of Drew and Shayla's house. Drake never spoke about where he lived. She presumed he had a condo or something more toward the hip communities, closer to the nightlife. To her surprise, Drake pulled into the same gated community as Drew and Shayla's house.

"Why are we here? Do you need to stop by Drew and Shayla's?"

"No. My home is also in this community."

"Really . . . but why? It's just you. All these homes are quite large and full of families."

"I like my space, and who knows, one day maybe I will share my home with someone."

Lila was surprised when he pulled up to a beautiful white Southern-styled version of a cape cod. It had a huge front porch and was not what she expected.

"This is beautiful. I did not picture you in this type of home."

"I like Southern charm. It relaxes me and reminds me of a slower pace. A good contrast to the rest of my life."

Drake pulled into one of the garage doors and grabbed Lila's bags. They entered through a side door inside the garage which spilled into a large mud room, similar to Shayla and Drew's. The mud room connected to a beautiful kitchen. Lining the walls were tall white cabinets; some of the cabinets had glass fronts, a huge island centered the room and was a deep dark wood. Light gray quartz countertops graced all the cabinetry. The kitchen was beautiful, a dream kitchen along with top of the line appliances. Lila would love to cook in this kitchen.

Drake, observing her facial expressions, asked if she likes the kitchen.

"Oh, yes. It is beautiful. Cooking would be marvelous in a kitchen like this, so much space. Perfect for baking."

"Well, we will probably order out tonight as I don't have much here. Follow me."

Lila nodded and followed Drake down a wide hall to a set of stairs by the front door. A beautiful curved staircase with wrought iron spindles and dark wood floors with white contrast curved to an open area at the top. Drake went to the right and entered an immensely large bedroom. It looked to be the master bedroom, so Lila asked.

"Is this your room?"

"Yes."

"I don't want to take your room."

"You're not, you're sharing with me."

"What, but . . . why? I can use a guest room."

"Lila, no arguments. You will sleep here and get used to me being close."

Lila mumbled something under her breath, which did not go unnoticed by Drake.

"What did you say?"

"Nothing."

"Don't lie to me little girl. What did you mumble?"

"I said I wonder how many women have been in this bed," she said a little too forcibly.

"None. Until now."

Lila was momentarily speechless. How could that be? Drake was not a saint and had to have been with a lot of women.

"You seem surprised."

"I am. It's . . . it's just . . . I suspect you have had your fair share of women."

"I have, Lila, but this is my home. I have not wanted to bring a woman back here."

"But I'm here."

"Yes, yes you are."

After that comment, Drake went inside a large closet and started to unpack her clothes. Lila followed.

"I can do that."

"No, I got it. This side will be yours. Why don't you put away your toiletries? You can have the right sink and drawers. They should be empty."

Lila grabbed her small bag and headed through a set of doors which led to the master bathroom. It was spacious and as beautiful as the kitchen. Dark cabinets with the same gray quartz countertops adorned the room. Light tiles and walls created an elegant contrast. There was a separate shower with multiple shower heads on both sides, which looked like it could hold a lot of people, and a large deep soaking tub made for two. Lila started putting her stuff away. Well, at least Drake is neat and tidy like me, she thought as she looked around.

"Hey Lila, how about a pizza tonight?"

She jumped at the sudden intrusion. "Oh God, you scared me."

"Sorry. Pizza?"

"Sure. That's fine. Just no anchovies or pineapple. Anything else is fine by me."

"Good. I'll order. Why don't you shower and relax until the food gets here. The towels are in here," Drake said opening a linen closet door.

"Okay."

Lila took a nice long shower. It was wonderful using the various settings in water pressure and sprays. Very fancy dancy, like she was at a luxurious spa. She could get used to this. A beautiful home, gorgeous man, a family, Lila thought, letting her mind wander. Realizing she was just standing under the stream of the shower daydreaming, Lila shut off the valve and dried off. Combing out her damp hair, she kept it down to air dry. She put on a comfy pair of shorts and a tank top and left the bedroom. Since she could hear Drake downstairs, she took a moment to snoop through the rest of the upstairs. On the other side of the staircase were three other bedrooms. One was furnished with its own private bathroom. The other two were unfurnished and shared a Jack and Jill bathroom. A perfect family home.

Lila went downstairs and looked around some more. To the left of the front door was a large formal dining room. There was a large table with seating for ten with a hutch against the wall. The look was not formal nor casual. It was simple, but nice. Matched the house's southern elegance.

To the right was a large office with glass-front doors. Lila peaked through the glass and noticed a large dark wood desk with bookshelves behind it. The walls were painted a light gray with white trim. Again, a nice contrast in colors just like the rest of the house.

The wide hall led back to the kitchen where she found Drake. Off the kitchen was a huge great room with a large stone fireplace. The back wall was all windows, like Drew and Shayla's, and opened up to an expansive deck.

"Pizza will be here any minute. Here," he said handing her a beer. "Figured we can kick back, watch a movie, and relax a bit. We are going to have a lot going on very soon."

"Okay," Lila said just as the doorbell rang. Drake excused himself and paid for the pizza.

"Can you grab the plate?"

"Sure, but there is only one."

"We only need one," Drake said, surprising Lila.

Drake grabbed the pizza box, some napkins, and opened a door off the kitchen. It led to a basement. To the right, the basement opened up to a huge family room. A massive television was on the far end, surrounded by a huge sectional and a recliner. The other side hosted a bar and a pool table. Lila followed Drake to the sectional.

"Sit. Is an action movie okay?"

"Sure."

Drake selected a movie then got out a slice of pizza. Pepperoni and bacon. Yum.

"Open."

Drake put the slice up to Lila's mouth. She took a bite, and then he did off the same piece. He was feeding her. Why did this seem so intimate, so personal, something two lovers would do. Drake kept giving her bites, a couple times wiped her mouth with a napkin. Some women would be offended by this act, feel like they were being treated like a child, but for some reason it made her feel special. Taken care of and cherished.

"Let me know when you have had enough."

"Okay."

They continued this process for a little while until Lila motioned she was full. Drake ate another piece then got up to put the pizza away and grabbed another beer. He patted his lap and encouraged Lila to lay down.

"Thanks for dinner."

"You're welcome."

They stayed like this, Drake stroking her face or hair, while they watched the movie. Next thing Lila knew, she was being carried up the stairs to the bedroom.

"What's going on?" she asked.

"You fell asleep. I am putting you to bed."

"I'm sorry."

"No apology necessary."

When they got to the bedroom, Drake put Lila down, pulled back the covers and looked at Lila. "Arms up."

"What?"

"Please lift up your arms."

She did, and Drake removed her tank top, then pulled off her shorts and panties until she was standing there fully naked. Drake's eyes gazed over her body. She was bare down below, just like he liked it, and a desire to bury his face into her sweet center rushed over him.

"You need to use the bathroom?"

Shaking her head no, Drake gestured toward the bed. Lila climbed in. Drake went into the bathroom and came out in only a pair of boxer briefs. God, that man was built like a god. Perfect. Not an ounce of fat. He got into bed, pulled her to him, and turned out the light.

"Goodnight."

"Goodnight," Lila replied wondering how she would fall asleep being naked next to Drake. Why did he get to keep his briefs on if she was naked? Figuring she needed to stop questioning everything, Lila snuggled in closer and quickly fell back to sleep.

8

H ands were all over her body, touching all the right places. Lips licking and sucking her breasts, slowly moving south, down her abdomen, closer, closer, closer to that sweet—Gasping, Lila sat up with a start.

"Have a nice dream?"

Startled, she turned to see Drake, almost forgetting where she was. "No," she replied grumpily. This was all she needed, to wake up turned on and unsatisfied. How could he sleep with her naked all night and not touch her? It was torment, cruel even. Lila knew he was the reason for her vivid dream.

"You got thirty minutes, then we are heading in. We'll grab breakfast on the way. Wear training gear. That's today's plan."

"Fine."

Laughing internally, Drake could tell she was pissed. He knew Lila was aroused. She was talking in her sleep, mumbling his name and where she wanted him to touch her, squirming and touching herself. It took everything in his power not to touch her all night, especially when she started dreaming. It was pure hell. Drake just wanted to bury himself deep inside her hot channel, but knew he couldn't. He needed to be patient, needed her to be worked up by tomorrow night. Lila needed to be able to let go, lose control when they visited *Pleasure Palace*. Convince everyone she was his sub.

Lila came downstairs in exactly thirty minutes. Her expression tense. She followed Drake to his truck, not saying a word as they headed to the office. They went to a local coffee house and got a breakfast sandwich. Lila was surprised when Drake handed her a tea, just the way she liked it. How does he know what I like? He must pay attention more than she realized. It shouldn't surprise her; keen observation is a necessary skill in his line of work.

They arrived at the office, and when Lila went to head to her desk, Drake told her to follow him. They went to his office, put down their bags, just as Drew peaked in the doorway.

"Y'all ready?"

"Yes," Drake responded.

"Lila, don't worry about any of the office stuff until the op is over. Shayla's got it. Just follow Drake's lead and work on prepping for tomorrow."

Lila just nodded.

"We're working with Rocco, Dallas, and the twins today while the rest get the surveillance equipment set up and ready."

"Sounds like a plan," Drew said.

"You ready?"

"Yes, sir. Just need to use the restroom."

Drake was waiting by the door when she exited, a serious look spread across his face.

"We're going to work on multiple attackers training, just in case you get put in this type of situation. We will be with you the entire time, so I doubt it will occur, but if we are ambushed, you need to know what to do. I would rather you be prepared if something goes awry."

They went to the Dome where the rest of the guys were waiting. Lila was a little withdrawn, worried about how the others would act around her after yesterday's striptease in the conference room, especially Rocco. They had a father/daughter type relationship, and she did not want him to feel awkward.

"Hey y'all. You ready for some fightin' darlin'?" Dallas said as he approached them.

"Yes," Lila said softly.

Dallas came up to her, kissed her on the cheek, and whispered in her ear. "Don't be embarrassed about yesterday. You know it was necessary, and you were a beautiful, perfect little sub responding to her Dom. You're a natural."

"Y'all done flirting?" Drake asked sternly.

"Aw shucks, I'm not flirtin'. I know she's claimed," Dallas said with a grin.

"Hey, sweet girl," Rocco said. "You ready to take on these buffoons?"

"You know it." Lila was always relaxed around Rocco. Rocco and Drake gave her some direction on dealing with multiple opponents and started putting it to practice. They started out slowly, going over different scenarios with Dallas, Jax, and Jace. After a few hours of training, they all took a break as the intercom went off and Shayla announced lunch had arrived. The group went up and met the rest of the crew in the lunchroom.

"So, how's it going?" Trent asked.

"She's doing well. It would be ideal to have more practice, but time is something we do not have," Rocco said.

"She'll be fine. We won't leave her alone," Drake added.

"I'm just in awe, Lila. I could not do what you are doing," Shayla said.

"Yes, you could."

"No, Lila. You have instincts I don't."

"Where are we with the equipment," Drake asked.

"Everything is falling into place. Matt and Garrett have the van almost finished. I am finalizing the final piece and will be hacking into the *Palace's* security system soon," Trent replied.

"Is everything staying on track with the training? What are you going to work on this afternoon?" Drew asked.

"Restraints," Drake said.

"Restraints?" Lila questioned.

"Yes, restraints. Worst-case scenario preparation. If you get restrained, what would you do and can you get yourself out."

"I thought the sub was not supposed to get out of her restraints."

"We are not talking about my restraints."

"Oh."

Finishing lunch, they cleaned up, and everyone resumed their work. Lila went back to the Dome with the group to go over restraints. First they started with rope. Rocco and Drake showed her different ways to position her body to allow her to get out of the ropes. Dallas, Jax and Jace then tied her up as if they were trying to contain her. It took several tries before Lila grasped what to do.

After being successful with rope, they went over a few other types of restraints an assailant may use. A few more hours passed; Lila was exhausted so they called it a day.

On the short drive to Drake's house, Lila was already dozing off. Drake took this opportunity to just look at her, really look at her. She amazed him and scared him at the same time. How could someone so strong, stubborn, and smart also be soft, sweet, and desirable? She was the complete package, and this draw to her, this need to be with her, scared the shit out of him. He had never allowed a woman to get close. It was not ideal in his line of work, nor had he ever met a woman who fit the perfect profile of what he would want in a woman, until Lila. Sure, she frustrated the hell out of him at times, but it just made him want her more. Drake pulled into the garage and tapped Lila on the shoulder.

"We're home."

Slowly coming to her senses, Lila stretched. "Goodness. Sorry I fell asleep."

"You worked hard today. Why don't you go up, take a bath, and relax. I will grill out tonight, and you can get to bed early. Tomorrow is going to be a long day."

Following Drake into the house, Lila went straight to the master bathroom. A bath sounded divine. Adding some bath salts to the tub, Lila turned on the tap. Once there was enough water, she slid in, laid back, and just soaked. It was very relaxing, and the bath salts helped ease her sore muscles.

Shivering, Lila startled herself. She must have fallen asleep again. Looking at her wrinkled fingers, she figured she must have been in the tub for a while. Getting out, she dried off and put on some comfy clothes and went downstairs to find Drake. Drake had the doors to the deck open, and the aroma of something delicious filled her senses.

"Hey."

"Oh, hey there. Did you fall asleep again?" he asked.

"Apparently. What smells so good?"

"Some pork chops and vegetables. You have good timing. It's almost done," Drake said as he was pulling the food off the grill.

Lila's mouth started to water breathing in the succulent aroma. Following Drake into the house, she waited as he started cutting up the chops, once again grabbing one plate.

"Could you grab a glass of iced tea?"

"Sure." She grabbed some tea and followed Drake into the great room. He turned on the television and put on re-runs of *Friends*. Drake kept surprising her. She never thought he would like the show *Friends*, one of her favorites.

"Come here," Drake said as he patted the cushion next to him. Without a word Lila sat next to Drake and they started eating, just like the night before. He would give her a bite, then take one for himself. They finished dinner and watched a few episodes before calling it a night. Drake loaded the dishes into the dishwasher, and then they both went upstairs. When Lila went to get into the bed, Drake told her to stop.

"Strip."

"Excuse me?" Lila questioned.

"I said strip. No clothes, just like last night."

When Lila once again started to protest, Drake just said her name. That was all she needed to stop her from arguing. She removed her clothes. Drake looked her over for a moment then went into the closet. He came out with something that looked like straps.

"What are those for?"

"Tonight, I am going to bind you to the bed."

"How will I be able to sleep?"

"Don't worry. I will make sure you are comfortable. Now get into bed."

Lila laid on the bed, and Drake placed the soft bindings on her wrists then attached them to the spindles in the headboard. She had slack in the bindings so she could move her arms some.

"What if I need to use the bathroom?"

"Wake me, and I will release you."

"Do you think this is necessary?"

"Yes."

Yes. That's all he said as he covered Lila with the blanket, hopped into bed, and turned off the lights. She must have fallen asleep quickly as she did not remember much after Drake got into bed.

Lila was surprised she was able to sleep given the bindings. She woke up when she felt Drake roll over and put his arm across her body. He snuggled close. Lila felt his erection. His large, rigid cock pressed against her hip. If she was not bound to the bed she would roll him over onto his back, straddle him, and ride him until she exploded. Suddenly he started rubbing her rib cage. Goose bumps formed all over from his touch. It was glorious and torture at the same time. Lila glanced at the clock, 5:30am, almost time to get up. She laid as still as possible, trying to ignore the sensations; but the combination of her nakedness, the rubbing, and Drake's large erection, set Lila's libido on fire. She needed to move, to get some space away from Drake or she would soon be begging him to take her.

"Drake? Drake?" Lila said softly. She had to nudge him with her knee to get him to wake up.

"What? What's wrong?" Drake finally said."

"I need to use the bathroom."

Coming to his senses, he realized he was practically on top of her.

"Sorry," he said as he released the bindings. Lila quietly got up, grabbed the clothes she had on last night, and went into the bathroom. After taking care of business, she decided to take a tepid shower. Maybe the shower and some distance would tone down her desire. She needed to be able to focus on this operation. Tonight was the first night.

After Lila finished her shower and was getting ready to exit the bathroom, she ran smack dab into Drake. Her arms instinctively raised, landing on his bare chest. Hesitating briefly, Lila slowly slid her hands down and off his chest. So much for the tepid shower.

"I'm going to go make us something for breakfast since we are already up and have plenty of time. Is that good with you?"

"Sure. If you can find enough stuff."

"I'll see what I can come up with."

Lila quickly left the bedroom and went down to the kitchen. Cooking something would distract her from thinking about Drake's half naked, hard body. She looked around and found enough in the refrigerator to make omelets. Ten minutes later, Drake appeared dressed for the day.

"What smells so good?"

"Just spinach and feta omelets. Sit down, it's almost ready."

"You want a drink?" Drake said as he went to grab a glass.

"Sure, water will be just fine." Lila served up the omelets, and they ate at the large center island.

"This is wonderful."

"It's just a simple omelet, Drake."

"But you cooked it perfectly. Thanks."

"No problem."

"Why don't you go ahead and get ready. Grab anything you will need for tonight while I clean up the dishes."

"Okay," Lila got up and headed to the bedroom. This was a strange, very domestic-in-nature interaction with Drake. Don't get comfortable, she said to herself as she got dressed and grabbed her makeup, items for her hair, and a few other things she may need for the first visit to the *Pleasure Palace*. Shayla was taking her shopping today to get outfits for the op. Shayla said she needed to play the part, thus the need for appropriate clothing. Who was she to argue? She was new to this, and Shayla lived the lifestyle.

As Lila and Drake headed to the office, he asked, "So what's your agenda before we prep for the op tonight?"

"I have a little bit of paperwork I am going to help Shayla with, then we are going shopping for 'appropriate' clothes," she said using her hands to make quotation marks.

"Shayla does have a sense of what would be appropriate for the club. Are you ready?"

"Sure. It shouldn't take too long to get what's needed."

"I meant for tonight."

Hesitating just for a moment before responding, Lila looked at Drake. "Yes. Ready as I can be."

"We'll find out, won't we?"

Shayla took Lila to an exquisite boutique that had the most elegant and sexy lingerie, sexy dresses and outfits, and other fetish items suitable for the operation. From the outside it looked like a typical store front in the upscale neighborhood, but inside would surprise most. The boutique was by appointment only, and clients were buzzed in upon arrival. They catered to high-end clients and, by being appointment only, allowed their patrons privacy during their shopping experience. As they browsed the boutique, they picked out several outfits and Lila started trying them on. Shayla insisted they get several outfits and appropriate lingerie to match.

"You look good in everything," Shayla said as Lila modeled the last dress. "I think you should wear this one tonight. We should also get you the red and silver dresses. Do you need shoes to go with them?"

"I only have the black strappy stilettos I wore to *The Manor*."

"Those will be perfect with this and the silver dress. I think boots would be perfect to go with the red dress. What size?"

"Eight."

"Be back in a flash."

Shayla went off and returned a few moments later with over the knee, high heeled boots. Lila tried them on. The fit was good, and the boots were surprisingly comfortable.

"Perfect," Shayla said. "I think we have enough for now. Hopefully this op won't take long. If we need more, we'll get it."

Checking out, Lila was dumbfounded at how much everything cost. The bill totaled over $1,500, and Shayla did not even blink an eye. While Lila had money now, she still was frugal and had never spent this much on clothes. She still had not been able to get used to purchasing luxury items.

Returning to the office, they brought lunch for the crew as everyone had been busy preparing for tonight. After lunch, the team met to go over the plan one more time.

Drake started the meeting. "Jax and Jace, you two will be

on the outskirts. Blend in. Obviously you will draw attention since you are twins, but you know what to do. Mentally note anything that seems out of place. Be there before we arrive. Dallas, you will arrive about 30-60 minutes after we do. You will hang with us to show others we are acquainted. Trent and Matt will be in the van monitoring all the audio and video feeds. Garrett watch the outside, be a ghost.

"Roger."

"Rocco, you and Drew will be here picking up the video feeds and to be a second team monitoring, be another set of eyes."

"We have everything here and in the van ready," Trent said. "All your devices are also ready to go."

"Good, Lila?"

"Yes, sir."

Drake slightly grinned at her response. "I need you ready by 1900 hours."

"I'll have her ready," Shayla said.

"The van needs to be in place by 1700 hours to ensure Rocco and Drew are receiving the transmission."

"Got it," Trent said.

"Alright. I think we are set. Do what y'all need to do before show time."

Lila went to Shayla's office, kicked back, and tried to relax. "What time do you think we should start getting me ready?"

"I say you have about an hour. Then you can shower, and we will get you perfect. All eyes will be on you. We want you to stand out. Not like you don't already."

"I don't stand out. You do. Grecian Goddess."

"Oh, please. Do you still not realize how beautiful you are? Trust me, you will have the eyes of many Doms tonight, and I guarantee you will make some subs jealous."

The ladies talked for a bit until it was time to get ready. Shayla insisted on doing Lila's hair and makeup. They started getting Lila ready around 5:30pm to ensure they had plenty of time. Shayla carefully dried Lila's curls to guarantee they stayed perfect ringlets cascading down her back. Next came the makeup. Lila really did not need much, but Shayla said she needed a bold statement.

She kept the eye makeup minimal except for her luscious lashes topping everything off with a bold, scarlet lip. Lila's lips would be the focal point of the look. That was not quite true as her light, ocean blue eyes shone brightly as well.

Lila dressed in the new undergarments and dress. She was not wearing a bra as the design of the dress did not allow for one. Once everything was put together, she did a spin for Shayla's approval.

"Perfect. You look stunning," Shayla said. "Everyone will be eating out of the palm of your hand."

"I thought as a sub they would have me in their palms."

"Oh, sweetie. You do realize the sub actually has all of the control."

"What do you mean?"

"You know your safe words, right?"

"Yes."

"Well, if you use one of your safe words, everything stops. A Dom should only give or do what you can take within your limits. You, Lila, actually have the ultimate control."

"Interesting. I never thought about it from that perspective. By giving up control, I am actually in control?"

"Exactly. Now are you ready to go?"

Lila nodded, and Shayla and Lila exited Shayla's office and walked down to the tech room. When the door opened, all eyes went straight to Lila. Drew, Rocco, Dallas, and Drake were in the room.

"Yowza. Aren't you a hot tamale," Dallas said.

"Thank you Dallas, you're looking mighty spiffy yourself," Lila said as she noticed both Dallas and Drake had changed.

Drake's eyes bored into Lila. Could she get any sexier? he thought. She wore a skin-tight, short, black dress with multiple shear panels strategically covering the most intimate parts of her body.

Her long, beautiful legs led to a pair of "come fuck me" stilettos. An abundance of curls fell loosely over her shoulders and down her back, and her lips, those lips, deep red. All he could picture was those lips wrapped around his cock.

"Lila, you think you have everything down? This is the real deal," Drew said breaking Drake away from his thoughts.

"I believe so."

"No, you're missing one thing. Rocco," Drake said.

He handed Drake a longish black object. "This is a collar. As my 'sub' you will need to wear this to let others know you are taken, already spoken for."

"But I already have on the one you gave me previously."

"This is a new one."

Drake showed the collar to Lila. It was about a ½" wide, black, and had what appeared to be four rhinestones across the front.

He held it up. "This is more than a collar, Lila. Each stone is actually a piece of equipment. The far right is a tracker. It will beacon your location. The second to the right is a small camera, third is audio, and the last is a battery. To activate them, all you need to do is click the back of each one, except the battery, of course. It will vibrate to let you know it was activated. Here let me put it on you so you can test it."

Lila turned, and Drake placed the collar on her neck. His hands paused on her shoulders, then rubbed down her arms.

This moment seemed real, not just for the operation.

Turning back around facing Drake, their eyes met and they shared a brief moment before anyone spoke.

"Try the buttons so we can make sure you can activate them."

Lila clicked them, starting in the order explained. She pinched the first one and felt a small vibration. Within seconds she heard a beep from one of the computers.

"Tracker's working," Rocco said.

She followed the same process with the remaining two. Images of Drake's body appeared on the large screen, coming from the camera on the collar.

"Can you go over to the other side of the room and whisper something so we can see if the audio is working?" Drew asked.

Lila did as requested and received a thumbs up. Walking back over to the group, Drake asked if she was ready. Lila confirmed with a nod. Shayla grabbed her in a hug. "You will do great. Just listen to Drake."

"I will."

"Exactly. Listen to Drake. Tonight is only to make yourselves known at *Pleasure Palace*. You do not need to look for anything suspicious. The guys will do that. You need to look like the sub he is training," Drew said.

Rocco came up to Lila. "You look beautiful, sweet girl. Relax and listen to Drake."

"I promise," Lila said, hugging then kissing Rocco on the cheek.

"See y'all there in a bit," Dallas added.

"Affirmative. Let's go."

They headed out, but instead of going to his truck, he led her in the direction of a sleek sports car. "Whose is this?"

"We keep a variety of vehicles available as needed. Don't want to use our personal vehicles. Plates and registrations are under fictitious names just in case someone wants to run the tags. Oh before I forget, I have a fake driver's license for you. We are still using our first names. Just different last names. It should not be necessary, but you will be Lila Smith. Easy to remember."

"Okay, that's easy enough."

They headed to *Pleasure Palace*. The club was located in the heart of Dallas, in an area mixed with bars and nightlife. It took them about a half hour to get there. Drake pulled up in front, exited, and came around to open the door for Lila. He handed a man the keys and in return received a valet ticket. Entering the club, first through metal detectors, Drake handed the attendant a $100 entry fee and their driver's licenses. Lila could already hear the pulse of music. The attendant welcomed them, handed back their identification, and then buzzed the door for their entry.

Drake guided Lila in. He whispered in her ear, "Follow my lead. Don't talk to anyone unless I nod. I want you to relax and blend in as much as possible. Tonight is to be seen only. Okay?"

Lila nodded in agreement.

This place was nothing like *The Manor*. There was a small lounge area. To the right a sign said employees only. To the left, signs indicated private rooms, restrooms, and an emergency exit. Straight ahead was the main room, or as their sign indicated, Dungeon. They entered the Dungeon and like *The Manor*, there was a bar, main play area, and seating around the room. The similarities ended there. Where *The Manor* was elegantly adorned, *Pleasure Palace* was the opposite. It fit the stereotype those not part of the scene would imagine a dungeon to be. It was black and red and tacky.

Drake led them over to the bar. He got them both a beer, Lila lifting up her eyebrow at his order. "Tonight I want you to relax," he whispered. "Don't worry, you won't get much," he said as he escorted her toward some chairs. Drake once again had Lila sit on his lap. She noticed Jax and Jace at the far left of the room chatting with a few women.

"Subs without a Dom will come out looking for fun for the night. That's who is talking to the guys."

"Okay," Lila said without looking back at them.

Only one couple was up on the main play area. It was still a little early, just about 9pm, but people steadily arrived.

Lila watched the couple. The guy was taking a whip to the woman, hard. She cried out with each lash, her body quickly turned red. The man pulled out his penis and forced it into the woman's mouth holding her head still as he pounded relentlessly. The brutal assault shocked Lila. She was doing everything she could not to react to the onslaught she was witnessing.

"Everyone is different Lila. She is fine and probably is into pain and degradation. You notice she hasn't used her safe word."

"Do you like that type of . . . interaction?"

"No, not like that. A little sting to wake up the senses is fine, but I prefer both parties to enjoy the act. A very heavy hand is not my thing."

The man removed himself from the woman's mouth and began the same assault on her mound while twisting her nipples at the same time. A few minutes later she heard the man yell "now" and the woman screamed out in orgasm. The man followed.

Lila was dumfounded. Just as the couple left the play area, Lila still processing what just occurred, a man approached them and introduced himself.

"Hello. I'm Marcus. I don't recall seeing you two here before."

Shaking his hand, Drake responded, "I'm Drake, and this is Lila."

"Nice to meet you, Drake. He moved his hand toward Lila. She looked at Drake for direction. Drake nodded, and Lila stuck out her hand. "Nice to meet you, Marcus."

Marcus kissed her hand. "Ah. Aren't you a good little slave, getting permission from her Master."

Lila instantaneously got a sick feeling in her stomach but did not let it show. She was not sure what it was, but this man made her immediately uneasy. Sitting down without an invitation, Marcus started asking questions. "So, you two new here?"

"I've been here before, but it has been some time. Lila is new to the scene. It's her first time here."

"Ooh, fresh meat." Marcus rubbed his hands together. "Do you ever share?" he asked not taking his eyes off Lila.

"Not usually. Sometimes, with significant limits. She is in training, so I am taking my time."

"You must be a patient man. I'm sure most here would not be able to contain themselves with this beauty."

"Maybe not."

"You going to play later?" Marcus asked just as Dallas approached with two beers in his hands.

Probably," Drake said turning to greet Dallas. "Dallas. Hey man. Glad you could stop by. This is Marcus, and this is Lila, the sub I told you about."

"Well, hey there Marcus. Nice to meet you. May I?"

Drake nodded at Dallas.

"Hello there, darlin'. Aren't you a ray of sunshine," Dallas said, using his usual line again on Lila.

Not missing a beat, Lila looked to Drake for permission.

"You can say hello to Dallas."

"Hello, Dallas. Nice to meet you," Lila said playing along.

Dallas took and kissed the back of Lila's hand. "I look forward to getting to know you better, Lila."

"Likewise."

Marcus sat and chatted a bit with Drake and Dallas. While she knew Drake, Dallas, and the other guys were Doms, Lila got a totally different vibe about Marcus. The first word that came to her mind was snake. Sleazy, slithery, untrustworthy snake. She would act normal and hold her thoughts until later, when he was gone.

"Well, gentlemen, it was a pleasure meeting you. I see the people I am meeting have arrived. Drake, all I will say is you are a lucky man. Hope to see you play tonight and see you around here often."

"Nice to meet you, too," Drake and Dallas said, each shaking Marcus' hand.

"Lila, such a beauty. Nice meeting you as well," Marcus said as he touched the side of her face. It took everything in her power not to smack his hands off or shiver from his touch.

Drake repositioned Lila on his lap as Marcus walked away. "He seemed nice," Dallas said.

"I agree, maybe we should get a little closer to see if he has any information," Drake whispered. "Jax, Jace you copy? Good." They must have responded through their ear buds, Lila thought.

"I don't like him," Lila said.

"Why? He seemed fine."

"Just a feeling. I immediately felt uncomfortable around him."

"Nah. He's probably fine. You just have not been around people in this lifestyle," Dallas said.

Lila kept her mouth shut and didn't say anything else. She still had a negative feeling about Marcus. Maybe he just was one of those creepy Doms that liked weird stuff, thus the funky vibes he exuded. Getting him out of her mind, Lila watched two men who were now to the side of the main play area. She was mesmerized as she had never seen two men together in an intimate setting. Well, if you can call performing sexual acts in front of a group of people intimate. The men were kissing and caressing each other's bodies. One man was already undressed, only in his underwear. The taller man with a beard pulled away and said something to his partner. The man turned around and the man with the beard bound his wrists, turned him around, and ordered him to his knees. Unbuttoning his trousers, he removed is already growing cock. Grabbing it firmly, he told his partner to open and entered his mouth. Slowly, in long smooth strokes, he moved in and out of his mouth. His partner, eager to quicken the pace, was reprimanded by the bearded man who grabbed each side of his face to control the pace.

Lila was awestruck. She did not see two men, just two lovers pleasing and loving each other. Truly connected. The bearded man, who she presumed was the Dom, held tight on his partners head, quickening the pace of his strokes. A few moments later he groaned, pulled away from his partner's mouth, and spilled himself all over his chest. Lila watched the Dom clean up his partner, still entranced in the moment; she almost did not hear Drake call her name as she was focused on the intimacy of the two men.

"Lila."

"Yes, sir."

"Stand up, please."

Lila stood; Drake gently grasped her elbow and led her toward the main play area. Dallas followed behind them.

"What's happening?"

"No questions, Lila. Just do as I ask and follow my lead."

As they approached the main play area, Lila started to get nervous. Drake turned her so she faced everyone in the room. All eyes were on her. Drake came in front of her temporarily blocking her view and caressed her hair.

"Relax little girl. You knew you would be on display," Drake said. "This is all about you tonight. Follow my lead and listen to my voice. You remember your safe words?"

"Yes."

"Good girl. Dallas is going to assist me."

Lila's eyes widened, her nerves igniting. She had not even had any sexual contact with Drake except for the few kisses and his making her undress. Now she was expected to have sex with him *and* Dallas at the same time, in public. Oh God! I don't know if I can do this, she thought. Dallas was her friend, but she did not desire him, not like Drake.

"Lila, look at me."

Lila stared into Drake's eyes.

"I know what you are thinking. Everything will be fine. I want you to enjoy this. Do you trust me?"

Lila did trust Drake. Shayla, Drew, they all told her to trust him. She did. She will. Sucking in a big breath, letting it out slowly, Lila then nodded at Drake. Suddenly, she felt hands on her shoulders from behind startling her.

"Just me, darlin'," Dallas said rubbing her shoulders. Then he whispered in her ear. "Lila girl, trust Drake, trust me. We got you. Relax and just embrace what is going to happen. Remember you're his sub. They all need to see that. Let go, give into the feelings and focus on Drake. You will be rewarded nicely. Okay?"

"Okay, Dallas. I trust you, too."

Dallas kissed her on the cheek and started rubbing his hands up and down Lila's body, but never touching intimate areas. Lila focused her gaze on Drake. He nodded, and Lila felt the bottom of her dress lifting; curbing her instincts to push it down was challenging.

"Arms up," Drake said, and Lila complied. She noticed Drake held something in his hand. Upon closer look, she realized it was a crop. Drake paced in front of her gazing over her body. The sudden exposure breezed over Lila's body, her nipples hardening.

"Beautiful," he said as he started to trace around her chest and breasts with the crop.

"Arms overhead. Dallas is going to bind you." She felt Dallas grab her left arm, attaching leather straps, raising it over her head, and attaching the strap to a chain hanging from the ceiling. He did the same with her right arm. Lila's breasts were more pronounced with her arms raised. She was surprised they left her legs alone, leaving her free to move her lower body.

Drake circled her body, came back around and faced her. He stared deep into her eyes. At that moment, Lila's mind cleared, and she forgot about everyone else, any other noise except Drake. She felt something go up and down her spine, breaking her gaze . . . Dallas.

"Lila, look at me," Drake said firmly. "If you feel Dallas, think of it as an extension of me, understand?"

"Yes, Sir," she said, her breath already catching.

Drake grabbed her neck and kissed her, deeply. Lila softened into the kiss, giving back everything he was giving her. Their tongues wrestled with urgent need. The kiss broke suddenly, and Drake kneeled, planting a kiss to her stomach. Slowly he removed her barely there panties, leaving her completely exposed; the only thing left were the stilettos. Standing, he brought the panties to his face and inhaled.

"Mmm. You smell so good, Lila," Drake said as he put the panties in his pocket.

A rush of liquid instantaneously flooded between Lila's legs. God, she was so turned on. Drake leaned down and took one nipple in his mouth. The sensation was glorious. Lila thought she was going to explode until she felt a sting on her backside. Drake went to the other nipple as Dallas landed another smack on her ass. Drake and Dallas continued their pursuit, Drake alternating between her nipples, sucking and savoring while Dallas landed light blows, always on a different spot.

"You like that, Lila?"

"Yes, Sir," she said breathlessly.

Drake stepped back and looked at Lila. "My God, you are so wet. I can see your honey glistening on your legs." Just as he said those words, Drake took his crop and tapped her breast, then the other. Lila could not believe how the sting of the crop was making her hotter and hotter, her desire building.

Dallas continued to use the crop on her backside as Drake fondled, kissed, and moved the crop to her breasts. Drakes hand traveled down her stomach to her folds. Slowly he traced the outline of her folds, finding her opening, rubbing back and forth, feeling her juices on his fingers. Drake found her center and circled his fingers, bringing out a cry. Lila tipped her head back and embraced all the different sensations Drake and Dallas created. The contrast between pleasure and pain aroused her even more.

Drake removed his hand, to Lila's disappointment, only to be immediately followed by a slight sting of the crop directly on her bud. The feeling shocked her. How could this feel so good? A succession of fast taps on her bud consumed her as Drake continued to feast on her breasts, Dallas' light stings going up and down her backside.

Lila's arousal continued to climb. Drake noticed the change, and then he gave the command. "Come." Instantaneously, Lila cried out, her orgasm overtaking her, the pleasure exploding throughout her entire body. It was nothing she has ever experienced, an everlasting orgasm. Drake continued his onslaught until Lila started to come down.

Drake and Dallas dropped their cops. Lila was spent and felt herself slipping, her legs weak. Drake caught her before she collapsed. Dallas quickly unhooked the bindings, and Drake picked her up and carried her back to the chairs. Dallas followed with her clothes and then fetched a cool rag. Drake gently cleaned Lila and restored her clothes. He held her close across his lap, stroking her hair. No words were spoken; they were not needed. Lila just stayed in Drake's arms for what felt like an eternity.

Lila's trance was broken when she heard Dallas' voice. "Lila, darlin', here's some water. Why don't you take a drink?"

She grasped the glass and took a sip, then another. Glancing up, she looked into Drake's eyes. There looked to be a combination of desire and . . . something else she could not quite pinpoint. They held each other's gaze for some time until Drake spoke, still caressing her hair.

"That was beautiful. Perfect. How are you feeling?"

"Lots of things."

"Did you enjoy it?"

"Yes, Sir."

"Good girl."

Clapping suddenly alerted them to Marcus' approach. He appeared in front of them. "Well done. Well done. Drake you are a very, very lucky man. Such a responsive little slave."

Drake just nodded and squeezed Lila a little closer.

"And Dallas, what an honor to participate. Maybe next time you want a second, you will grant me the pleasure."

Repulsed by the thought. That man will never touch me, Lila said to herself, still keeping herself close to Drake, not acknowledging Marcus.

"I'm very selective, Marcus, but will keep your offer in consideration."

"Very well. You guys going to play some more tonight?"

"No. We are probably leaving soon. I think she has had enough training for tonight."

"Too bad. I would love to see her being taken. Have a good evening. Hope to see you all soon."

"You too. We will be back. Probably this weekend," Drake advised. With that, Marcus went away and mingled with others.

"Snake," Lila whispered.

"What did you say, little girl?"

"I said he was a snake."

"Ah. He seems alright, just not your type."

"Hmph."

"You ready to go?"

"Yes," Lila said, still a little worked up from their play. She was not fully satisfied. While she had an orgasm, one like no other, she wanted more, secretly hoping Drake would take her to his house and fuck her senseless.

9

L ila and Drake arrived back at his place and went straight to the bedroom. It was already past midnight. They needed to go into the office early in the morning so the group could go over the previous night's events, but Lila was not even close to being ready to sleep.

Hoping Drake would continue their fun, Lila slowly started removing her clothes, making sure she bent over, exposing her backside when taking off her heels. Drake did not respond and just went into the bathroom.

Quickly, Lila got in the bed and tried to lie down in a provocative position before Drake came out. Drake returned, glanced at Lila, then got in bed and turned off his side lamp. Confused, Lila tried to instigate a response by asking, "Are you going to bind me tonight?"

"Nope. Just go to sleep. We have to be up in a few hours."

Frustrated, Lila stormed off, used the facilities, and returned to bed. Turning off the light on her side, she rolled over facing away from Drake. The furthest away from him she could get. She could swear she heard him chuckle. Bastard. Sleep eluded her and Lila tossed and turned all night.

At 6am the next morning, Lila decided just to get up and get ready. It was not like she could try to go back to sleep. Showered and dressed, Lila exited the bathroom and noticed Drake was awake. Ignoring him she went downstairs to make something for breakfast. Lila banged around the kitchen preparing omelets. "I shouldn't make him one," she said as she still prepared breakfast for both of them. Ten minutes later, Drake made his way downstairs. He watched Lila for a few moments before he entered the kitchen.

"Something smells good," he said.

Lila just glared at him and clanked a plate down on the center island in front of Drake. He knew she was pissed at him.

"What has our panties in a wad?"

"Oh, let me see . . . nothing. I'm fine," Lila said as she ate her food, standing on the opposite side of the counter. Scoffing down her food, Lila cleaned up the dishes. "Hurry up. We need to leave. Please put your plate in the dishwasher when you are done," she said then briskly left the room.

Smirking, Drake leisurely ate his breakfast. He did clean up his plate and took his time getting ready to leave. Lila was already in his truck waiting. They did not speak on the way to the office. Drake visualized if she was a cartoon character, steam would be coming out of her ears. The image made him chuckle

Lila did not wait for Drake and went straight to her workstation. She quickly passed Drew in the hallway, said a brusque hello, and kept going. Drew stood there flabbergasted. He had never seen Lila pissed before. Drake walked in and approached Drew.

"What pissed her off?"

"Let me give you one guess."

"Ah," Drew said, motioning Drake to follow him to his office.

"So, what did you do? Get her all worked up last night then deny her?"

"Yes and no."

"Yes and no? Explain."

"Oh, she had a great experience, but little girl wanted more and I didn't take the bait."

"Alright, so she got a little tickle, wanted more, you said no, and now she is sexually frustrated and pissed at you."

"Yes, basically."

"You bastard," Drew said, laughing.

"Proud of it."

Shaking his head, "Y'all ready to brief on last night? We all need to sync up and discuss what occurred and if there needs to be any changes to the plan."

"Yep. I'm ready. I would like to hear if the others saw anything suspicious or out of place. I was a little distracted by you know who."

Slapping Drake on his back, Drew claimed, "Oh little brother, you are in deep, deep in trouble."

The rest of the team arrived, and they gathered in the conference room. Shayla noticed Lila was out of sorts. She sat next to her and whispered, "What's wrong?"

"Nothing. I'm fine.

"I know you. You are not fine. What happened? Who pissed you off?"

"Who do you think? I'll tell you later."

"Okay."

"So, Trent, Matt, Garrett, you all see anything out of the ordinary?" Drew inquired.

"Negative," Matt said. "All seemed like normal coming and goings."

"Garrett, how about you?"

"All quiet. Kept out of sight. Nothing out of the ordinary."

"We were able to get in and monitor their cameras in the

lobby and halls. Nothing on our end, either. We could not get any feeds to their playroom. Either they do not have them in there, or we need to do better to gain access."

"I did not see any signs of cameras or other equipment in their dungeon," Jax said.

"He's right. No signs inside," Jace confirmed.

"Did you two see anything out of place, suspicious, or just did not seem right?"

"No. Just normal club activity, even though it can't hold a candle to *The Manor*," Jace said.

"Most places can't," Drew replied.

"How was your interaction with others?"

"We mingled, talked to some regulars. Let them know we were new in town and checking the place out. Had multiple offers. Do you know how hard it was to turn them down?" Jace said.

"I'm sure. How about y'all, anything stand out?" Drew said directing the question to Drake, Dallas, and Lila.

"Same as the twins. Nothing out of the ordinary, but we were focusing elsewhere last night," Drake said, Dallas agreeing with him.

"You've got to be kidding me," Lila blurted.

Everyone turned and looked at her.

"What do you mean, Lila?" Drew asked.

"One word: Marcus."

"You still flapping on about Marcus," Drake replied.

"Excuse me ass . . . Drake. Yes, Marcus."

"Who is Marcus, and what is wrong with him?"

"Marcus is another Dom, just not Lila's type so she does not like him."

"Oh, shut up, Drake. Marcus is a creep."

"Ooo, she told you," Matt teased as Drake's eyes pierced Lila.

"Don't get testy with everyone else because you're mad at me."

"Focus, Lila. What's with Marcus? Why did you call him a creep?" Drew asked.

"Because he is. He's a sleaze, untrustworthy. I just have a bad vibe about him. He seemed a little too interested in us. In me."

"Uhm, have you looked at yourself, and after that little show last night, I am sure all the Doms were interested," Dallas said.

"Dallas is right. Great performance by the way," Jax added, making Lila blush.

"She is just not used to the scene and is overreacting," Drake said.

"No, I'm not. I have a gut feeling about him, and it is not positive. You know the old saying, trust your gut instincts."

"Marcus is fine," Drake said.

"Whatever. You would not believe me anyway. I am not a 'sub' and new to doing an op," Lila said as she sat back in her chair, crossing her arms.

"Enough, Lila. We need to move forward," Drake said.

That only pissed her off more. Drake knew he would need to deal with Lila later. Lila just sat back and listened, not giving any additional input.

The group continued the strategy for moving forward. "Okay. So everyone goes back tomorrow night. This time we try to put the bug in a few ears," Drew said.

"Affirmative. We will just be observers. Get to know some of the regulars and staff. See if anyone will open up," Drake declared.

"Sounds good. We will also work on face recognition on those in and out of the *Palace* last night," Trent said. "So we can point out anyone suspicious."

"Alright. We are good to go for now. I think this meeting is adjourned," Drew stated.

Shayla grabbed Lila's arm and walked out with her. Lila willingly let Shayla guide her to her office and flopped down in a guest chair in frustration.

"So, are you going to tell me what has you so worked up? I am presuming Drake did something."

"God, this is so embarrassing," Lila said covering her face. "It is what he did not do."

Shayla came around her desk and sat next to Lila. "Tell me what's wrong. Apparently things went well at *Pleasure Palace*."

"It was after, that was the problem. Yes, at the club things went well. Drake had Dallas up there with us."

"Oh my God, Dallas had sex with you too. On your first time?"

"No. Oh, no. Actually there was no sex."

"Okay. Now I'm confused."

Lila filled Shayla in on what happened at the club.

"So did you enjoy it?"

"Yes. I was surprised how I could tune everything else out and how turned on I got from the contrast of pleasure and pain. The orgasm was incredible."

"So what happened after that upset you?"

"The issue was I was still worked up. I was hoping . . . hoping Drake would just take me.

The prior two nights he made me strip and sleep naked. The second night he bound me to the bed, but he has yet to touch me other than last night at the club. So when we got home, I stripped, he ignored me. Then I tried to lie on the bed inviting him. He ignored me. I asked if he was going to tie me to the bed, he said no, turned the lights out, and went to sleep. I just thought with the kiss, how he demanded he would be the Dom and what you keep saying, that he wanted me. Guess I was wrong. Kinda makes a girl insecure, being rejected."

"Oh, Lila, honey. I can tell he wants you. Drake must be in conflict with his emotions. I don't think he knows how to handle you."

"That does not help my body right now. I think I am going to go down to the Dome. I need to work out some of this frustration."

Lila got up, changed and headed to the Dome. Garrett was there, along with Rocco.

"Hey, sweet girl. What you doing here?"

"Need to work out some of this tension."

"Want me to go through some drills with you?" Garrett asked.

Surprised, Lila gladly accepted. Garrett, the quiet standoffish one of the group, was the only teammate she had yet to figure out. She was happy he engaged her on his own. Garrett and Lila started going through drills and some light sparring. Few words were exchanged, but the silence was soothing. They actually worked well together, like they communicated telepathically. Words were not necessary. She knew what Garrett wanted and vice versa.

Lila and Garrett worked together for almost two hours. Garrett surprised her again by putting his arm around her, kissing her on the top of her head, and telling her she did great. Lila thanked him, said her goodbyes to Rocco, and went to seek out Drake to find out when they would be leaving. She found him in his office with Drew.

"When will we be leaving today, Sir?"

The guys turned their heads and looked at Lila.

"Where have you been? The Dome working with Rocco?"

"Yes the Dome, and no, Garrett."

"Garrett, huh," Drake said, surprised.

"Actually we worked well together. So, back to my question, when will we be leaving? I need to know if I should go ahead and shower here or wait until we get to your house."

"We can leave in about a half hour."

"Okay. I will be at my desk until you are ready. Sir," Lila said, turning on her feet and leaving Drake's office.

"Oh, Drake, you better fix this before tomorrow. She needs to be able to focus, be on her game."

"I know. I know. I've got it handled."

"Sure you do."

The car ride back to Drake's place was quiet, just like the morning. Breaking the silence, Drake asked, "Would you like to go out and grab some dinner?"

"I don't care. You decide. I just need to shower."

"Alright. Maybe we'll go out in a bit."

They arrived at Drake's and Lila went straight upstairs and into the bathroom. She started the shower and undressed. Staring at herself, naked, in the mirror, telling herself she needed to get a grip and stop thinking about Drake, just do your job, the one you volunteered for.

Stepping into the shower, Lila started to wash her hair when she suddenly felt hands touch her shoulders. A scream was about to escape just as she heard Drake's voice.

"It's just me."

She opened her eyes and looked over her shoulder. There was Drake. Naked. In all his glory, and what a glorious body it was.

"What are you doing in here?"

"Something I should have already done, something long overdue," Drake said. Taking Lila's shower puff, he grabbed her body wash and slowly started washing Lila's back. Goose bumps started traveling down Lila's body, arousal was immediate. She could not believe Drake was washing her. Gliding down from her back, Drake headed to her backside, then her legs. Without warning, he pressed his body up against hers, pulled her hair to the side, and kissed her neck.

Lila could feel his erection pressing against her lower back.

He was so hard, solid, and from what she could feel, not lacking. Drake gently turned Lila to face him. He continued to bathe her. Moving toward her breasts, he continued to slide the shower puff from one to the other. Using his other hand, Drake started lightly pinching and rubbing her nipple. Pure desire filled his eyes.

Courageously, Lila slyly glanced down and got her first peek of his manhood. Her eyes widened as she looked back up at Drake.

"Like what you see?"

"Yes," she replied, mesmerized by the size of him. She had never been with a man so big, so hard, standing straight up, just waiting to be touched.

"Spread your legs," Drake requested. Lila did as asked and Drake started washing her most intimate spot. She could not tell if he was washing her or caressing her, it felt so good. Her head fell back as Drake continued to clean her center. Next thing she knew, Drake's mouth was on hers. A scorching kiss, hot, uninhibited. Lila did not want him to stop. Drake broke off the kiss, grabbed the handheld sprayer, and rinsed Lila.

"Out." That was all he said, and Lila walked out of the shower. Drake grabbed a towel and started drying Lila before drying himself. She was in his arms, being carried to the bed. Lila laid there, fully naked, spread out like a feast for Drake. His gaze traveled up and down her body. Her beautiful, natural breasts and bare womanhood, just the way he liked it. Drake could not wait to taste her.

"This is so, so long overdue," Drake said, just before taking her mouth in another steamy kiss. Lila reciprocated with full fury, wrapping her arms around his neck. Their tongues tangling, Lila desired more and more of his touch. Drake started to travel the kisses down her neck, sending chills up her spine. Her breasts were next on his feast. Drake was taking his time, giving each breast his full attention, sucking and licking, tormenting Lila. His tongue circled around her nipple before pulling it into his mouth and sucking. Pleasure now radiated to her core. Her arousal increased. She felt coolness across her breasts from Drake's retreat, to be followed by kisses and licking in a path down her stomach. Drake planted a kiss on her belly button then each hip before kissing the top of her mound.

Looking up at Lila, "I can't wait to taste you. God, you are so wet," he said as he touched her with his fingers. Moving his hand around her mound, but never touching where she desired the most, had Lila squirming, wanting. Drake's mouth then met her bud. Lila screamed out in pleasure as Drake devoured her. Licking then sucking her bud into his mouth, Drake continued this pattern, filling Lila's pleasure, her honey wetting his chin.

He inserted one, then two, fingers inside Lila, her body arching in pleasure with the new invasion. The stroke of his fingers in sync with his tongue. Lila's body tightened, and Drake knew she was close. She felt the glorious pleasure within her body build, reaching and reaching. Drake reached up and rolled both nipples with his fingers, and Lila exploded. So many sensations encompassed her body all at once. She did not think an orgasm could be better than last night, but she was so wrong. Drake kept his mouth locked on her bud, licking and sucking until Lila came down. Kissing his way back up her body, Drake took her lips. She could taste herself in his kiss.

"You taste sweeter than I imagined. So sweet, so responsive."

Lila could not believe what Drake could do with his mouth. The exquisite pleasure he brought her was something she had never experienced. Grabbing her legs, Drake positioned himself between them and slowly entered. He was large. Lila did not know if he would fit. One final push and Drake fully seated himself inside Lila. She gasped at the full sensation.

"God, you are so tight," Drake said as he started to move his hips, undulating his cock inside her. The long, smooth strokes moved in and out of her channel, sending sparks, tingles, and many other pleasurable sensations through her body. Their eyes locked, holding with every movement.

Drake's pace quickened as did Lila's breaths; pleasure filled her body. Instinctively, Lila wrapped her legs around Drake and tilted her hips up, reaching for more. Drake moaned at the change of position then took her mouth with searing heat. Lila kissed him back with the ferocity of a wildcat while running her fingers up and down his back, with a final destination on his backside.

The sensations running through Lila's body built higher and higher, slickness increased, her inner walls contracted around Drake's cock. She felt him harden even more, if that was even possible. Feeling her orgasm approaching, she closed her eyes, tilting her head back.

"No. Look at me Lila. I want to see you come."

Lila opened her eyes. The look on Drake's face set off a series of explosions. She screamed out as her entire body tightened around Drake. His pace increased, relentlessly pushing deeper and deeper as Lila's orgasm peaked. His body could no longer hold out. The pleasure was too intense, and his release was imminent. Drake roared as he spilled himself into her. His hot, wet seed releasing with each final stroke.

Drake collapsed on top of Lila, her body still pulsating around his cock. A rush of emotions started to engulf him. No orgasm has ever felt so exquisite nor had he ever felt like this with anyone. Lifting his head, Drake slowly and gently kissed Lila. Suddenly with a start, Drake quickly sat up.

"Shit! Fuck! I can't believe I did that!"

Dread instantaneously flooded Lila. Was Drake upset by what they just experienced together? Gaining courage, she asked, "What's wrong?"

"I didn't fucking use a condom!" Drake was worked up. He had never been bare back. Never. He knew he was safe, but that's not the only reason he always used protection. He also did not want a kid from some random hook up.

"It's okay, Drake."

"How is it fucking okay?"

"Well, I am on the shot to prevent pregnancy, and I am clean. Was tested after the last guy I dated and have not been with anyone until now. So, unless you have something, we are fine. I apologize, too. I should've said something, but I got distracted."

"I'm clean and get regular check-ups and always use a condom . . . that is, until tonight. There is no need to apologize. It is my responsibility."

"No, it is both of ours. You okay now that you know we are safe?"

Stroking her cheek as he calmed down, he replied, "Yes, sorry. Didn't mean to blow up just after such an amazing—"

"Yes, it was amazing," Lila whispered. "Thank you. I was a little," she smiled a guilty smile, "worked up."

"I know. You have been through so much in such a short period of time. I'm impressed Lila," Drake said as he placed a soft kiss on her lips. "Hold still. I'll be right back."

Drake got up and went into the bathroom. A short moment later he was back, wash cloth in hand. Gently he wiped Lila clean and tossed the washcloth in the laundry basket. The rest of the evening was low key. They decided to stay in. Lila rustled them up some stir fry, and they watched a few episodes of *Friends*. Drake made love to Lila two more times that night, or at least in her mind it was making love. Once on the sectional and another in the middle of the night. Lila would savor each moment with him while she had him. Soon enough everything would go back to normal, if that was even possible.

10

S aturday arrived. Lila was satiated. They had a remarkable night. Something she could treasure when her life returned to normal and she had to give him up, even though she wondered how she could. Tonight they were going back to *Pleasure Palace*. She had time this morning to relax, was meeting Shayla for lunch, then would head to the office. Drake was already up and working out in his home gym. Lila decided to sit out on the deck for a bit until she had to get ready for lunch. The morning was beautiful, not too hot and the humidity was low. She grabbed a book and headed outside to a lounger. It was nice just to be able to relax and enjoy the quiet. She read for a while, then closed her eyes and soaked up the morning sun, not hearing Drake approach.

"Lila. Wake up. Aren't you meeting Shayla soon?" Drake said, lightly shaking her shoulder.

Slowly opening her eyes and stretching, she looked at Drake. "Oh. Thanks. I must have dozed off. I seem to be making that a habit lately," she said with a smile.

"Well, I did interrupt your sleep a little last night."

"True, but I'm not complaining."

"Better not."

Laughing at Drake, Lila got up and headed inside. "I'm going to take a shower. Shayla will be here in about an hour. We're meeting at the office later, right?"

"Yes."

"Okay. I'll make sure I take my stuff with me and get ready there."

"Sounds like a plan. I need to shower, too. I think I'll join you."

"You'll make me late."

"Nah. I'll behave myself," Drake said as he followed Lila up the stairs.

Of course he didn't behave himself. As soon as he saw her naked, standing in front of him, he grabbed her, his hand like a magnet immediately pulled toward her clit. Kissing her neck, he felt her heat instantly. She was ready for him that quickly. Drake entered her from behind in one quick stroke. He was on a mission. Slamming into her relentlessly over and over, they peaked together, both letting out a scream. Drake had to grab Lila under her arms as her knees weakened from yet another intense orgasm. Drake let her go when she gained her balance, grabbed a washcloth, and smacked her on the ass.

"Here," he said giving her the washcloth. "See, I'm not going to make you late."

"But you didn't behave."

"I didn't hear any complaints."

Lila giggled and finished washing. She got out of the shower before Drake and started getting ready. She put on a sundress, a pair of sandals, and pulled her hair into a simple ponytail. Grabbing a bag, Lila gathered what she needed for the night just as the doorbell rang. Drake let Shayla in just as Lila was coming down the stairs.

"Ready?" Shayla asked.

"Yep. I have what I need for later. You're dropping me off at the office right?"

"Of course."

Turning to Drake, "I will be there no later than four. Just in case there is anything to go over before we head to the *Palace*."

"Alright, that will work."

"Bye."

"Later, Drake," Shayla said.

"Bye, ladies."

Shayla drove them to a little bistro in the town's historic district. Since the weather was still nice, they decided to sit outside. After ordering, Shayla started the inquisition.

"So, you seem *a lot* more relaxed than you were when you left work yesterday."

"I am."

"That's all I get? Come on. Give me the dirty details. Obviously something happened between you two. It's written all over your faces."

"We had a nice evening."

"Great. You're killing me here,"

"Okay, okay," Lila said laughing. "Well, something did happen. Four times in fact."

"Woo-hoo. I knew it. It's about time."

"That's basically what Drake said, the first time. Actually he said it was long overdue."

"So how was it? Is it kind of weird asking this question since Drake's my brother-in-law? But you're my best friend, and best friends share."

"It was spectacular. That's the best way I can describe it. Just raw, pure sex. No spanking, no binding, just us," Lila said, her facial expression suddenly looking grim.

"What's wrong? Why do you suddenly look sad?"

"I don't know. It's just everything was perfect. We completely meshed, like a perfect fit, but I know it all changes when this op is over. I move into my own place. We go back to our own lives," Lila said as tears started to form in her eyes.

"Oh honey, don't cry."

"Trying not to. I'm just scared Shayla. Even though he drives me crazy, I think I am already too attached. Not sure how I will be able to handle working for him and not be with him when this is over, especially after last night."

"Maybe you won't go back to before."

"Drake does not want a relationship. He told me himself he likes his freedom. Last night just sealed the deal for me. I went over the cliff," she said, putting her head into her hands.

"Lila, don't worry about the unknown. You never know what life brings you. Personally, I feel Drake has similar feelings but is scared. You just need to focus on tonight and trying to find Caroline. You and Drake will figure it all out later."

"You're right. Finding out who is taking these women is what is important. My love life can take a back seat."

Lila and Shayla enjoyed their lunch then browsed some of the shops nearby. Their friendship grew more solid every day. Lila had never had a girlfriend she could completely trust, until now. They may not have known each other long, but Lila felt like she'd known Shayla her entire life. She trusted her, truly enjoyed her company, and they confided in each other. A precious relationship.

A few hours later they headed over to the office to prep for the op and go over any last minute changes. Lila dropped her bags off at her desk and immediately sought out Drake. He was in his office talking to Drew. Once he saw her, he stopped talking, fixated on Lila. Drew looked back and forth between the two before breaking their trance.

"Lila, you look relaxed. Y'all have a nice lunch?" Drew asked, knowing something happened between Lila and Drake.

"Yes, thank you. So what's the 411? Anything I need to know before we go tonight?"

"Yes. A few things. We're all meeting in about 30 minutes. Trent made some last minute adjustments on the van equipment. Just giving him time to finish."

"Sounds like a plan. See you in a bit."

"Lila," Drake called out.

"Yes, sir?"

"Time to focus."

"Yes. I understand."

Lila needed no other explanation. She knew he meant for her to clear her head regarding last night and focus all her energy on the op. Thankfully, Lila was always able to block things and focus when needed. She strode down the hall toward the Dome, then to the vehicle bay, a place she discovered after their first visit to the *Palace*. Donovan Security had several vehicles, surveillance vans, cars, and trucks. They never used their personal vehicles for ops.

"How's it going guys?" Lila said as she approached Trent and Matt.

"Good. Almost done. We wanted to add additional back-up servers so if one went down, we had back-up for the feed."

"Sounds like a good plan. You don't want to miss anything."

"Exactly," Matt said, exiting the van. "You ready for round two?"

"As ready as I can be."

"Well, ladies," Trent said.

"Such a comedian," Matt replied.

"We better get back for the pre-op meeting. After you, my lady."

Lila, Trent, and Matt headed to the conference room just as everyone else was arriving.

"Have a seat everyone," Drew said. "Trent, Matt, is everything set?"

"All's ready. We are covered," Trent replied.

"Garrett, same plan, just a different day."

"Affirmative."

"There are only a few changes for inside *Pleasure Palace*. Drake will fill you in."

"Dallas, you can continue to interact with me and Lila, but mingle some tonight. Jax, Jace, try not to stay together all night like last time. Charm the fairer sex and see if you can get any information. Lila, we are not playing tonight, just observing. Everyone needs to keep a close eye on everything. Lila can you maintain the role and still keep your eyes and ears open?"

"Yes, I can."

"Good. You need to be another set of eyes and ears. We need to stagger our arrivals again, but a little closer together. It should not look suspicious since it is Saturday and the club should be busy. Is the van ready to leave when we are done?"

"Yes. Ready to go," Trent said.

"Excellent. Everyone make sure you test your mics and earpieces before going inside. Okay. Let's get moving. We need to get this wrapped up, stop any more disappearances, and find the Senator's daughter."

"Roger." a few of the guys responded

As everyone got up and started to leave, Lila approached Drake. "I'm going to go ahead and get ready. Just making sure there isn't anything else you need from me."

"No. We're set. Be ready in an hour."

"Will do."

Lila stopped by Shayla's office before getting ready. "Hey there, you going home?"

"Yes, in a bit. What are you wearing tonight?"

"I think the silver dress."

"Good choice. You'll make Drake drool."

"Drooling over me is not the goal tonight."

"True. Lila . . . ," Shayla said, then paused.

"What is it Shayla?"

"Be careful."

"I will. What do I really need to worry about with all the guys?"

"I know. I just have a weird feeling."

"Don't worry. All will be fine," Lila said as she gave her friend a hug and left to get ready.

Lila was putting the finishing touches on her makeup when there was a knock on the restroom door.

"Almost done?" Drake yelled in.

"Yes. Be out in a few seconds."

Taking one last look at herself, Lila exited the restroom to meet Drake. He was in the hall by her desk and looked delicious in a pair of dark jeans, a black button up shirt, and boots. God, he was sexy.

"Ready," Lila said.

Drake soaked her in, filling his eyes. He would take this one moment to enjoy looking at her. He had to focus as soon as they left.

Lila wore a short silver dress with thin straps. The front was normal, a little higher, encroaching her collar bones, but when she turned around to get her clutch, Drake noticed the back, or lack of it. It was open and so low, just above her bottom exposing the dimples of her lower back. Her hair was down, long and flowing, makeup was simple except for her scarlet lips.

Stunning.

"You look . . . delicious. Trying to make it hard for me to focus?"

"Oh, you'll be fine. You're the professional. Anyway, you told me to play the part."

"And that you are."

Drake and Lila stopped by the tech room to quickly speak to Drew and Rocco.

"We are heading out. Everything working?"

"Yes. Van's in place. Trent and Matt already hacked into

the security cameras at the club, and the feed's coming through. We're ready to roll."

"Good. Lila, let's go," Drake said.

Rocco got up, hugged Lila. "You look beautiful. Be careful tonight. Remember what I taught you, and don't forget the collar, worst case scenario."

"Thank you, and I will. Love you, Rocco."

"Love you too, sweet girl."

Drake did not understand the twinge of jealousy that occurred with Lila and Rocco's exchange of 'love you.' It was not like he was seeking Lila's love, was he? They headed to the garage and once again took the Lexus LC. Drake's expression changed on the ride over. Lila observed his intense focus, switching gears for the op.

"Lila, we already discussed we are not going to play tonight and you should also keep your eyes and ears open.

"Yes."

"Just make sure you look natural in your role and follow my lead. You're smart. You'll understand what to do."

"I will. Promise. I just have a feeling tonight is going to be the pinnacle in this investigation. It has to be. We need to stop them and find Caroline before anyone else gets hurt."

"I agree. Thus we all need to focus."

"Precisely."

They pulled into *Pleasure Palace*, and once again Drake handed over the keys to the valet. Drake paid, and they were buzzed in. The gentleman in the lounge area greeted them and asked if they had any special needs or wanted to reserve a private room.

"No. Not tonight. I think we are just going to go into the Dungeon."

"Wonderful. Let me know if you need anything," the young man said as he eyed up Lila.

Heading into the *Palace's* dungeon, Drake guided Lila over

to the bar. He ordered a beer and a Diet Coke. Just as soon as he ordered, Lila felt someone's hands on her shoulders and instantly cringed.

"Well, hello there, you two. Glad to see you back so soon."

Marcus, creepy Marcus. Like a moth to light as soon as they arrived. He had his arms around both of them. Drake turned to greet Marcus.

"Hey, Marcus. Nice to see you again."

Marcus did not take his hands off Lila even while he shook hands with Drake.

"And you, beautiful lady. Don't you look stunning," he said as his hand traced down Lila's bare back. It took everything in her power not to grab him and snap his wrist. Creep.

Drake nodded to Lila, "Thank you, Marcus."

"Pleasure is all mine. Being in the presence of a beauty like you is an honor." Turning back to Drake, he said, "You two playing tonight? I would love to join in."

Lila felt bile start to travel up her throat.

"Not tonight. See, little Miss here needs to learn a lesson on patience, thus she gets to watch tonight. Nothing more."

"Oh, how disappointing. You need to behave, my lady, so I can play with you."

Fuck off, she said to herself before she responded, "I will."

"I see your friend, is it Dallas, has arrived," Marcus said raising his hand to get Dallas' attention.

Dallas sauntered over, looking like a super sexy cowboy. "Howdy y'all. Lila, Lila, Lila. Aren't you a ray of sunshine," Dallas said and kissed her cheek. "Drake, Marcus," he said shaking their hands. Dallas nodded to the bartender to get a drink. "How's it going? Anything special going on tonight?"

"We just got here," Drake said.

"Ah."

"Oh, I'm sure there will be plenty of play tonight. Looks like it's getting busy already," Marcus said.

"I see that. Lila, let's go find somewhere to sit."

Lila nodded as Dallas said he would join them for a bit. They found a couch to the right side of the room. It gave them a pretty good view of the entire room. Good choice, Lila thought. Lila was sandwiched in between Drake and Dallas, Drake draping his arm around her shoulders. She noticed Jax and Jace arrive, go to the bar and then split up and mingle with some of the women.

Drake and Dallas talked, and they all appeared to be watching the activity going on in the play area even though they were truly trying to pick up signals from others. Suddenly, a pretty brunette came over and flirted with Dallas.

"Hello there, pretty girl. Why is someone like you here all alone?"

"Hi, handsome. I'm here with a friend. She's the one in the play area. My name is Trina. What's your name?"

"Dallas. Come on over here and sit down and join us."

Trina hopped up on his lap and put her arm around Dallas' shoulders. My, my, how forward, thought Lila.

"So Trina, aren't you an outgoing little thing."

"Thanks. Gets me in trouble with most Doms. I never know when to stop talking."

"I don't mind talkers as long as they also like how I play."

"I'll play any way you want, sexy."

"This is Drake and Lila," Dallas said, motioning his arm in their direction.

"Hi, guys."

"Hello," Drake said.

"Something wrong with her?" Trina asked. "She can't talk?"

Slut, Lila mused.

"She's being punished," Drake said.

"Oh, okay. Sorry."

The guys and Trina talked a while before Dallas started his

discreet questioning. "So, you and your friend come here often?"

"Yep, a few times a week."

"How come you have not found your own Dom yet?"

"Oh, you know. I like to keep my options open. Maybe after we get a chance to play, you will be my Dom," Trina said as she rubbed her hand up and down Dallas' chest.

"Maybe. You never know. You know, you girls should be more careful. I've heard a few girls have gone missing recently."

"Oh, yes. I know. The one that went missing recently, Kimmy, we played some together. She was fickle. Would come and go. Who knows if she is really missing."

"I heard there were others," Drake added.

"True. There was one girl I was asked about by some investigator. What was her name, Carol? No Caroline, something like that. I think I saw her a few times. Did not really know her. Was too busy having fun."

"Really. An investigator. Wow." Dallas said. "Did she hang around anyone here much?"

"I'm not sure. She was friendly with Marcus."

Marcus, creepy Marcus. I told them something was not right with him, Lila thought.

"Trina, I see you have met my new friends here," Marcus said putting his hands on Lila's shoulders.

Speak of the devil. Lila cringed internally from his touch but did not let it show.

"Oh, hi, Marcus. Yes, I have. They are great," she said snuggling into Dallas. "Trying to get to know this handsome man better."

"I'm sure you have plenty of time for that. Amy asked for you. Wanted me to relay the message."

"Thanks." Turning to Dallas, "I'll see you in a bit. Need to see what my friend needs."

"Hurry back."

"Looks like you will get a little play time later," Marcus said grinning at Dallas.

"Maybe. How about you? Gotta hot little thing lined up for tonight?" Dallas asked.

"Yes. I have my eye on someone," Marcus said and squeezed Lila's shoulders. "I'll see you all later."

"Later, Marcus," the guys said.

"Fuck, what a creep. Did you notice how he appeared as soon as Trina was talking about the missing girls?"

"That's just a coincidence. How could he know that's what we were talking about?"

"Drake's right. He would not have been able to hear us. He was over by the bar," Dallas seconded.

"Well, I still think something is up with him. If he knows Trina is a chatter box, it was a way to stop her from spilling anything. And he keeps touching me, yuck."

"Lila, he just finds you attractive. He wants you. That's all."

"He will NEVER have me."

"Twins. You picking up anything?"

"Not much. Similar to what that Trina girl said," Jax said, moving away from the group he was speaking with.

"You can talk to them?" Lila whispered.

"Yes."

"Why didn't I get one?"

"You didn't need one. The fewer on the frequency, the better the reception and recording abilities."

"Oh, fine. If you will excuse me, I need to use the restroom."

"Okay. Make it quick," Drake said.

Lila got up and headed to the ladies room. It was located outside of the Dungeon, down the hall from the lounge by the lobby. She nodded at the attendant in the lounge and went in to take care of business. Adjusting her clothes and checking her makeup one last time, Lila went to head back to the guys. As soon as she opened the door, she ran directly into someone.

"Sorry," she said, then looked up and saw Marcus.

"No apologies necessary, Lila."

"If you'll excuse me, I need to head back to Drake."

Not moving out of her way, Marcus took her by the elbow. "While you are here, why don't I show you the rest of the club? Sometimes those in the private rooms allow people to watch."

Trying to pull away from Marcus, Lila told Marcus Drake was waiting for her. Marcus did not let go.

"Marcus, please. I'm not interested tonight. I need to get back to Drake."

In a split second, she saw the look on Marcus' face change. Evil was staring back at her. Lila knew Marcus was shady, but the guys did not believe her. Suddenly Lila felt a sharp pain in her neck. No, it was a stick. The fucker stuck me with something. Seconds later, Marcus was dragging her down the hall. Lila started to scream to get someone's attention, but he covered her mouth. Instincts kicked in and Lila started to fight back. Turning, Lila landed a jab to his nose, blood spurting on contact.

"You little cunt," he said, grabbing his face with his other arm.

Lila went to make a move to get free from his grip when a sudden heaviness overtook her body. She could not move her arms, her legs, nothing. Her body was going limp. Fuck, he drugged me, Lila realized just before everything went black.

11

Trent could not believe his eyes. "Code Red! Code Red!" he yelled into the mic. Matt looked over at the screens and froze. There was Lila, limp, being carried down the hall of *Pleasure Palace* toward the side emergency exit.

"Garrett. West side door. NOW! They got Lila!"

"Shit. I'm all the way on the other side," he said as he took off in a sprint. Matt ran out of the van to also try to get there in time, gun in hand.

"Drake, Dallas, twins, Code Red. Move it, NOW!"

It was like everything was in slow motion. Trent watched, feeling helpless, as Lila was put into an SUV by the man who was carrying her. They took off just as Garrett and Matt rounded opposite corners.

"Fuck. She's gone. They got her!"

Drake, Dallas, Jax, and Jace scrambled out of the dungeon into the lounge. Drake spotted the attendant.

"Where is she? Did you see my date? She was using the restroom."

"I saw her head down the hall, but she has not come out. Maybe check the restroom."

Drake rushed toward the restroom, flung the door open, looking for something, anything. He knew what Trent said over the transmitter, but did not want to believe it. Maybe they saw someone else. Not his Lila. His Lila. Yes, she was his. He needed to get her, find her.

"Get here. To the van, stat!" Trent said in the transmitter.

They quickly rushed out of the *Palace*. Drake pushing the valet ticket into the attendant's chest. "Get my car, fast. Have it here running for me." The attendant, stunned at first, made a mad dash to retrieve Drake's car.

Sprinting to the van, Drake threw open the door. "What the fuck happened" Where is she? How did you let this happen?"

"We didn't let it happen. It took all of 30 seconds, and they had her. I have already sent the replay to Drew and Rocco and they are trying to pick up something, anything. Here, watch what happened and the timeline."

They watched Lila exit the restroom and run into Marcus. A few words were exchanged. When she turned, he had a syringe and stuck her. Lila tried fighting, but whatever he had was potent and worked quickly. Marcus picked her up, ran to the side emergency exit door where an SUV pulled up just as Marcus opened the door, and then took off.

"Do you have a visual on the SUV? A tag? Anything?"

Trent pulled up the other angle. They timed it perfectly. The SUV pulled up only two seconds before Marcus was at the emergency exit. They're smart. They either took the plates off or had them covered.

"Fuck. Fuck. Show me the other angle, of the hall. How did the alarms not go off when he opened up the emergency door?"

The video replay displayed and Drake saw the lounge attendant peak around the corner and hit something on the wall as soon as Marcus had Lila out the door. Immediately

Drake sprinted back to the club. Storming in, he found the attendant, grabbed him, and slammed him against the wall.

"Okay, Mother Fucker. Where is she? Where are they taking her? You better fucking tell me right now, or I am going to kill you!"

"I don't know. I swear."

"You lying piece of shit. You better tell me, NOW!"

Security came out of the dungeon and were closing in on Drake. Dallas, Jax and Jace stopped them.

The attendant, scared shitless, tried to speak. "I, I don't know where they are taking her or who else is involved. I only know that Marcus paid me to turn a blind eye."

"What kind of low-life, piece of shit are you. To sit back and allow this to happen, for money."

"I told him no. I wanted no part of this," the attendant said, shaking. "One night a few months ago two men came to my apartment, beat me up and said if I did not do what Marcus said, they would kill my family first, in front of me, then kill me. I was scared. Told me I would pay if I went to the cops. It has just gotten out of hand."

Matt ran in, "FBI's on their way. ETA five minutes. I'll stay. You all get back. I'll be there as soon as possible."

Drake let the attendant go and hurried to his car. Dallas grabbed his arm.

"Let me drive. You should not be driving."

"Fuck off, Dallas."

Instead of getting in the truck he arrived in, Dallas got in with Drake. Everyone raced back to the office. Drake called Drew while he was on his way.

"Drew, you have anything yet?"

"Negative. Cannot pin anything on the SUV. We are trying to get into the traffic cameras to see if we can trace their movements. How far out are you?"

"Ten. Keep working. We have to get her."

"I know, Drake. I know."

Hanging up, Drake sped to the office at a supersonic pace, the others on his tail. Tearing into the office, everyone convened in the tech room. By the time they got there, Drew and Rocco were able to pull the traffic cams and follow the SUV.

"What you got?" Drake demanded.

"Look."

They all watched as the SUV took a non-direct route. Typical scenario to make sure they were not being followed. The vehicle pulled into a private airstrip. The traffic cameras were a little far back, but they could see the SUV pull up to a plane, the people exit, and get on the plane. Moments later it took off. She was gone.

"Mother Fucker. Get the numbers on the plane, a flight plan, something. We can't let them get away."

"Working on it," Trent said.

Trent and Rocco went to work on identifying the plane. Jax, Jace, and Dallas re-reviewed the surveillance footage to see if they could find anything they missed. Garrett was on the phone with Matt.

"Matt and Agent Harris will be here in a few. Agent Harris has his team handling the club," Garrett said, watching Drake pace back and forth.

"Fine. Anything yet?" Drake barked.

"Negative," a few voices echoed.

"Hurry the fuck up."

"Drake, you need to get your head on straight," Drew said.

"Fuck you, Drew,"

Pulling him to the side, "Look. I know you care about Lila. We all do; but if we are going to find her, you need to get your shit together and focus. You're the best at this. We need you. Lila needs you. I know it's hard. If it was Shayla, I would be the same way. You can lose it later. Lila needs you to be at the top of your game."

"You're right. You're right," Drake said.

"Shayla. Oh shit. I better call Shayla. She would never forgive me if I did not tell her what happened."

Drake took a few deep breaths, cleared his head. Drew was right. Losing his shit would not help find Lila. This is what he did best, find and help people. Time to do his job. One last deep breath and the warrior took over. He calmed, went over to the guys and went to work.

Drew called Shayla and told her what happened. She broke down, started screaming and crying. Drew tried everything he could to calm her.

"I'm coming."

"No. Just stay home. I'll keep you posted."

"There is no way I can stay here. She is my best friend. I'll go crazy waiting on news. I would rather be there with you all."

"Don't drive. Please. Get a cab, Uber, something. You are not fit to drive. I don't need to worry about you being distracted and getting in an accident. Promise me."

"I promise."

Hanging up, Shayla called a cab and told them she would pay double fare if they were there in 5-10 minutes.

The tech room was a hot bed of activity. Everyone was doing something to try to trace the kidnappers. They all knew the first 24-hours were crucial. Matt arrived with Agent Harris, Shayla only a few minutes behind.

"So, what do you have?" Agent Harris inquired when they walked into the tech room.

"We tailed them to an airfield in the southeast part of the city and are still trying to get an image of the plane's identification numbers. They have had her now about 45 minutes," Drew said looking at his watch.

"She was right," Dallas said distraughtly.

"What?" Drew asked.

"Several times Lila said how suspicious she was of Marcus. If that is even his real name. Even tonight when that girl Trina started talking about the missing women, she tried to tell us something did not add up. We just blew her off, and she was right all along."

The room was silent for a few moments until Drake finally spoke. "You're right. I blame myself most of all. I told her to trust me. I told her she would never be alone, but I failed her."

"We all failed her," Jace said. "Now, let's go get her.

"Damn right. We need to find my baby girl," Rocco said sternly.

A CONTINUOUS HUM filled Lila's ears, only to be followed by pain in her temples. She heard voices around her but could not focus, could not see anyone. Was the place dark? Were her eyes open? she questioned as she suddenly recognized one of the voices. Marcus. That creepy fucker. Then it struck her. He'd drugged her, bastard, but where was she now? While her senses were coming around, Lila remained still and listened. She did not want them to know she was alert.

"Boss man's going to love this one. What a beauty. I can't wait to get my hands on her," a man with a Spanish accent said.

"Yes she is, but you better keep your hands off the merchandise. He may want her for himself," Marcus replied.

"Hope not. I want to test her out. See what she is made of."

"You want to test out all of them."

Lila heard movement. Someone was approaching. Shutting her eyes, peaking just enough so she could slightly see, a man filled her vision. While not that tall, he was clearly strong as evidenced by his physique. The man started fondling her body, his hands traveling to her breast.

Before he even knew what was happening, she grabbed his wrist and bent it backwards, then punched him in the balls, jumping on top of him. Lila, punched, kneed, did everything she had learned against this animal.

The guy was strong and was able to get up, punching Lila in the face several times. She stumbled back and fell. The man then kicked her in the ribs. The kick knocked the wind out of her. Focusing, Lila swept her leg at his knees, dropping him. Space was limited, and Lila realized they were on a plane. They both got up to square off when Lila felt the sting of the syringe. Fuck me, she thought.

"Julio, settle down. You always let your temper get the best of you," Lila heard, just before everything went dark, again.

HER BODY WAS HOT. She felt sweat droplets running a marathon in all directions. She could not see. Everything was dark, black. Pain seared throughout her body. What happened? Where am I? Suddenly everything came rushing back like a tsunami. She was taken. Another victim. The operation failed. Will he find me? Will I ever be free again?

Starting to regain her vision, she saw a sliver of light high up to her right. Starting to get her bearings, Lila was finally able to focus a little as she looked around the room. She saw a few cots lined against the walls, one overhead light where a ceiling fan hung, barely making any impact on the heat. There was a toilet and sink in the corner, no walls for privacy. There were several windows, high up on the walls, which were open, but had bars on them. Trying to sit up, Lila noticed slight movement from the back corner. Her vision had yet to fully restore, but she realized it was another person.

"Are you okay?" a quiet feminine voice asked.

Squinting, trying to focus better, Lila finally saw her. "Caroline?"

The woman moved forward, looking at Lila. "How do you know my name?"

"We've been looking for you. I can't believe I found you."

Caroline approached. "Well, looks like they got you, too. Are you okay? They hurt you," Caroline said, noticing cuts and bruises on Lila's face.

"I'm okay. Fucker hit me when I went after him on the plane. Then they drugged me again, and here I am."

"They are cruel, cruel people. Especially if you do not do exactly as they say, Julio in particular. I unfortunately have felt his anger," she said, dropping her head, a lost look on her face.

Lila took a long look at Caroline. She was petite, but looked very frail, defeated and childlike. Her clothes were minimal, and she looked as though she was unkempt. The startling part was the emptiness in her eyes. Lila ached for her, wondering what she had been through. Lila finally responded. "Yeah, he's the one. I did get a few blows in, though," she said coughing and grimacing from the pain. "We've got to figure out how to get out of here."

"It's hopeless. They all have guns."

"Nothing is hopeless, Caroline. Shit," Lila said remembering her collar. She reached up. Thank God. It was still there. They did not remove it, and Lila smiled.

"DRAKE, DRAKE," Trent yelled.

"What?"

"I've got a beacon on Lila."

Everyone rushed over to Trent. Sure enough, there was a beacon. Next thing they knew, a screen came alive with the camera view. All they saw was another woman. Ripped clothes, dirty, then the audio engaged.

"There you go, my sweet girl. Didn't forget to active the trackers," Rocco said.

"Got a location yet?" Drake asked.

"Closing in. Give me a minute, and I should be able to pinpoint her," Trent said, right before they heard talking.

"Caroline. I'm Lila. We will get you out of here. I swear. Drake and the boys are on it. They are the best of the best," they heard Lila say.

"She found Caroline. Oh my God," Drew said.

"No one can help us. There have been others since I have been here. No one comes to help," the other woman, Caroline, said.

"What happened to the others? How many have you seen?"

"Two. Julio likes to 'test the merchandise.' If they comply, apparently they are auctioned off."

"Mother fuckers. Why are you still here Caroline? You've been missing almost two weeks."

"I don't . . . don't comply."

Lila waited for Caroline to continue.

"I scream, fight each time Julio 'tests' me. I heard them say no one will purchase me if I am not obedient," she said softly, her eyes downcast.

Lila understood what she meant. That evil fucker had raped her, repeatedly. Lila could not imagine how Caroline had withstood being repeatedly raped. Sure, Lila had experienced trauma at the hands of a man, but being beat up does not even come close to being raped. She knew at that moment there was no way she was going to allow them to hurt her ever again.

"Well, we are getting out of here."

"Good girl. Keep her talking Lila," Agent Harris said. "You're recording all of this right?"

"Yes," Matt replied.

"Good. Gives us more ammo when we catch them."

"Got it!" Trent yelled. "They are on a private island off the coast of Houston. Fuck me."

"What?" Drake asked.

"That island is owned by the Perez cartel. Guess he is expanding his business from the international drug trade to sex trafficking."

"Wonderful, just wonderful. This makes things a little more complicated. We have to assume they have strong firepower," Drew said. "Agent Harris, can you get a warrant secured? We should have enough already."

"Yes, right on it," he said as he started to walk away, grabbing his phone.

"If you want your team to go, have them here in thirty," Drake told Agent Harris. "We will be heading out. Garrett, Dallas, get the gear. Jax, Jace, get the firepower. Rocco, please call Stan and make sure the plane is fueled and ready," Drake commanded.

Everyone stopped when they heard Caroline speak.

"Quiet. They're coming," she said, and they could see her scurry back to a cot in the back corner. They could see Lila turn toward an opening door. Lila leaned back and they got a view of his face. Smart thinking on her part.

"Trent."

"On it." Trent knew Drake wanted him to do facial recognition.

"The puta is awake," the guy who entered the room said.

"Oh, look, its Satan's spawn," Lila spewed.

"Fuck, Lila, don't egg him on," Drake yelled out loud.

"Ha ha ha. The little whore thinks she's funny. Maybe it's time to show you who's boss. You'll be begging me for mercy and learn to keep your smart mouth shut," Julio said as he grabbed Lila, throwing her on the cot, pinning her down. Lila struggled underneath him, trying to figure out how to get out from his grip. "I'm going to show you how to behave. You will listen when I am done with you. Show you what a real man is," Julio said as he was trying to remove her panties. Once he let go of one arm, Lila slammed an elbow in his face. The blow stunned him enough Lila was able to push him and get up on her feet.

"You little bitch. You are going to pay for that."

"Bring it on, pond scum."

Drake and the team were on edge watching everything go down and not being able to do anything to stop it. A cross between being pissed she was not keeping her mouth shut and proud of her fighting back struggled in their minds. They all knew what would happen if Lila didn't fight.

Hearing Shayla quietly crying behind them, Drew turned to her. "Shayla, you need to leave. You shouldn't be seeing this," Drew said, trying to guide her out of the room.

"No," she screamed. "I love Lila. She is my friend. I know I can't help her, and seeing this is destroying me, but I sure as hell can at least be here rooting her on, even if she is unaware."

"Fine, but if it gets worse, if anything . . . happens, you're leaving. No questions." Shayla nodded in agreement.

Looking back at the screen, they saw Julio try to punch Lila. She backed up just as he skimmed the bottom of her face, blood spurting from her bottom lip. She ducked then landed an upper cut, rocking Julio's head back, following up with a kick to his gut.

"Fucking, puta. I'm going to kill you."

Something snapped in Julio, and he unleashed a full force assault against Lila. He came at her like a lion attacking prey. Landing numerous punches to her face, he continued punching and kicking her ribs. Lila did everything she could to defend herself, but Julio was strong and large. The madness that engulfed him was overpowering. Caroline screamed, telling him to stop.

"Oh my God," Shayla choked, tears streaming down her face as the group watched in horror. Drake went white. This guy was going to kill her while they watched. Suddenly, the door flew open and a shot rang out. Marcus and another one of Perez's men ran in. Julio stopped, hovering over top of Lila, heaving heavy breaths.

"What the fuck are you doing, Julio? You trying to kill her?" Marcus yelled.

"That fucking puta hit me. No one hits Julio."

"And I'm sure you weren't trying to *test* her out even after the boss said not to."

"Fuck you, Marcus. I do as I please."

"Tell that to the boss man. Leave, now!"

Caroline rushed over to Lila and grabbed and held her.

"Is she okay?" Marcus asked.

"What do you think? Please get the doctor."

Marcus nodded to the other goon and just shook his head. "The doc will be here soon," he said as he turned and left, the door locking behind him.

Drake let out his breath. She's alive. Thank God they walked in. A few minutes more and she would not have made it. He could not imagine life without Lila.

Life without Lila.

It struck him that moment he had fallen in love with her. She was his life. Everything he had ever desired, searched for, he finally found, in Lila. He could not lose her now. She brought him a happiness he had never before experienced. She was his equal, if not more. Drake would do anything for her, and everything depended on this moment.

"Are we ready?"

"Affirmative. Van is loaded," Garrett said.

"Plane's ready," Rocco added.

"Already got the transfer to the portables so we can monitor her on the plane," Trent added.

"My team will meet us at the hanger. A Houston crew will be at the rendezvous point with the warrant. We can coordinate plans on the flight," Agent Harris said.

"Well, let's get the fuck out of here," Drake demanded.

Drew went to kiss Shayla and tell her he would keep her posted.

"Oh, no, you don't. I'm going," she said.

"Shayla. You can't. I can't have you in harm's way."

"I'll stay with the plane. I have to be there for Lila when you find her. You can't stop me!"

"Hmph. Fine. I understand. Just do what I say, okay?"

"Yes, Drew. I understand. I cannot stay back. Not this time."

"I know, love. I know."

They took off and headed to the hanger. As promised, Agent Harris' team was waiting. Quickly, the equipment was loaded onto the plane, the systems were up and running, and they were ready to go. Drake kept looking at the monitors to see if there were any changes in Lila. Caroline was still sitting there, holding her.

12

W here was the doctor Marcus promised? Caroline thought. She did not know what to do for Lila but hold her. She knew Julio was violent, but she had never seen him like this. Pure evil radiated and was reflected in his eyes. She truly thought he would kill her. It was the one and only time she was thankful someone else entered the room.

Clanking came from the door, and in walked Dr. Menendez. Dr. Menendez was kind to the girls. Caroline could not wrap her head around how he got involved with these people. How gentle and caring he was did not resonate with someone involved in sex trafficking. Did they pay him so much he just overlooked the horror and torment experienced by the women? Dr. Menendez was an oxymoron. It just did not add up.

"Jesus," he said when he took his first look at Lila. He mumbled something under his breath and then drew cross over his heart. Dr. Menendez walked to them and bent down to check Lila.

"What did he do to her?"

"He beat her, badly, just because she punched him when

the bastard was trying to rape her. She fought back, and this is the result."

"Has she lost consciousness?"

"No, I haven't," Lila suddenly said in short breaths.

"Oh, Lila. Thank God. I thought you were unconscious. This is Dr. Menendez. He is a nice man. Let him help you."

"How can I trust someone associated with these evil people?"

"Lila. May I call you Lila? I am not one of them. I'm not here by choice. Just like you. Let me take a look at you, try to get you patched up, then we can talk. Okay?"

Interesting, Caroline thought.

"Fine."

"Now, besides what I can see, please tell me where it hurts and where he hit you."

"My face, obviously. My wrists, but they should be fine. I took quite a few punches and kicks to my abdomen and ribs."

Dr. Menendez first examined Lila's face. He got some warm water and a clean rag and started wiping the blood off her. "Your lip will heal. I think I need to put a few stiches in this cut on the back of your head. Do you have any blurriness in your vision, feel dizzy?"

"No."

"Good," he said, taking a light and checking her eyes. "I don't think you have a concussion, but you will have some significant bruising and swelling. Now, Lila, I'm going to need to remove your dress to be able to examine you. Is that okay?"

"Yes."

"Caroline, can you grab a sheet so I can put it over her?"

"Yes, Doctor," Caroline said as she quickly got up to grab a sheet. She returned and helped Lila remove her dress and draped the sheet across her.

Pulling the sheet up enough to expose her abdomen, Dr.

Menendez slowly started to press. "Tell me if anything hurts and if so, describe the pain."

"That hurts, but just feels sore. Not when you press hard, just as soon as you touch it."

"There's a bruise forming." Dr. Menendez continued to check her abdomen. Lila had similar responses. He then took his stethoscope and listened. "I do not think you have any internal injuries, just a lot of bruising. I am sure it will get worse before it gets better. Now can you take in a deep breath?" he asked as he moved the stethoscope to listen to her lungs.

Lila gasped and coughed. "Ouch, that hurts."

"Can you show me where?"

Lila points to her left middle rib cage. Dr. Menendez felt around, and Lila suddenly jumped.

"Sorry, Lila. I know it hurts. I think you may have cracked ribs on top of the contusions. Your breathing sounds good, even though it hurts." Dr. Menendez listened to her heart and checked her extremities. "You are a lucky lady."

"I don't consider this lucky."

"True. So true. Bad choice of words. From what I can see overall you should heal. Probably have a cracked rib or two, but all I can do is tape you to help with the pain. I need to stitch the cut on your head, and the rest are a lot of contusions. I will see if they will give me some ice to help reduce the swelling, but you will need time to heal."

"Good, but I doubt I have a lot of time."

"Can I go ahead and tape you and address these wounds?"

"Yes, go for it."

Dr. Menendez took some wide tape from his bag and asked Caroline to help. He taped up Lila's ribs to help make her breathing less painful. She felt immediate relief. Next he took out a needle, stitches, and a syringe. Lila shifted back slightly.

"My dear Lila. This is just to numb the gash so you don't feel me stich you up. It's not to drug you. I swear."

Lila relaxed and lets Dr. Menendez stitch her wound. He put some bandages on a few others and then grabbed some medication from his bag. "Here, take this. It will help with the pain."

"What is it?"

"Tramadol."

"Nope. No way. Not taking anything that causes impairment."

"Lila, you are really going to feel the pain. It will only get worse."

"Don't care. I need my mind to be clear. Got anything else?"

"How about some ibuprofen."

"Sure, but that's all."

"Yes. I understand."

Lila took the Advil and Caroline helped her back into her dress. Suddenly the door opened and Marcus walked in. "You about done in here, Doc?"

"No, Marcus. I need to stay for a while, at least a few hours, to monitor her for a concussion and internal injuries. Also, can I get some ice for the swelling?"

Marcus did not look pleased.

"I'm sure Julio will appreciate it. If something happens to her, he will have to face Perez. Don't think he wants that. I doubt he would fare well."

"Fine. Juan will bring the ice. You're right. I'll check back in a while," Marcus said, closing and locking the door behind him. A few minutes, later Juan returned with the ice.

As soon as he left, Lila sat up and looked around. She started to get up, but Dr. Menendez protested.

"Lila, you need to rest."

She did not listen, but picked up her stilettos. Turning the shoe around she grabbed a cot, stood on it, and smashed the camera that was above the door. She looked around and saw one more in the back, the same area she initially found Caroline, smashing that one as well. Lila then started searching the room, even though with every move, pain shot throughout her body.

"What are you doing, Lila," Caroline asked.

"Getting rid of the cameras and any bugs." She only found one in the light, hoping there weren't any more hidden in the room.

Sitting back down on the cot next to Dr. Menendez, talking low, "So, you seem nice, seem to care. How in the hell did you get involved with these guys?"

As soon as her question was out, the door clanked and opened. In walked Marcus and another goon.

"What did you do? The cameras are not working," Marcus said, looking around to see the debris from Lila's destruction.

"You may be holding me prisoner, but you sure as hell do not need to sit and watch me suffer. It's not like I am going anywhere," she said, pretending to get dizzy to cover for Dr. Menendez.

"Fine, but they will be replaced," Marcus said as he and the goon left.

"Okay, back to my question," Lila said.

"Like I said earlier, I am not one of them. I am not here by choice; like you, just different circumstances," Dr. Menendez said, sighing.

"Tell me."

"I am a surgeon out of San Antonio. My family is still down there. One day some of Perez's *representatives* visited my office and offered me money for my services, and I refused. I was told I had no choice. I told them I did not want any part of their business. Next thing I knew, the following week, I received a text message with a picture of my family, gagged and bound, guns pointed at their heads. In walked Perez's men. They asked me now if I would work for them or would I watch my family be murdered, and here I am. I have not seen my family since. He keeps them fed and a roof over their heads in exchange for my services. You see, I would not let him kill my family. He could have taken me, but I could not sacrifice my family."

"Oh my God, Dr. Menendez. I'm so sorry.

"Call me Javier," he said with a slight smile.

"Javier, do you know what they are drugging the women with? Well, I guess I am one of the women too."

"It's a very strong, fast-working sedative. Usually used on large farm animals. I feel so guilty because I am the one who prepares the syringes for them. It sickens me."

"I don't blame you, Javier," Lila said, and she meant it. She knew he was telling her the truth. Poor man. Leaning back, Lila started to think. "Do you have any of that sedative with you?"

"Yes, why?"

"I have an idea, and we all are getting out of here."

"We're what?" Caroline asked.

"Getting out of here. My guys will be coming, looking for us, but I don't think we have any time to waste. We need to get out ourselves."

"It's too dangerous. We will be killed."

"Caroline. Think about the alternative. You will either be killed anyway or be a sexual slave, sold to God knows who, and suffer for the rest of your life."

"You're right, but I'm scared."

"So am I."

"You don't look scared."

"Look, being scared and being brave to get ourselves out of asituation are different. What I need from you now is to be brave."

"I'll try."

"No. You will. I know you can do it. Javier, I'll need a syringe of the sedative," Lila said. She then filled them in on her plan.

"Lila, they will know how you got the sedative and they will kill my family," Javier said.

"I am aware of that. Already thought of an alternative. I'll tie you up so they think we overtook you. They will never know you were aware of the plan. When this is over and we arrest these bastards, you will be free from being under Perez's control. Drake will make sure of it."

"Who's Drake?" Javier asked.

"He's my . . . I work with him. I swear, Javier. I will do everything I can to help you and your family."

"I believe you will, Lila. I do. I know it sounds crazy just meeting you, but I trust you."

"Thank you, Javier. I trust you, too. Let's get moving. Caroline, can you rip up some sheets please," Lila said as they were getting ready to work on their plan.

"FUCK, LILA. DON'T BE A FOOL," Drake yelled into the monitor. "She has a death wish. She knows we'll be coming and has to wait."

"I feel the same, but I can't really blame her after what she just went through," Dallas said. "We don't know what they may do to either of them before we can get there."

Drake did not even want to think they may not get there in time to save them.

"Buckle up. Touching down in about ten," Garrett said from the cockpit.

He was their main pilot. All of them knew how to fly, but Garrett handled most of the flying unless it was an emergency.

"My guys are ready and waiting with the rest of the equipment. Are we all good with the plan?" Agent Harris asked.

"Yes," Drake and Drew both said.

"Good. We will go over it briefly when we hit the ground then get moving. I don't think those two have much time left, especially if your girl's plan goes afoul."

"She's smart. She's a good shot, if she moves forward before we are there, they have a chance as long as she can get a hold of a weapon," Rocco interjected.

The plane landed on a strip right on the waterway. As promised, Agent Harris' Houston team was ready and waiting. Boats were docked and ready to go. The team quickly started unloading their equipment, the guys having already changed on the flight.

"Drew, Drake, I would like you to meet Agent Simmons. He is the lead of the Houston team."

The men all shook hands. "So everyone up to speed on the plan," Drew asked.

"Yes. We've mapped out the compound and have targeted the best entry points," Agent Simmons said.

"Let's gather everyone so we can get this show on the road. Lila is about to make a move on her own," Drake said.

They called everyone together, Donovan Security crew and the FBI teams.

"We are all on the same page on everything so far. Here is a map showing where we are, the compound and the route is outlined. There are three entry points. Two have armed guards. They are here, here, and here," Agent Simmons said as he pointed out the landing targets. "This one here has a small tower by the dock."

"Yes, we saw that on our satellite pictures," Drake said.

Agent Simmons just looked at Agent Harris.

"They have clearances."

"Okay, I think it's better to break up into three teams. The house entry points are here," Agent Simmons said.

"Jace, give me our house plans," Drake asked. "We have it, along with the layout. Looking at the plan, our best guess is the ladies are here. Lila's beacon confirms they are somewhere in the southwest corner. This is where Perez and his family congregate. The back of the complex, where the ladies are held, is where his men's quarters are. We need to have one team infiltrate the family's part of the compound and the remaining two come in on each side of his men's quarters. We will presume they work in shifts and need to surprise them as much as possible," Drake said.

"I agree. This looks like a good plan. Your map gives us a clearer outline of the structure. Men, come forward and study this, commit it to memory," Agent Simmons said.

"How long will it take us on the skiffs to reach the compound," Drew asked.

"About three minutes, nineteen seconds."

"Okay. Let's make our teams and load the skiffs. I want at least one of my men on each team," Drake said.

"Roger."

They identified the teams, each one's landing point, rules of engagement, and went over the plan one more time.

"You all have seen the pictures, but here they are once again. Lila is the blonde and Caroline is the brunette. Eyes open for any other women you may come across. They could also be victims. Everyone ready to rock and roll?" Drake asked.

As soon as he asked that question, they all heard Shayla screaming.

"Drew, Drew. Come here now!"

Drew, Drake, and Agents Harris and Simmons ran onto the plane. On the screen they saw Lila against the wall, syringe in hand, ready to make a run for it.

"Fuck," Drake yelled.

"Shayla, keep watching. Tell us what you see in the mic. We will hear you. Can you do that?" Drew asked.

"Yes."

"It may not be pretty. You will not like what you see, but what you tell us will help us find them. Are you sure you can handle it? I can leave someone back."

Straightening her shoulders, she said, "Yes I can do it. I'll do anything for Lila."

"Okay, we're out," Drew said as he kissed Shayla, and they all dashed to the skiffs.

13

L ila was armed with the syringe. Dr. Menendez was tied up on one of the cots, and Caroline was ready to make noise to get the guard's attention. Lila nodded and Caroline started banging on the door. The door opened slightly, "What's with all the racket?" It was Julio. God, Lila hoped he was alone.

"The doctor needs assistance," Caroline said.

"Move out of my way," Julio said as he flung the door open all the way, pushing Caroline along with the door. He did not see Lila behind him. She pounced, quickly injecting the sedative. Julio had just enough time to see Dr. Menendez tied up, turned and looked at Lila before he stumbled and went down. Caroline shut the door and they quickly scurried to secure Julio. Lila searched him. She grabbed his AR15 and ammo strap. He also had a holstered handgun, and in his back pocket was a knife and keys, and a walkie talkie was attached to the gun belt.

"Do you know how to use a gun?" Lila asked Caroline.

Shaking her head no, Lila then placed the knife in her

hand. "Just in case. Go for the soft spots, eyes, throat, stomach."

Lila strapped on the holster and slung the AR15 ammo across her shoulders, and grabbed the AR15. Pain shot through her body, but Lila had to force herself to block the pain. She had no choice. "Caroline, we need to get moving. Stay directly behind me unless I instruct otherwise. Keep alert, and be ready for anything okay. You can do this. You just need to trust me."

"Okay. I trust you, Lila."

Lila then went to Javier. "I promise we will be back for you. My team will be here. I know it. I will make sure your family is safe," Lila said then kissed his forehead. Javier gave her a look. She knew it was him saying "good luck." She nodded then headed to the door. Opening it slightly, she listened. Not hearing anything, Lila opened the door, gun raised, and looked each way. The hall was clear. She went left, moving slowly down the hall, Caroline right on her heels. Slowly and quietly, they crept down the hall.

Javier had described the layout and what he knew of the compound in order to help them try to get to the best exit point. Unfortunately it would involve many turns and doorways, increasing their chances of running into one of Perez's men.

They cleared the first hall, stopping at a corner. Lila pushed Caroline back against the wall as she heard footsteps approaching. It sounded like only one person. Trying to be silent, Lila prayed he went straight and did not turn in their direction. The footsteps grew louder. Lila anticipated when the man would get to the hall opening. Three, two, one, she counted to herself. The man passed the opening and continued straight. Lila slowly let out her breath. Peaking around the corner, the hall was clear.

Making another left, they approached the area which

unfortunately took them past the men's sleeping quarters. As quietly as possible, they advanced. There was no way to avoid passing the men's quarters as it was in the direction of the quickest and most accessible route out of the building. As they approached the first door, Lila noticed it was shut. Listening closely, she didn't hear any movement. They moved past the first door, following the same precedent as they approached the second door.

Just as they were getting ready to move past, the door opened and two goons exited, spotted Lila. Taking the butt of the gun, Lila slammed it into the head of the first man. He dropped like a brick, out cold. The second man came at her. Lila could not bring the AR15 up fast enough. The man lunged, tackling Lila, and they both went down. A struggle ensued. Lila reached for the pistol while she wrestled with the man. She was finally able to get her hands on the pistol. A shot rang out, hitting the man in his side. He slumped on top of her, his blood starting to seep onto Lila. With some difficulty, Lila pushed him off and grabbed Caroline's hand.

"We've got to move, and fast. They will be on top of us before we know it with that gunshot." Pulling Caroline behind her, Lila fled. They had one more hall to conquer until they reached the outside, which opened up a whole new set of problems with being exposed. Lila heard feet scurrying toward them.

Lifting the gun, Lila screamed 'Get down' at Caroline. She got down just as a group of men rounded the corner. Lila let off a few rounds, hitting two of the men. The others fired back as they retreated behind the corner. Lila knew she had seconds to get Caroline out of harm's way.

"Go, go!" she said, encouraging Caroline to run in front of her. A few additional shots rang out in their direction, one just missing Lila, as she sprinted toward the last hall. As they approached the outside door, it suddenly opened, one of Perez' men entering. He did not see her in time. Lila pointed and fired. Another one down.

Caroline froze, the dead body directly in front of her. "Ignore him. Step over. We've got to move, get outside. They'll catch up to us any second. We've got to try to get to the docks."

Running full steam out of the building, Lila was taking shots at some of the men approaching from different directions. It seemed like the men were everywhere. How many men did Perez have? It felt like one against a hundred.

Lila heard other gunfire from afar, wondering briefly if the guys had made it. She did not have time to think about that. She had enough on her hands at the moment and had to get Caroline to safety, which was proving to be challenging.

Suddenly a shot rang, coming from behind. Tackling Caroline to the ground to protect her, Lila felt it, a punch in her back, followed by a burn and sting. Grabbing the pistol, she rolled over to see Julio staggering and pointing his gun at her. Lila pulled the trigger.

Everything slowed, and she saw the bullet strike him in the forehead, Julio fell back. Dead. A strange sense of satisfaction that she was the one who took him out engulfed her right before the pain and weakness became apparent. Reality sunk in. She had been shot. Julio got her, but he paid the ultimate price with his life.

Calm spread over Lila as she laid there. The last thing Lila remembered was Caroline screaming her name, then she saw him. His face. Drake. Right before losing consciousness.

"LILA'S ON THE MOVE," Shayla said looking at the map of the complex Drew left her. "She's moving left. I think that's east. She has a weapon, got it from that Julio guy. She pulled it off, was able to drug him and tie him up."

"Keep the info coming in, Shayla," Drew said.

"Looks like they are taking another left, the southeast corner. If I'm right, it looks like she is approaching the sleeping quarters. Seems like they are trying to head in the direction of the exit on the east side, Drake's crew's landing point. Oh, God!"

"What? What's happening," Drake said.

"No, oh no," Shayla said, pausing. "Whew, thank goodness."

"Tell me, Shayla," Drake demanded.

"Two men came into the hall. She hit one in the head with the butt of the gun and shot the other.

"Fuck, our ETA is about two minutes. Her shot will alert everyone on the complex. Teams, you all getting this?"

"Roger," said Drew, followed by Garrett.

Gasping, Shayla started to speak. "There's a group of men. They're firing at her and Caroline. Looks like she got a few. They came from the direction Lila was being held. They're running toward the outside door. Shit! Shit!"

"What, Shayla? We are landing now," Drake said.

"Someone came in from the outside. Whew, she got him. I have no idea how. It was so fast. Y'all better hurry. They are at the door, running. No!," Shayla screamed and started crying and yelling "no" over and over.

Drake saw it all. They were already on the compound and heading in Lila's direction, taking out anyone who got in their way. Julio, with some men behind him, approached the open door. Lila dove on top of Caroline but did not get down fast enough. She was hit but turned and fired, killing Julio. Drake ran to Lila while his team took care of the remaining men. Caroline already rolled her over and was screaming her name when he got to Lila, blood oozing out of left side of her back. They locked eyes for just a moment before Lila's eyes fluttered and closed.

"Stay with me, Lila. Please, please stay with me."

"We're secure," Garrett said.

"Us, too. What's happening?" Drew asked.

"Lila's been hit. She's bleeding, bad. Jace, get here. We need to get her extracted, fast."

"Roger. On my way," Jace replied.

"Lila, stay with me," Drake said putting pressure on her wound.

Finally finding her voice, Caroline grabbed Drake's arm, "Sir, sir. Dr. Menendez was in the room we were in. He is a good man. Not part of the group. He can help."

"What?"

"Dr. Menendez, he can help."

"Garrett, you copy?"

"Yep. On it."

Jace ran up and noticed blood everywhere. He rolled Lila to see the wound. The bullet went all the way through. It must have hit something due to all the blood. Pulling items from his pack, he cut Lila's dress to expose the area. He tried to clean the wound to get a better look just as Garrett approached with another man. This must be the doctor.

"Let me see, give me some room," the doctor said. The man swore in Spanish. "He hit an artery. I need a clamp." Jace just shook his head no. Dr. Menendez knew that meant he did not have anything like a clamp. "I think her lung is collapsing. Her breathing is erratic. We need to keep pressure on the wound and get her out of here, and fast."

Drew and Rocco ran up; Rocco's face turned white.

"Plan?" Drew asked.

"Get her to the skiff. Get a Life Flight at the airstrip pronto," Jace said.

They did not see Agent Harris approach. He was already on the phone calling in the emergency and the urgency. "Life Flight is five minutes out."

The rest of the guys approached, all with grave concern for

Lila etched on their faces. Dr. Menendez and Jace wrapped Lila as tightly as possible, keeping as much pressure on the wound as they could.

"We don't have a lot of time. She is losing a lot of blood. Let's move," Dr. Menendez said. Drake picked her up to carry her to the skiff. Dr. Menendez and Jace followed.

Caroline just sat there, Lila's blood covering her, shaking, shock setting in. Trent bent down in front of her. "Caroline," he said trying to get her to acknowledge him. "Caroline, I'm Trent, a good friend of Lila's. It's over. You're safe. I promise. Will you come with me? You need to get checked out at the hospital," he said softly. "Your parents are already on their way." That comment broke her trance and made her finally look up at Trent. What he saw killed him. This beautiful woman before him with such torment in her eyes.

"They're coming?" she asked, desperation in her voice.

"Yes. They will meet us at the hospital."

"Promise?"

"Promise. Now will you come with me? I'll protect you. Swear on my life."

Nodding, Caroline said, "Please take me where Lila will be. I need to be close. To make sure she is alright."

"I will," Trent said extending his hand.

Instead of taking his hand, she reached out with both arms, locking eyes with Trent. He took the clue and reached down and picked her up, cradling her in his arms as he took her to another skiff. "Don't worry, lovie. I've got you," Trent said as Caroline relaxed in his arms.

14

A n agent raced Drake, Lila, Jace, and Dr. Menendez back to the dock at the airfield. They were met by a bevy of emergency personnel, the Life Flight crew already waiting. Dr. Menendez advised of Lila's condition. They loaded her up on the stretcher, secured her, and headed to the helicopter.

"We only have room for one," the flight nurse said.

"I'm going," Drake barked.

Jace grabbed his arm, "Look man. I know how you feel about her, but let Dr. Menendez go. They need him. He's been keeping her as stable as possible."

It was the hardest split-second decision he had ever had to make, but he nodded in agreement. Drake did not know if this would be the last time he would see Lila alive. Drake never prayed, but today he did, asking God not to take her from him when he just found her.

"Where are you taking her?" Drake asked the flight team.

"Memorial."

Drake and Jace backed up so the helicopter could take off. As they turned around, they noticed another skiff approaching.

It was Trent with Caroline in his arms. Running over, Drake helped get Caroline out of the boat. She immediately reached for Trent as soon as he was on shore. Trent carried her to the closest ambulance, Drake walking alongside. The crew met them and got Caroline on the stretcher.

"You have to take me to where Lila is going. You must!" Caroline demanded.

Trent, at the doorway opening, once again reassured her. One of the EMTs came out to speak to them.

"Who's Lila?"

"She is the one who was taken on Life Flight. Caroline needs to be taken to Memorial. Her parents will be meeting us there," Trent said.

"We have to take her to the closest—"

"No, you will take her to Memorial. Her father is Senator Henderson."

"Oh. Okay. Do you know if she has been injured?"

"The blood is Lila's. Caroline is in shock, but she has been . . . repeatedly assaulted."

"Bastards."

"Trent!" they heard Caroline scream.

Dashing immediately inside the ambulance, he grabbed her hand. "It's okay, lovie. I'm here."

"Please stay with me. Don't leave me."

Trent looked at Drake. Drake nodded.

"I won't leave you. I'm right here."

The EMT's tended to Caroline, starting an IV while Trent gently wiped the blood off her. Just as they shut the back doors, Drake heard Shayla yelling his name, running full speed toward him.

She leaped into his arms, crying. "Lila, where are they taking Lila?"

"Memorial."

"We need to leave. We need to go now! What's her condition?"

"I'm not sure. It's not good," Drake said just as Drew, Rocco, and Agent Harris walked up.

Shayla flew into her husband's arms, repeating, "We need to get there. Get me to her, Drew."

"Take one of our SUV's," Agent Harris said, motioning to one of his guys. "I'll take care of everything here. Lila's more important. We will meet up later. Some of your guys are still here to help. I'll get them to the hospital when we secure everything."

Not hesitating, Drake grabbed the keys when the young agent held them out in his hands. Drew quickly grabbed them from Drake.

"I'm driving. No arguments."

Drake knew not to argue. He was not in the best mental state to be behind the wheel. The four of them darted to the SUV and took off to the hospital, all of them saying silent prayers in the process.

THE FLIGHT TEAM and Dr. Menendez were trying to keep Lila stabilized. The paramedic inserted an IV and was giving her fluids at a fast pace. Her bleeding continued, not seeming to slow.

"We're losing her," the paramedic said.

"No. I can't let that happen. We need to clamp her. Fuck!" Dr. Menendez said as Lila's vitals stopped.

The flight nurse immediately started compressions as the paramedic and Dr. Menendez scrambled to get her as sterile as possible.

"Give me a scalpel. Quick."

Dr. Menendez opened the area and searched through all the oozing blood for the source. He found it. "Clamp, now."

He grabbed the clamp, the nurse stopping compressions so he could clamp the bleed. Once clamped, she resumed compressions.

Beep . . . beep . . . beep they heard from the monitor. "She's back. The clamp is helping bring her blood pressure up," the paramedic said.

"Her breathing is still shallow." Listening to her lungs, Dr. Menendez said, "Her lung is collapsing. We need a chest tube or she will not make it to surgery."

Quickly grabbing a kit, they doused Lila again to keep her as clean as possible, and Dr. Menendez inserted the chest tube in seconds, blood quickly flowing out, restoring lung function. Lila's vitals and breathing improved.

"They have an OR ready?"

"Yes, Doctor."

"Good. Please tell them I'm going in with them."

"But sir—"

"I am Dr. Javier Menendez, a trauma surgeon from San Antonio General. Lila is my patient, my friend. I can't leave her now. She just saved Senator Henderson's daughter and I need to save her. Too many people are counting on me."

"Okay, doctor. Trauma has copied and are waiting on us. One minute out."

As soon as the Life Flight landed, the trauma team was waiting, ready to rush Lila off to the operating room. A nurse escorted Dr. Menendez to a locker room to change and clean up for surgery.

Dr. Menendez quickly changed and prepped for surgery, knowing Lila needed immediate attention. That clamp was a temporary fix, giving them precious minutes to get her into surgery. He met Dr. Jacobs, briefed him on what occurred, what was done on the Life Flight, and then they went in to save her.

DRAKE, Drew, Shayla, and Rocco arrived at the hospital. Swiftly entering the emergency department, Drake dashed to the information desk.

"Lila Norris. She arrived on Life Flight. What's her status?" Drake demanded.

"One moment, sir," the clerk said typing on the computer.

"I need to know if she is okay."

"What is your relationship to Ms. Norris?" the clerk asked just as Shayla, Drew, and Rocco caught up.

Hesitating only momentarily, "She's my fiancée."

Clicking her keys a few more times, the clerk looked up at Drake. "She is currently in surgery Mr.?"

"Donovan."

"Mr. Donovan, if you go down this hall, make a left, you will see the OR waiting room. I will put a note in the system that family has arrived."

Drake and the others followed the clerk's directions and went to the waiting room. Shayla sat down; Rocco sat next to her and grabbed her hand. Drake could not relax. He would sit, then get up and pace the room, only to continue to repeat the process.

Drew's phone buzzed. It was Agent Harris. "It's Harris. I'm going to take this in the hall." Drew was gone about twenty minutes. He came back with drinks for everyone.

"Thought you all could use a drink," he said as he passed them out, Drake still pacing the room. "Any updates?"

"Not yet. What's taking so long? They should have had her in surgery for some time now," Drake said.

"Come on man. You wearing a groove in the floor is not going to make it go any faster."

"I know. I know. What did Agent Harris say?"

"They got Perez, Marcus, and five of his men. Found the woman taken after Caroline, Kimmy. Perez had decided she would be his. Thirteen DOA's. Looks like Lila took several out herself.

"Oh, thank goodness they found the other girl," Shayla said.

"Unfortunately it looks like there were many before them. Preliminary reports show at least 100 or more. They found files and records at the compound of other women. Auctions and purchases. Most were false names, so there is a lot of work to do to figure out who else is involved. It's looking like it will turn into an international investigation."

"Oh, my God," Shayla said.

"Also found thirty kilos of cocaine. We should have enough to put them away for life."

An hour passed, and the rest of the team from Donovan Security arrived, except Trent as he was still with Caroline.

"Any news yet?" Dallas asked right as Dr. Menendez rounded the corner.

Drake rushed over, grabbed him by the shoulders. "Is she alive? Is she okay? Please tell me she is okay."

"Drake, is that correct? Let's sit," Dr. Menendez said.

He did as asked, and they sat down across from Shayla and Rocco. The rest of them gathered around.

"Lila is alive. The bullet nicked an artery as you probably figured. I was able to clamp it on the flight over until we could get her into surgery. Dr. Jacobs and I were able to repair the artery. The bullet had gone all the way through. No organs were damaged. The soft tissue injuries should heal fine in time. Her lung unfortunately did collapse on the flight, so I also had to insert a chest tube. Her breathing has been restored, and we were able to remove the tube."

"So she's going to be fine?" Drake said.

"The major concern now is the blood loss. She lost a lot. We had to give her three pints. The next twenty-four hours will tell us more. She is still sedated from the surgery, but don't be surprised if she is still unconscious when it wears off. With the trauma and blood loss, the body sometimes slows itself down in order to heal."

"When can I see her?"

"In about an hour. She will be in the ICU until she gains consciousness, at a minimum. I will do everything in my power to help Lila. She wanted to help me and my family who are also victims of Perez. I only had a few hours with her, but I know how special she is."

"She sure is," Dallas said.

"She's tough too. I've never met a woman who would take on a cartel all by herself after she had already taken a beating. She's remarkable, so strong. If anyone can pull through its Lila. Well, I'm going to check on Caroline. I will keep you updated and let you know when you can see her, even if only for a few minutes.

"Thanks, Doc. Keep us posted," Drew said.

Drake sat down and put his head in his hands. She was alive. Relief flooded his body. While she was not out of the woods, the first obstacle was over. Drake knew firsthand many people with gunshot wounds never made it out of surgery. He was still worried. He saw how much blood she lost and suspected she lost a lot more before surgery was over. Sometimes the loss of blood was what took them, even if the doctor's repaired the damage. Dr. Menendez confirmed his concern was the blood loss. Drake knew the next twenty-four hours were going to be the worst of his life. Not knowing if Lila would pull through was going to kill him.

"I'm going to go check on Caroline and Kimmy. They were brought here to be examined. I also want to see if the senator has arrived," Drew continued. "Him and his wife were on their way. You want to come with me? Give yourself a break until you can go in and see Lila?"

"No. I'm not leaving . . . just in case."

"I am going to stay with Drake," Shayla added.

Drew kissed Shayla and headed over to the emergency room.

15

The emergency room was a hot bed of activity. On top of the normal abundance of staff, patients, and relatives, there was a bevy of law enforcement and security for the senator. Drew went to the desk, flashed the clerk his contractor IDs for the Federal Government, and told the clerk Agent Harris and Senator Henderson were expecting him.

The clerk called the back to confirm prior to granting him access.

"Okay, Mr. Donovan. Take a left, go to the end then take a right. Follow to the end of the hall. I am sure you won't miss them. They are in Rooms 21 and 22."

The door clicked, and Drew followed the clerk's directions. He saw Agent Harris and Trent right outside the doorway to the rooms.

"How's Lila?" Trent asked. "Is she going to be okay?"

"She made it out of surgery, lost a lot of blood. She will be in the ICU. Doc said next twenty-four hours will determine a lot," Drew said.

"Damn. Keep me updated. I don't know much about her, but from what I saw, she is a tough one," Agent Harris said.

"She sure is. So how's Caroline, Kimmy?"

"Medically they both are cleared. The doctors are running blood work, testing for STDs, given the situation, as well as the standard rape kit."

"That is expected; sad, but expected."

"Yes. Kimmy seems to be doing a lot better emotionally. From what we got from her so far, she witnessed Julio rape Caroline. When Perez called for her to be brought to him to preview, he decided he was going to keep her as his, at least for the time being. She complied. Kimmy said that she would just try to think of it as role playing to be able to get through being kidnapped and raped. She did not want the brutality Caroline experienced to happen to her. She will need counseling for sure but seems to be handling things better than it could have been. Just thankful we found her. She said Perez actually treated her well because she was obedient. Caroline on the other hand—"

"What about Caroline?"

"Well, you heard what she told Lila. While it does not appear that they beat her, they forcibly held her down and repeatedly raped her, as evidenced by the bruising on her arms and legs and other signs of forced contact." Drew knew exactly what he meant. "She would scream, cry, and try to fight them off each time. On more than one occasion, there would be several men holding her down while she was raped. They would take turns trying to make her comply. Needless to say, she is not faring well. She jumps whenever a male nurse or doctor enters her room; they had to switch over to an all-female staff treating her."

"Poor girl. She clung to you though Trent. Even wanted you to stay with her in the ambulance."

"Yeah. I can't explain it. As soon as I saw her, I felt a need to help her. I assured her that she would be safe; I would make sure of it. I guess she believed me, especially after Lila told her that we would help them. She must trust me because of Lila."

"Maybe. When someone experiences trauma, we do not know what will trigger them and what will not. She must have a sense of security with you."

"I wish I could help her more. Make all this go away."

"We all do. Is the senator in there with her?"

"Yes, he and his wife. I felt it best to leave the room, give her time with her family. She protested, but I told her I would be right here, she needed to be with her parents."

At that moment Senator Henderson exited Caroline's room. He immediately came up to the group. Sticking out his hand to shake the senator's hand, the senator bypassed the shake and grabbed and hugged Drew, patting him on his back.

"Thank you, thank you so much for finding my little girl. There is no way I can truly repay you all for bringing her back to us."

"You're welcome, senator, but Lila was the one who truly saved your daughter."

"Yes, Caroline told me what she did for her. That she was shot protecting her. How is she doing?"

"She's out of surgery and lost a lot of blood. Only time will tell, but we are hopeful. Lila is strong, much stronger than most of us gave her credit for. I know she will fight to come out of this, I'm sure."

"We will be praying for her. If there is anything, I mean anything, I can do to help, get her the best medical care, anything, please let me know. We owe you, owe her. She will always have a place close to our hearts for saving our Caroline."

"Thank you senator. We appreciate it."

"Stu honey, Caroline is asking for you, and you as well, Trent," Senator Henderson's wife said as she peaked out of Caroline's hospital room door.

"Gentlemen, I better get back in there. Please keep me informed. You have my cell number, and we will check in on

Lila's recovery," Senator Henderson said just before he went back into the hospital room.

"I will be down there shortly to check on Lila. Let me see what Caroline needs," Trent said as he turned and headed back into her room.

"I better get back to Shayla and Drake. See if there is an update. You know how to find me."

"Affirmative. Keep me posted also," Agent Harris said.

Drew found Shayla and Rocco still sitting in the waiting room holding hands. Drake was still pacing back and forth. Jace, Jax, and Matt were sitting around a table quietly playing cards, while Garrett stood leaning up against the wall watching them. Dallas was sitting on the opposite side, eyes closed, head back against the wall. He was not sleeping, the distress on his face all telling. In actuality, the distress and concern for Lila shrouded all of their faces.

Drew walked over to Shayla, "Any news yet?"

"No. Not yet," Shayla said softly.

"I don't know what is taking them so fucking long. Why haven't they come to get me so I can see her," Drake demanded.

"Drake, it has not been even an hour. Dr. Menendez said it would be at least an hour."

Making a growling sound at Drew, "I don't care. I want to —I need to—see her now," he yelled.

Dr. Menendez arrived in the waiting room just as those words were out of his mouth. Drake sprinted to him.

"She is in the ICU now. I can take two of you in to see her. No more than two at a time."

"Let's go," Drake said.

Drew looked at Shayla.

"I'm going, too," Shayla added.

Drew looked at Dr. Menendez. "Can, just this once, we have three people?"

Dr. Menendez understood what Drew was saying. He knew Drew needed to be there for his wife and his brother the first time they saw Lila. Seeing her was going to be difficult.

"Just this once. Others will have to come in twos. Visitation is very limited in the ICU."

"We understand, and thank you," Drew said.

"Well, let's go," Drake demanded.

"Why don't all of you follow me? There is a different waiting room for the ICU."

Everyone got up and followed Dr. Menendez. He led them to the ICU waiting room, then turned to the group.

"If you three will follow me, I will take you to Lila. You can switch out with the others so they all get a chance to see her. It will need to be quick. The next visiting times are at 4pm and 8pm. You only get about 30 minutes each time."

They entered the ICU floor, following Dr. Menendez, as staff was moving about. It was relatively quiet except for the hums and beeps of medical equipment. Since these were the sickest patients, noise was kept at a minimum in order to encourage healing.

Dr. Menendez walked them to the corner room and held the door open. What they saw shocked them. Shayla almost immediately collapsed and would have hit the floor if it was not for Drew being there to catch her.

Lila was pale, extraordinarily pale. So many tubes connected to her lifeless body, multiple machines monitoring anything and everything. There was no movement, except for the very small rise and fall of her breaths.

Drake just stood there, at the end of her bed, staring. He could not move, just looked at her, like his feet were made of cement. His vibrant, stubborn Lila, laying there helpless, fighting to stay alive.

Shayla pulled away from Drew and moved to Lila's bedside. She found and held her hand.

"Lila. Lila. It's me, Shayla. I'm here. We are all here. We love you. You need to get better. I need you to get better. You're my best friend. I need you to keep these boys in line," Shayla said as tears streamed down her face.

Drew came up behind Shayla and put his hands on her shoulders, rubbing. "Shayla is right," Drew said. "Shayla can't keep these boys in line without your help. Especially Drake. You have to keep giving him shit. It provides me with a lot of entertainment."

It was quiet for a few moments until Dr. Menendez, who was standing at the door, spoke. "If you want any of the others to have a minute to see her, we better do so now. Since this is not normal visiting time, we only have a few minutes."

"I'm not leaving," Drake said.

"Understood," Drew said. "Shayla, let's go so someone else can come in."

Shayla kissed Lila, Drew did the same, and they left the room with Dr. Menendez. The doctor returned with Rocco and Dallas, Drake never moved from the foot of her bed. Rocco immediately went to her side and grabbed her hand, like Shayla.

"My baby girl. Oh, my sweet baby girl. You did so good, so good. You saved Caroline, got her out of there. I could not be more proud of you. Now you just get yourself better. I need you back in that Dome showing these buffoons how it is done," Rocco said.

"He's right sunshine. Looks like you can show me a thing or two. You better get yourself up and out of here. Who will I flirt with and drive Drake nuts if you are not around."

"Oh, Dallas, you flirt enough with everyone. Lila will just shoot you down like always. Don't listen to him, sweet girl. He's a fool. Well, do listen to him because you need to wake up and get back to me. Love you, sweet girl," Rocco said kissing her on the cheek.

The guys got up and left so the others could come see Lila. Jax and Jace next, then Matt and Garrett. They all only stayed a minute.

After Matt and Garrett retreated, Dr. Menendez told Drake they needed to leave until the next visiting time.

"I told you, I'm not leaving."

"Drake, they won't let you stay. This is the ICU, the rules are different."

Drake just stood there, at the end of the bed, ignoring the doctor. Dr. Menendez went to get Drew. Maybe he could help get Drake so he did not cause a scene. Drew came back to the room with the doctor.

"Come on, man. You know you can't stay. Let's go grab something to eat, and before you know it, the next visiting time will be here."

"No. I'm not leaving. Not sure why you all don't understand."

The door opened and Drew dreaded it would be security coming to haul Drake out of the room. This would not go very well. He turned around to see Senator Henderson and Agent Harris at the door.

"He does not have to leave. He can stay with Lila as long as he wants. I, we, made sure of it," the senator said referring to him and Agent Harris.

"We talked to the staff and administrator of the hospital. They understand that Lila is important. Part of an FBI investigation and someone is to be with her and protect her at all times," Agent Harris added.

"Thank you gentlemen. I do not think it would be easy trying to get him to leave," Drew replied.

"I agree."

Senator Henderson approached the side of Lila's bed and just looked at her. "What a brave young woman. I owe everything to her. Caroline is here because of you, young lady. You better heal, get better, so I can thank you properly." Turning to Drake, said, "Take care of her. She is important to our family."

Drake just nodded at the senator.

"Drake, if you need a break, food, anything, let us know. Someone will be in the waiting room and can come sit with Lila."

"Won't need one."

"Drake . . . Fine. Get me if anything changes, okay?"

"Okay."

Drake was finally alone with Lila. He was at the foot of the bed a few moments longer, then finally went to her side, sat down, and grabbed her hand. Gently he rubbed his thumb across her knuckles. Drake looked at her face; swollen and bruised, a cut on her bottom lip. Bruises also ravaged up and down her arms. He could not imagine what the rest of her body looked like. Slowly he pulled back the covers. She was in a hospital gown, but he could see the bandages of her gunshot wound peaking around her left side. Cuts, scrapes, and bruises covered her legs. Gently putting the covers back into place, he bowed his head, emotions overtaking him.

"I need you, Lila. You need to come back to me. You can't leave me now, just as I found you. You better fight, damn it! You fought your way out of that place, saving Caroline and Kimmy. Yes, we found her too. Now you need to fight for yourself, fight for us. We all need you Lila, especially me. Open your eyes. Please. Open your eyes Lila . . . something. Squeeze my hand, and let me know you are with me. Let me know you are still here. Please. Please. I need you," Drake said, pleading to Lila.

A loud beep interrupted Drake's words. The beep did not stop. He was afraid to know what that meant. Suddenly, the door flew open and hospital staff rushed in.

"Sir, you need to step out of the room," a nurse said.

Immobile, Drake just stood there in shock starring at the nurse.

"Sir, I said you need to step back."

"What's wrong?"

"She stopped breathing. Now step back so we can help her. Now!" she demanded.

Drake stepped back and stood in the doorway while the nurses and doctor worked on Lila. Dr. Menendez flew through the ICU room's door and straight to Lila's room. Drake heard someone say they needed to intubate her. A lot of fast-paced activity filled the room, everyone doing something, until the beep finally stopped. It was replaced with another sound and the words "she's stabilized" echoed by someone.

16

Morning came. Drake held a vigil at Lila's bedside. Continued talking to her, praying, something he never did, and holding her hand. He finally fell asleep sometime in the early morning hours, his hand still in hers, his head resting on the side of her bed.

Drake was dreaming, reliving the events of yesterday. It was like it was happening all over again, seeing Lila running away, Caroline in front of her. The gun being raised, fired, hitting her.

He was screaming her name when he felt something squeeze his hand. He was running toward her when he felt it again, jolting him from his dream. Quickly sitting up, he saw it. Lila's eyes were open, looking at him. She squeezed again, holding his hand firmly.

"Lila. Lila. Oh, my God. You're awake. Thank God. How are you feeling? Are you hurting? Shit, you can't talk. Wait a minute," Drake said as he raced out of the door to the nurse's desk.

"She's awake. Come quick," he said then rushed back to her side.

"I got the nurse. She's coming. Oh, Lila I was so—" Drake was cut off by the staff coming into her room. He was pushed back as the nurses went to each side.

"Mr. Donovan, could you please step outside into the waiting room to give us some space in here with the patient," one of the nurses asked.

Drake took one last look at Lila, nodded acknowledging the nurse's request. As he was exiting the ICU, Dr. Menendez was entering.

"See, Drake, prayers work. Let me get in there, and I will be out as soon as possible to update you."

"Sure. Thanks, Doc."

Drake left the ICU and went to the waiting room. Almost everyone was already there. Shayla, Drew, and Rocco approached him quickly.

"What is it? Is she okay? We saw Dr. Menendez running into the ICU," Shayla said in fast succession.

"She woke up."

Hoots and hollers filled the room. Shayla hugged Drew, then Rocco. Dallas approached Drake and patted him on the back.

"I told you she was tough and would pull through," Dallas said.

"So, what happened? What did the staff say?" Drew asked.

All eyes and ears on Drake, he filled them in on the little he knew, leaving out that he was reliving the shooting in his dream.

"I fell asleep then felt a squeeze on my hand. I woke up and Lila was looking at me. I asked her a few questions and realized she could not talk, due to the intubation, and then I went and got the nurse. I was asked to leave the room. That is all I know. Dr. Menendez said he would come out as soon as he could to update us."

"I knew my sweet girl would pull through. This is what Dr.

Menendez said. Getting her through the night would be the toughest part. She is now awake; that's all that matters."

"Yes, it is the first step. We just need to wait to see what he says," Drew said.

"I know, Drew. It has just been a long night. The unknown has been hard to deal with. Now that she is awake, I just want answers."

"We will get answers," Drew said as he put his arm around Shayla, pulling her to his side.

"You need coffee. I'll be back," Garrett quietly said to Drake then disappeared around the corner.

Drake sat down and put his head in his hands. His emotions, once again, all over the place. She made it through the night. His Lila was now awake.

His Lila.

Realizing he really needed to tell her how he felt about her, but he was scared. This feeling was new to him. He did not know how to express his emotions as he had never felt like this about a woman. It had been ingrained in him for so long to push his emotions as deep and far away as possible. Drake knew that was no longer an option. Lila brought out the best in him, made him feel love for the first time. Not the love you have for family or close friends, but in a life partner, a soul mate. Something he'd never thought he would ever find.

Drew came over and sat down next to him. "How are you doing?"

"Don't know."

"I understand. Experienced that early on with Shayla."

"Yeah, I guess you do."

"You going to tell her how you feel, or are you going to be a stubborn ass?"

"I'm going to tell her. I just need the right time, right place. Now is not the time. She needs to heal, to rest."

"Don't you think if you just told her, it would actually help her recover quicker?"

"How do you know it will help? It could set her back with the added stress."

"Why would she have added stress?"

"You know . . . maybe . . . maybe she is not on the same page as me."

"You've got to be kidding me."

"What?"

"I don't think you have anything to worry about in that department. All I can say is don't take too long, brother," Drew said, just as Dr. Menendez came out to the waiting room.

Shayla dashed toward the doctor, questions once again flying out of her mouth. "How is she Dr. Menendez? Is she going to be okay? When can I see her?"

Laughing, "Slow down, Shayla. Have a seat, and I will fill you all in."

Everyone moved to the chairs, Dr. Menendez sitting down next to Drake and Drew.

"Lila is awake, as I am sure you have already heard. We removed the intubation tube. She was quite adamant about that," he said smiling, shaking his head. "Lila is doing great. It is a huge turnaround. Her color is good, her breathing is good. She said she has some pain, but asked that we not give her anything very strong and is talking, even though a little scratchy. The prayers worked. If she maintains this over the next few hours or so, we will probably move her to a regular room. She wants to see you."

"I'm going in now. Can I? Do I have to wait?" Shayla said.

Dr. Menendez looked at Shayla then to Drake. "Um, sure you can go in now if you like."

Shayla did not hesitate. She bolted toward the ICU room door. Drew stood up, put his hand on Drake's shoulder, and then followed Shayla. He knew Dr. Menendez meant she asked for Drake. Drake knew how hard this had been on Shayla and let her have her time with Lila. He would get alone time with her soon enough and make sure she knew how he felt. He gave Shayla and Drew a few minutes before he went to her room, knowing everyone would want to come in and see her.

"Lila! Thank God. I have been so worried," Shayla said as she swiftly went to Lila's bedside, grabbing her hand as Drew came around, standing behind Shayla.

"Good to see you're awake, Lila. You gave us all a scare."

"So how are you feeling? Are you in much pain?"

"Surprisingly, not much. I definitely know the injury is there, but I don't hurt as much as I would expect. Just a little tired and weak feeling. Dr. Menendez said that's due to the loss of blood, but I should feel better quickly."

"You did lose a lot of blood. It really worried us, but we knew you were tough and would make it through. Just glad you are back with us. You know Drake held a vigil at your bedside," Drew said.

"He did?"

"Yes. He has not left your side unless they forced him to, like they did when you woke up."

"I'm surprised they allowed him to be in here all that time. Aren't there rules?"

"I think they knew better than to tell Drake he could not stay in here."

"Guess you are right."

"I am so proud of you and mad at you at the same time," Shayla said. "What were you thinking trying to get out on your own? You had to know the guys would be coming for you."

"I knew they would be, but some things happened, and I did not feel like we had much time. I had to do something.

While I felt the vibration on the collar when I went to activate it, how did I know for sure it was working?"

"I know . . . I saw," Shayla said softly.

"You saw what?"

"Everything. Everything once you activated the collar."

Lila was silent for a moment, taking it all in. The collar worked. They saw Julio attempt to rape her, the fight, everything.

"Are you okay, Shayla?"

"You're asking me if I'm okay? Don't you have that turned around a little bit?"

"We're best friends. I know it could not have been easy to witness everything that happened."

"No, it was not. That is why I am mad and proud at the same time. Mad that you didn't wait for the guys, but proud for being so brave and getting both you and Caroline out. Knowing what happened to you and what could have happened, oh, God, I just could not imagine . . . ?

"You don't need to imagine. I made it out. I'm alive."

"Hurt, shot, beat up."

"All in a day's work," Lila teased. "Sorry . . . look, I am here, Caroline is safe and I will be fine. Did we get them? That's all I want to know."

"Yes, we got them," Drake's voice echoed in the room.

Lila turned to see Drake standing in the doorway. They locked and held eyes for a few moments, many unspoken words expressed through their gazes. Everyone was silent until Rocco burst into the room.

"My sweet girl. I just could not wait any longer," he said as he pushed through, went to her side, and kissed her on the forehead. "I am so relieved you are going to be okay. You had me so worried."

"Hey there, Rocco Taco. I'm fine. Just needed to take a little nap, that's all."

"You think this is funny? Just wait until you get better. I'll make you pay for that little comment."

"I bet you will. I know it is not funny, but what's done is done. I'll be fine, Caroline is safe, we got them. Mission accomplished."

"Even tougher than we thought. I'm so, so proud of you. You remembered your training."

Glancing down, a slight distraught look on her face, "It did not fully pay off. If Julio was not interrupted—"

"Don't think about that, sweet girl. It is in the past, as you said. You got out and took care of that bastard. He will not be hurting anyone else again."

"Thank the fuck not. Does it make me a horrible person that I am happy he is dead?"

"No," they all said simultaneously.

"Lila, you did what you needed to and feel the way anyone of us would about that fucker," Drew said.

"If you didn't shoot him, I would have. You just beat me to it," Drake said.

Drake. She just wanted to have a moment with Drake. Alone. He was the last person she saw before everything went black and the first person she saw when the light returned. Lila wanted to tell him how she felt. That it was him she thought about the entire time. How she just wanted to get back to him, in his arms. Facing death, Lila decided she was not going to hide her feelings, not anymore. He may not feel the same, she would get over it if that was the case, but being shot puts a lot of things in perspective.

"I know you would have, Drake. Can't lie though, I am glad it was me. What that man has done . . . he was pure evil."

"Yes, he was. I heard what Caroline told you. How he would force himself on her and the other girls. What he tried to do to you. I've never really wished death on anyone, until him," Shayla said.

"I feel the same way. You could see the change take over in his eyes. It was very unnerving at first, but then I was able to use it to my advantage."

"What do you mean?" Rocco asked.

"While he was strong, very strong, I saw a weakness in him when he was in a rage. His focus was very centralized, and he was not prepared for anything else, nothing coming from the sidelines. That's what helped me with the plan. He would not, and did not, expect anything but a front-on attack, and he paid the price."

"Such a smart cookie. To endure what you did and still see a weakness and act on it. Can't say it enough how proud I am of you," Rocco praised.

"Smart, yes, but foolish," Drake added.

"Excuse me?" Lila said, irritation in her voice.

"Maybe foolish was the wrong word to use. You should have waited for us. You knew we would be coming."

"Yes, I knew you all would be coming, but like I said, and given the circumstances, I had to make a decision. It all worked out.

"Worked out? You got shot Lila."

"And?"

"And? And? Isn't that enough? You would not have been shot if you would have waited."

"So let me get this straight, me getting shot is all my fault? Did you see the video feed?" Drake nodded. "Then you saw what was happening. You knew I did not have long. I would have either been raped, killed, or both. Then Julio would have taken it out on Caroline. Is that what you wanted? Did you want to see that happen? Tell me Drake, if it was you, what would you have done? Would you have *waited* for someone to save you or would you have saved yourself? I knew the risks going in. My job was to save Caroline no matter what happened to me. It was the same risk all of you would have taken. So don't patronize me for getting the job done!"

Beeping went off on her monitor. The nurse came in. "Ms. Norris, your heart rate and blood pressure is up. How are you feeling? Is everything okay?"

"Yes, ma'am. Just got myself a little worked up."

"You need to keep yourself relaxed. Maybe too many visitors at once," the nurse said, eyeing all of them.

"Don't worry, ma'am. Some were just leaving," Lila said looking at Drake.

Drake turned on his heels and stormed out of the room. Closing her eyes and taking a deep breath, Lila tried to stop the tears in her eyes.

"Don't be mad at him, sweet girl. Drake was just worried. He does not know how to express himself very well. Most of us don't," Rocco said.

"Lila, Drake blames himself," Drew added

"Why would he blame himself? It's not like he was kidnapping women and selling them."

"He promised you would be safe, that you would not be alone, then he let you go to the restroom by yourself, and then you were gone. He feels if he did what he said, you would not have been kidnapped and have to go through what you did."

"I don't blame him."

"I know you don't, but that does not change the fact that he feels responsible."

"But we found Caroline. I have a feeling if all this did not happen, she would not be with us right now. They would have either sold her, or worse, before we could have tracked down the culprit. It's a blessing, in a way. Sure, I got beat up and shot, but I will heal. It's not like I haven't been through some trauma before. I will be alright. Heck, I have all of you for support"

"Yes you do," Shayla said. "We will be right by your side

until you heal and every day thereafter." She said as she grabbed Lila's hand, holding tight.

"Drake is just going to have to compartmentalize all of this before he realizes that it is no one's fault but Perez and his hired help. Just ignore his outbursts and be a little easy on him. Give him some time to move past this."

"Why is he so upset? I know he has been through tough situations before. Lost friends. He seems to be able to continue moving forward."

"It's different with you."

"Oh, because I am a female? That's comforting," she said sarcastically.

"No, because he is in love with you," Drew said.

Stunned silent for a moment, Lila looked between Drew, Shayla, and Rocco. "That can't be true. He didn't act like someone who was in love."

"I told you, Lila. Drake has never cared about anyone like he does you. He does not know how to handle these new feelings," Shayla said.

"I agree. I saw it from the day he returned. The cookout just confirmed it for me. Sweet girl, he is one of the tough guys. Always taught through his training to rein in and control his emotions. Something necessary for all of us to do the job. He just let it also seep into his personal life. Happens to a lot of us in this line of work. Just give it some time. You can then talk to him, let him know how you feel," Rocco said.

"How I feel? And how is that?"

"Don't play with me, sweet girl. I know you love him, too."

"Is it that obvious?"

"Yes," all three said in unison.

"Oh, God. What am I going to do? He confuses me so much. Thinks that I should have waited, but then blames himself. It's all too confusing."

"What you are going to do is try not to worry about it. You

need to take care of yourself, heal from all this first, then you two can work it out. It will give Drake time to settle down, come to grips with everything. You getting better is the main priority," Shayla said.

"You're right. I'll try not to worry about Drake. Unfortunately he is not that easy to ignore."

"Well, you need to. Drake's a dominant. He is used to getting what he wants, but he is also not used to failing, and he feels like he failed. Either ignore him or call him out on his bullshit. What is the old saying, you lash out on those you love the most," Drew said.

Sighing, "Fine. I will do my best to ignore him. I just want to get out of this place."

"They are moving you to a regular room today. We can talk with Dr. Menendez and see when he thinks we can take you home," Shayla said.

"That would be perfect. Any place other than a hospital."

LATER THAT DAY, Lila was moved to a private room, out of the ICU. All of the guys visited her once she got settled. Shayla stayed with her entire time, taking care of her like a mother hen. She had not seen Drake since he stormed off that morning. Drew stopped in briefly to let Shayla know he would be back by early evening to get her to go to the hotel. He was briefing with the FBI to finalize the reporting on the raid.

There was a knock on the door, and Drake appeared. Lila was happy and mad at him at the same time. Happy to see him, but mad he had not been there all day. She knew that he was with Drew at the debriefing, but that still did not curb her disappointment. She was just getting ready to ask Shayla if she would give them a minute when he spoke.

"I have some visitors who would like to see you," Drake said right before opening the door for Senator Henderson, who was pushing Caroline in a wheelchair. They were followed by an attractive, middle aged woman. Lila presumed she was the senator's wife. Trent was also on their heels.

"Lila. Oh, Lila. I'm so happy to see you. I was so worried once they took you away in the helicopter. I have been trying to get updates, but I kept being told you were stable and that I needed to worry about my health."

"How are you Caroline? You didn't get hurt when we fled did you?"

"No. No injuries. Other than . . . well . . . you know. They made me go in this wheelchair to visit even though I am fully capable of walking."

"Now, now, dear, you have been through a lot. There isn't anything wrong with a little rest," the woman said.

"Yes, Mother." Looking back at Lila, she asked, "So how are you really feeling? Are you in much pain?"

"I'm fine. The pain is actually minimal. Less than I would have expected. I'm just tired."

"That is to be expected young lady. You make sure you rest and do what the doctors say," the senator said as he approached Lila. "Margaret and I cannot thank you enough for what you did to save our Caroline. Putting yourself in the line of fire to protect her. It's admirable, heroic."

"Any of us would have done the same thing. She had already gone through enough. Caroline, you were very brave, by the way. I'm so proud how you handled yourself. We would not have made it if you did not do your part in the plan."

"My part?" she said grabbing Lila's hand. "My part was to listen to you and follow your directions. You were the one who got us out of there. You came up with the plan, got us out. I just did what you said. Lila, you took a bullet for me. I . . . I can never repay you for what you did. Ever," Caroline said as tears streamed down her face.

"Don't cry, Caroline. It's my job. I volunteered to go in and help you. After being taken and knowing what they did to you, to the other girls, there is no way they were going to touch you again, ever. You were not going to be sold."

"Your job?" Senator Henderson said. "From what I hear Ms. Norris, you are their executive assistant but had been training with the crew. You volunteered to help as you were passionate about stopping abuse on women. This was your first operation, and you played a major role.

"You're just their executive assistant? You have to be kidding me. But, how, I would never have guessed you were not a professional. You knew how to shoot, and you fought back, with skill. This is insane," Caroline said, flabbergasted.

"Well, I had been working with Rocco for some time. He taught me a lot of fighting skills. I grew up shooting, so I had some experience there."

"There is a big difference between shooting for sport and in battle. I doubt you were ever shooting at people," the senator said.

"Yes, sir, that is true. It's just, my instincts kicked in. I had been through some personal trauma in my life not too long ago and was not going to let them hurt either one of us again, or any other woman for that matter."

"Well, young lady, I am glad it was you who showed up. Sorry you had to go through what you did, but you gave us our daughter back. We will always be grateful," Caroline's mom said.

"Thank you, Mrs. Henderson. Caroline is a great girl. Much, much stronger than she gives herself credit. I will always be there for her." Turning to Caroline, "I mean it Caroline. Always."

"Me, too, Lila. We are bonded now. Nothing will change that," Caroline said, the two holding hands.

It was true. They were bonded. It was not just going through something so traumatic with someone which created the bond, but Lila's instincts; she knew immediately Caroline was special. A good soul, someone she would want in her life.

"So, when will you be getting out of this joint?" Lila asked.

"Today. The doctors have pretty much cleared me physically. The last of the blood tests should be back soon, then I will know."

"I understand," Lila said, knowing she was referring to the doctors checking for sexually transmitted diseases.

"The doctors want me to get counseling," Caroline said as she lowered her head.

"You must. Promise me you will. While I know you are strong, Caroline, you went through a lot. It will be for the best and will allow you to move forward, fully, without any hesitation."

"I know. I will. Promise."

"Well, we will get her the best counselor there is. Also, Trent here is coming along. I want her to have personal security until she and the counselor feel she is ready and we have cleared up any other possible threats. It's just not worth taking any other chances. Caroline seems to trust Trent and that is important to me."

Looking at Trent, Lila confirmed the senator's thoughts. "Trent is a good guy and a great agent. He will protect Caroline."

"I believe so, too," Caroline said, gazing up at Trent. "Hey, when do you think you will be discharged?"

"I hope I can answer that question," Dr. Menendez said as he walked into Lila's room.

"Hey there, Doc."

"How's the patient?"

"Doing well. When can I leave?"

Laughing, "Oh, my little spunky Lila. You never cease to amaze me. Let's see, if you keep doing this good, maybe tomorrow. I need to check you out first, see how you are responding."

"On that note, we will leave you. We will be in touch Ms. Norris," Senator Henderson said.

"Lila, please call me Lila, sir. Thank you all for stopping by. I really appreciate it."

"Of course. You take care of yourself."

"I'll talk to you soon," Caroline said as she kissed Lila on the cheek and let her father wheel her out of the room.

Drake went to follow them out of the room. "Drake, please stay," Lila asked.

He stopped in his tracks, turned around, and came back in the room. Drew arrived at that moment.

"What's going on? Just saw the senator and Caroline."

"Yes, they just stopped by to visit me. Dr. Menendez was going to check me and let me know when I can go home," Lila said with a little grin.

"Guess I better get to checking. All your labs are looking great. The monitor here is reading well. Have you had any episodes or issues breathing?"

"No, all is good. I feel normal."

"How's your pain? Give me a scale from 0-10. Ten feeling like the worst pain ever, zero no pain at all."

"I would say I am about a 3-4. It hurts but is bearable. Kind of like whiplash, you are sore all over after an accident."

"That's to be expected. Sit up for me. Let me listen."

Lila did as she was told. Dr. Menendez listened to her lungs, then her heart. He then started to gently feel around.

"Does this hurt?" he said pressing around her back.

"No, not really. I can feel it when you touch closer to the wound. Some discomfort in other places."

"Well, you are pretty bruised. Lay back down. Let me feel around your abdomen. How does this feel?"

"Pretty much the same. More muscle pain to me."

"Yes, the bruising as well. Just making sure you are not experiencing anything else in your organs."

"So, what's the verdict? Do I get to go home? Well, back to my hotel until I can get into my apartment."

"If you are the same or better in the morning, I would be inclined to discharge you, only if you are not left alone. You will need to be with someone, at least for a few weeks. I don't want you alone in a hotel room"

"She can come to my house," both Shayla and Drake said at the same time.

"Good. Good. I will check on you one more time tonight and then in the morning. If all is well, you can be released."

"Thank you, Dr. Menendez. I'll see you soon."

"That's settled. You are coming home with me," Shayla said.

"She can come to my house. All her stuff is already there," Drake responded.

"Drake, she is going to need help 24/7. It is much easier for me to work from home than you. I am sure you will also have some other things to clear up with Agent Harris."

Drake did not seem very amused.

"Shayla is right, Drake. You know they want us to help finish the job, work with them to find where the other girls are. You won't have time to help take care of her. Shayla can be at home with Lila."

"Fine. Fine." That's all Drake said before he left Lila's room.

"Drake, come back," Shayla said.

"Let him go. He's still worked up."

"I hope he is not mad at me."

"No, Shayla, he's not."

17

The next morning, Dr. Menendez examined Lila and agreed to discharge her with strict orders of rest and recovery. He was slightly reluctant as his preference was for her to stay an additional day or two, but he relented. He knew Shayla would not let her out of her sight, and Lila would most likely discharge herself as she was antsy to leave. Drew had arranged to fly him to Dallas for follow-up visits until Lila was fully healed. Dr. Menendez graciously accepted and offered to help in any way, especially since he and his family were now free and out from under the control of Perez. He owed his family's happiness to her.

"Drew said the plane will be here around noon," Shayla said. "You should be discharged by then. Garrett took everyone back last night except me, Drew, and Rocco. He told me he was not leaving without his girl."

Lila smiled, but disappointment filled her. She had not seen or spoken to Drake since he left after it was decided she would go to Shayla and Drew's house. Was he mad at her? Was he avoiding her?

"Thanks. I'm ready to get out of here."

"What's wrong, Lila?"

"Nothing."

"Tell me the truth. I know you better than that. Is it Drake?"

"He did not come back before he left. No calls, nothing. He seemed so mad the last time he was here."

"I'm sure he is just busy with the rest of the investigation. He knows I'm here to help you."

"Maybe."

There was a knock on the door and in walked Drew and Rocco. "Hey guys."

"My girl ready to blow this joint?" Rocco said, smiling at Lila.

"Sure am, Rocco. I need some fresh air."

"Garrett just called. He's landed. Was able to get out earlier than expected, so we are all set for whenever they let you out of here," Drew said.

"It should be any moment now. They want patients to rest in here, but it seems like they are in my room every hour. How can I rest? It's why I hate hospitals. I will probably get better quicker when I am out of here."

"I agree," Shayla added. "Hospitals help people, but it seems like you never get to sleep with all the interruptions,"

"You'll be out soon, sweet girl," Rocco said, as he grabbed and held Lila's hand.

Just then, a nurse walked in, papers in her hand. "Ms. Norris. You ready to be discharged?"

"Yes, ma'am."

"Let's go over your discharge papers, then we will get you dressed and on your way."

The nurse went over everything with Lila while Drew and Rocco secured their ride to the airport. Thankfully, Shayla bought some clothes for Lila, or she would have had to leave in a hospital gown. Shayla helped her dress, and then the hospital escort was there to wheel her down to the waiting vehicle.

The SUV pulled up just as they exited the entrance. Drew and Rocco got out and helped Lila into the vehicle. Moving was slow as the injuries were much more noticeable when she was up and walking. They made their way to the private air strip where Garrett was waiting. Gingerly, Rocco helped Lila out of the SUV and got her settled on the plane. He had pillows and a blanket ready to make her comfortable.

"There you go. Are you comfortable? Would you like some water?"

"I'm good, and thanks, Rocco."

"Anything for you," Rocco said and took a seat next to Lila.

Shayla sat across from them, and Drew sat up in the cockpit with Garrett. Quickly they were off, heading back to Dallas. The flight was relatively short and uneventful. After they landed, they drove straight to Drew and Shayla's house to get Lila settled.

"Where would you like to relax, Lila? You can have the guest room, but if you want, we can get you set up on the sectional."

"I'd rather stay downstairs for now, at least until bedtime."

"Of course. Why don't you take the chaise part? That way you can sit or lie down easily. I'll be back in a second with some pillows and a blanket."

"Thanks, Shayla," Lila said as Rocco escorted her over to the sectional.

"You going to be okay, sweet girl?"

"Yes, Rocco. I'm just a little tired."

"Relax, take a nap, and don't try to do too much."

"I won't, promise."

Shayla returned with the blanket and a few pillows. Lila got herself comfortable and Shayla handed her the remote for the television.

"Here you go. If you want to watch TV, you have the remote close. It's about lunch time. Are you hungry? I can see what we have."

"Thanks. I am a little hungry."

"How about I go pick up something. I have to go back to the office and get my truck anyway. If you place an order, I will get it. It will only take me 30 minutes tops," Drew said.

"Sounds good to me, then it will give me time to see what we need from the grocery store and make a list. One of us can go later this evening, if that is okay with you Lila."

"Of course. I can go with the flow. I don't want to make anything difficult or be an inconvenience."

"Difficult? Did you really say that? First, you are my best friend and I would do anything for you. Second, you just got beat up and shot, all during an op. We take care of our own. So, I don't want to hear anything about being difficult or an inconvenience."

"Yeah, what she said," Drew added.

Laughing at them and grabbing her side, Lila chuckled, "Okay. I won't say it again. Just don't make me laugh."

Rocco came over to give Lila a kiss goodbye, letting her know he would check in later. Rocco and Drew left so Drew could get his truck and lunch. Shayla started to busy herself in the kitchen making her list.

"Hey, Shayla. Do you think Drake could bring over some of my stuff later? It would be better to have at least some of my essentials here."

"I'm sure he would, or I will go over later when Drew is home and get them for you."

"Thanks."

"Of course. I would want my own things as well, even though you know you are welcome to anything of mine."

"I know and appreciate it."

Drew returned with lunch. They sat and ate with Lila in

the family room instead of the table. After lunch, Drew went back to the office to do a bit of paperwork and grabbed the grocery list from Shayla. He said he would stop on his way home then grill something for dinner. Lila took a nap after lunch. She awoke felling a bit rested as the travel home took a bit out of her.

"Shayla, do you think you could help me take a shower before Drew gets home?"

"Can you take one? What did the doctor say?"

"He said I could, just to be careful around the wound. I would have to clean it and re-dress it twice a day anyway. I just want someone there the first time at least. You know, just in case."

"Absolutely. Of course I will help you. I'll just give you something comfortable to wear until we get some of your stuff."

"Thanks, I appreciate it."

Slowly, Lila ascended the stairs, Shayla right behind her. They decided until Lila did not need help she would shower in the master bathroom. The walk-in shower was large, enough space for several people and would make it easier if she needed help. She undressed with Shayla's assistance. Shayla removed the bandages, and Lila went into the shower. She was able to wash most of her body, but Shayla washed her back and gently cleaned the bullet wound. When finished, Lila carefully dried off and sat on the stool Shayla had at the counter so Shayla could re-dress the wound and brush her hair. She helped her dress in a simple tank top and leggings.

They made their way downstairs. Drew would be home soon as it was approaching 7 o'clock.

"Do you know if it is nice outside?"

"I think so, why?"

"I'd love to sit outside for a bit, now that it is not the hottest part of the day."

"Sure. Let me check for you."

Shayla went on the deck and said it was nice as she came back toward the doors. "It's warm, but not hot. Come on out. We'll get you set up out here."

Lila followed Shayla out onto the deck and selected a chaise lounge to the side which gave her a full view of the deck and pool area.

"You want me to bring you a book or some magazines? I am going to make some tea and start prepping some sides. Drew sent a text. He should be here in about ten minutes then I will come out and join you."

"Magazines would be great."

Shayla brought Lila a few magazines of various genres and went back into the kitchen, leaving the doors to the deck open. Lila was perusing a few women's magazines when she heard Drew come in, arms loaded. She could hear Drew and Shayla talking as they unloaded the groceries. Lila loved to listen to them talk. They were so much in love and truly enjoyed each other's company. A few minutes later she heard another voice. The one that always sent shivers down her spine. Drake. He was here. Lila felt anxious and nervous, but happy to see him. She was still upset he did not come to see her in the hospital before he headed back with the others, but she also wanted desperately to talk to him. To finally tell him how she felt.

Lila heard some talking, making out a few words. Then she heard Shayla say, 'You want to stay for dinner? Lila's out there. You can sit and visit for a while before dinner is ready." She heard him say something to Shayla but could not make out the words. A few minutes later Shayla came out, two glasses of iced tea in her hands. She sat down next to Lila.

"Was that Drake? I heard his voice."

"Yes . . . it was."

"Where is he? Is he staying for dinner?"

Looking at Lila, trying to form her words, Shayla finally

responded. "Drake brought over some clothes and personal items. He said he could not stay for dinner."

"Is he gone?" Lila asked quietly.

"Yes. I'm sorry."

Tears streamed down her face. "He could not even take one minute to come out here and say hi. What is wrong with him? Why is he being such an asshole?"

Shayla grabbed Lila's hand to console her just as they heard Drew come out on the deck saying, "Wish I knew why he is being such an ass. I know he is mixed up over everything that happened, but this is inexcusable."

"I'd like to know what I did to make him so mad at me that caused him to ignore me."

"You have not done anything, Lila. This is all on him," Drew said.

"It doesn't seem that way."

"Lila, it's not you. Drake just does not know how to deal with his emotions. I know he loves you. He just can't compute it all," Shayla added.

"Yeah, yeah, you all keep saying that, but I am starting to doubt your presumption. This was probably just part of the job to him. He is going back to how he was when I first started," Lila said as she looked off, drying her tears.

Shayla and Drew just looked at each other. Drew was getting angry at how upset Drake was making Lila. Knowing she needed to change the negative atmosphere, Shayla slapped her knees and said, "Well, let's forget about him. We're going to have a nice dinner and a nice conversation between friends. We don't need that party pooper here anyway."

Lila could not help but laugh at Shayla. She was such a good friend, doing her best to make her feel better, physically and mentally. Drew had picked up some fish and shrimp and cooked them on the grill. The three enjoyed the meal and each other. They talked for a few hours before Lila was ready for bed. Drew gave her a kiss goodnight, and Shayla helped her get settled. She put her cell phone on the nightstand and told Lila to ring her, no matter what time it was if she needed anything, and not to be stupid and do things on her own when she knows better.

The next two weeks were a blur. Lila was healing well. All of the guys visited multiple times, Rocco daily. Everyone except Drake. He never even called to speak to her. Drew did tell her Drake had to go out of town to help Agent Harris at the Perez compound. They were gathering evidence to start piecing together the victims and their buyers. Identifying the buyers, the victims, and the money trail would be a difficult task. Even though Lila knew he was working, the more Drake ignored her, the more her feelings turned to anger. Lila could not comprehend how two people could go through an experience like this to suddenly act like it never happened. What kind of human being could be so heartless? How could a person whose career was to help others be so contradictory in his behavior toward a colleague, especially one he was intimate with. Well, if he was going to be a jerk, she was better off without him.

Dr. Menendez flew in that weekend and, after a thorough exam, gave Lila the all clear. He said she still had a few more weeks until she would be fully recovered but could resume some normal activities, ease back into physical training. He advised her to be smart, to listen to her body. Lila was relieved as she was so bored sitting around the house. She never liked being cooped up and wanted to get back to work and see where they were on the investigation. Shayla made her promise to only work half days at the beginning, knowing she would tire easily.

Monday morning, Lila decided to go into the office for a bit. Shayla, in all of her mothering glory, said they could work a few hours then go to lunch before Lila was to head back home to rest. Lila agreed as she did not want to argue with

Shayla after all she had done for her. Still only having some of her stuff, Lila put on a simple sundress and sandals and braided her hair. It made her feel good to wear something other than tanks and shorts. The ladies rode together, another one of Shayla's sneaky tactics to ensure Lila only worked a half day, as Drew had left earlier that morning for the office.

Lila and Shayla arrived just around 8 o'clock in the morning, and Lila headed for her desk while Shayla sought out Drew. As she approached her desk, she saw a huge bouquet of flowers and a card. Lila opened the card and all of the guys had signed it welcoming her back; all except Drake. Ass, she muttered then tried to get it out of her head. Neither Drew nor Shayla signed it so maybe it was just from the guys. Next thing she knew, Dallas popped around the corner.

"You're here! You like?"

"Yes, Dallas. They are beautiful. This was so thoughtful of all of you. But you didn't know when I would be back."

"Drew told us that you would probably be coming in for a little bit today so—"

"Sneaky guys. Thanks again. I appreciate it."

"I better head back to my desk. We have a status update meeting at 0900 on the Henderson case. Between that meeting and everyone who will probably be stopping by, I'm not sure how much you will get done in an hour. Just prepare yourself."

"I figured it would take at least today to get reacquainted. I'll see you at the meeting."

Dallas came around her desk and gave her a hug, then went to his office. As the others trickled in, just as Dallas had said, they all stopped to talk to Lila. She repeated her thanks for the lovely flowers and card. Before she knew it, it was five minutes to nine and then she sensed him. Drake was coming down the hall toward the conference room. He stopped when he saw her at her desk. Looking at her for what felt like an eternity, he finally spoke, just saying her name. She responded equally with "Drake." They did not have time for any other discussion as everyone else was heading to the conference room. She grabbed a pen and notepad and followed suit. As everyone entered the conference room and took their seats, Drew brought the meeting to order.

"First, I would like to welcome Lila back. We are glad you are doing better, but take it easy. We need you here, so no pushing it."

"Yes, sir."

Drake stiffened at her response. "Yes, sir." He missed hearing that from her. Those two words evoked a response so deep, so protective. She's mine, he thought and those words should be for him only. Drake did not like hearing her refer to Drew in that manner. This insane rush of jealousy was unsettling. She was only responding like any other professional would. Focus on the meeting, he told himself.

"So, we have been working closely with Agent Harris and his team with all of the data and records we found at Perez's compound. It appears his involvement in human trafficking has been going on about three years, and there have been approximately 150 women and young girls taken and sold all over the world. It seems to be a pretty tight network of some very wealthy and sick individuals. We think some are sold to be personal slaves to the buyers, others to be sent to brothels. What we have started doing is working on the money trail. The FBI's analysts have been working diligently on this part. If they can trace the financial chain, we may be able to locate the buyers. We are going to break into teams to help work on this project."

"I will help in any way. I'll be glad to review documents looking for any patterns, anything that stands out," Lila said.

"We will definitely need your help. That would be perfect while you are still recovering. Also, once we start pinpointing the buyers or the women, we will be assisting in the extraction.

This will involve joint efforts with the FBI, military, and foreign partners. We have been hired on to consult and assist as needed in the case. It will take time to try to track down all of the people involved. Right now, we will be working on any leads, focusing on the Middle East and Europe as we have a lot of experience in those regions."

"Yes, we do," Drake said. "Once we make a determination or confirmation of a target, we will work with the military on extraction, especially for Middle Eastern locations. As of our last conversation with Harris, they are estimating about 20-30 girls in the Middle East, specifically targeting Saudi Arabia, Jordan, Qatar, and the United Arab Emirates. In Europe, they suspect girls are scattered all over. We'll figure it out and try to locate and retrieve these women and put the bastards away."

"Has the FBI verified any locations yet?" Lila asked.

"Not at this time. These are estimates based on prior information from the FBI's foreign partners."

"I will need the updates as soon as they come in, and I can start working on breaking it down. Lila can help me," Dallas said.

"Works for me," Lila added.

Drew and Drake provided information to the team about what had been located and planned so far. They divvied up the responsibilities as the more time that passed, especially when buyers got wind of the Perez take down, the harder it would be to find the victims.

"Alright then, we will send out the intel we have to date and divide and conquer. If anyone has a question on their assignment, just come talk to us. Any questions for now?" Everyone shook their head in the negative. "Okay. Meeting adjourned."

Everyone started to rise to leave. Drake just looked at Lila then left the room. Shaking him out of her thoughts, she went back to her desk and Shayla approached.

"So, how about we leave around noon, go grab some lunch at the Bistro, then head home?"

"Yes, mother," Lila said, laughing. "That sounds like a plan."

Behind Shayla, she saw Drake leave his office, keys in hand, heading to the front entrance.

Realizing Lila was looking elsewhere, Shayla asked, "Has he spoken to you?"

"Yes and no. He came up to the conference room, looked at me and said my name."

"What did you say?"

"His name back. Everyone started coming, so he went into the conference room. It's like when we first met, cold, avoidance. I just don't get it."

"Me either. I know Drake is intense at times, and we know he is very dominant, but he is not normally an ass. His actions are actually very surprising to me. I have never seen him act like this in all the years I have known him."

"Well, if he does not at least start acting professional to me, I'm going to punch him. He may not want to be with me on a personal level, but he is not going to ruin my job for me."

"Good for you. Just make sure I am here when you sock it to him. I want to see that," Shayla said as she laughed and walked back to her office.

Two hours passed and Lila was almost finished going through the overabundance of emails when Shayla approached her desk.

"You ready to get out of here and grab lunch? I'm hungry."

"Sure. Give me like five minutes and I will be ready."

"Alright. I'll go say goodbye to Drew then meet you in the lobby."

Lila read the last few emails, responded to the ones that

could not wait or Shayla had not already addressed, logged off, and headed to the lobby. Shayla was already waiting.

As they walked out to Shayla's car, she asked, "Is the Bistro still good for you? We have not been there in a while."

"Sure is. We can probably sit outside. It's such a nice day today.

"It sure is. Sounds perfect."

Lila and Shayla headed over to the Bistro engaging in some small talk on the way. They were greeted by the host who escorted them to the outside terrace. Once they approached their table, Lila abruptly stopped, not sitting down, her face a combination of sadness and anger.

"What is it Lila? What's wrong?"

When she did not respond, Shayla turned around to see what she was looking at. Then she saw source of Lila's reaction, Drake at a table on the other side of the terrace, but he was not alone. He was with another woman.

"Oh, that bastard. How could he do this?" Shayla angrily said as she headed in his direction.

"Shayla, no. Please stop. Don't go over there," Lila said, but her words fell on deaf ears. Lila followed behind, still trying to stop Shayla from confronting Drake.

"Well, hello, Drake. What are you doing here?" Shayla said as she eyed up the woman at the table.

Looking past Shayla he saw Lila. The hurt in her eyes evident, and he put it there. Drake focused back on Shayla.

"I'm having lunch. Why?"

"That's obvious, but don't you have *other* obligations?"

Drake knew what she meant—Lila.

"Excuse me Miss, may I ask who you are and why you are interrupting? We are trying to have a nice lunch here," the bimbo said in a snotty tone.

Drake's lunch date was the epitome of a blonde bimbo. Fake everything. Fake breasts, plumped-up lips, a severely smooth Botox face, bleached-blonde hair, and to top it off, she was wearing a teeny, tiny outfit leaving nothing to the imagination. No wonder Drake was ignoring her. If this is his kind of woman, Lila did not stand a chance. She was natural, no extra enhancements. Lila preferred being real over the artificial Barbie-doll look. If Drake preferred a fake, plastic, doll-like woman, Lila knew she could never compete.

"Candace, this is Shayla, my sister-in-law. Shayla, Candace."

"Oh, oh. I'm sorry. It's nice to meet you, but please call me Candi. I prefer it," Drake's date said, her attitude doing a 180 and now very friendly.

Go figure, a porn star name for Bimbo Barbie, Lila brooded.

"Fine, Candi." Turning back to Drake, "I thought your schedule was full. I did not know you had time for such a casual lunch with all that is on your plate at this moment."

"Oh, it's my fault," Candi said. "I just got in town. I'm a flight attendant. Drake and I like to hook up, I mean get together, whenever I am in for an overnight stay."

"Really? Isn't that nice," Shayla said sarcastically.

Lila grabbed Shayla's arm again, trying to get her to go back to their table.

"Who is that behind you?" Candi said as she took her arm to push Shayla aside.

Bitch, Shayla thought, doing everything she could not to lash out at this woman.

"This is Lila," Drake said.

"Oh, my my, what happened to you? You get in a car accident or something?" she remarked, eying the remaining bruises on Lila.

"Something like that. Hazards of the job."

"You work with Drake then? Wow. I could not take that

kind of risk, just look at me," Bimbo Barbie said raising her arms out to her sides in a gesture to show herself off.

"I am. You're like a living Barbie doll," Lila commented.

"Why, thank you. Barbie was the inspiration behind my look."

Dumb, too. Doesn't even know it was not a compliment, Lila said to herself.

"We'll leave you two alone. Looks like you are on a date. Sorry for interrupting," Lila said, pulling Shayla along.

"Nice to meet you," Bimbo Barbie said as they walked away.

"You want to go somewhere else?" Shayla asked Lila.

"No!"

"But—"

"Shayla, if we leave, it will be very obvious this got to me. I am not going to give him that kind of leverage."

"Okay. I understand; I don't agree, but I understand."

They sat down at their table and looked at the menu. The waiter came over with two glasses of water and told them the specials of the day. The waiter left to give them time to decide what they wanted to order.

"So, I think I am going to have the shrimp taco special. What about you?" Lila asked.

"That does sound good, especially with the aioli sauce."

"Exactly. I think I will ask for a side salad instead of the rice. I'm sure they won't mind."

The waiter came back to take their order. Both of them ordered the special and a glass of wine. While they waited, Lila periodically glanced over at Drake and his date.

"Lila."

"Hmm?"

"It's me. Talk to me. Are you okay?"

"No, but I will be," she said as a few tears fell down her cheeks.

Shayla went to say something, and Lila waved her off as she discreetly wiped her tears. "Let's just enjoy our lunch. It is what it is."

Respecting her friend, Shayla changed the subject, and they talked about a new movie that was coming out. Before lunch arrived, Shayla excused herself to go the restroom. She was not really using the restroom but went to call Drew. She hated deceiving Lila, but she was at a loss and wanted his advice.

"What's up, darlin'? I thought you and Lila were at lunch. Is something wrong?"

"Yes."

Worried, Drew asked, "What is it? Is Lila okay? Do I need to come there?"

"No, you don't need to come, and no, Lila is not okay. Drake is here . . . with another woman."

"What?"

"Yes."

"How's Lila?"

"She is trying real hard to act fine. I tried to get her to go somewhere else, but she refused to leave. She said she did not want to give him the satisfaction by leaving, but she is clearly upset. To top it off, this woman Drake is with is the epitome of a blonde bimbo."

"What the fuck is his problem? He is going to seriously blow it with Lila. Everyone knows they are meant to be together. I just don't understand how he cannot figure out how to handle this? He needs someone to make him fucking realize what he is going to lose if he does not get his shit together!"

"I don't know what to do. What should I do, Drew?"

"Just support Lila. Be a friend. Let her talk if she wants to or don't say anything if she doesn't."

"Okay. You're right, Drew. See you later."

Shayla returned to the table. Lila tried to keep her composure, but the sadness Drake caused was etched all over her face. The toll of the encounter was affecting her self-esteem, making her wonder why she always seemed to get hurt by men. Was she just a magnet for the wrong men, men who always disappointed? This time hurt most of all. She may not have physically been hurt by Drake, but the pain in her heart superseded any physical trauma caused by the last guy she dated. She loved Drake, and he obviously did not feel the same, hence being here with Bimbo Barbie.

The waiter came with their meals. The food was delicious, but it was difficult for Lila to enjoy the meal while she was doing everything in her power not to look over at Drake and his date. Shayla was doing her best to keep the conversation light, and Lila appreciated it. Shayla was such a good friend. Lila didn't know what she would do without her.

When they finished lunch, Shayla paid and they got up to leave. Drake was still there. Lila refused to look at them when they left the bistro. That was not the case for Shayla. Lila glanced at her as they got up and saw Shayla look in Drake's direction, the expression on her face sending daggers. The drive home was short and relatively quiet. Walking into the house, Lila turned toward Shayla.

"I think I am going to go upstairs and take a nap. Dr. Menendez wasn't kidding when he said to take it easy, that I would get tired quickly. Please don't let me sleep past four okay?"

"No problem. I'll make sure you are up by four."

Shayla gave Lila some space. She knew Lila just needed some time alone to deal with her emotions over seeing Drake with another woman. How could he be so cruel to her? Shayla could not understand how Drake one minute was so distraught over losing Lila when she was shot, and then do a 180, ignore her, and be with another woman. She wanted to kill him.

Drake may be her brother-in-law, and she may love him, but right now she did not like him very much.

Heading to her room to change into something more comfortable, Shayla stopped in front of Lila's door. She could hear her crying. Deciding not to bother her, Shayla turned and went to change. She would give her the space she needed, for now. Shayla was so mad at Drake for causing Lila this heartache. This was just not like him. She hoped Drew could talk some sense into him.

DREW WAS FINISHING up a few phone calls before heading home when he heard movement in Drake's office. Still pissed from his telephone call from Shayla, Drew got up and went to Drake's office. Drake was logging back onto his computer, and Drew just stood in the doorway, arms crossed, staring at Drake.

Looking up, spotting Drew standing there, Drake asked, "Hey, man. What's up?"

"I should be asking you the same thing."

"What? Oh . . . let me guess, Shayla called you."

"Yep, you want to explain?"

"What is there to explain?"

"Don't pull that bullshit with me, Drake. What the fuck are you doing?"

"I was meeting a friend."

"Yeah, I know exactly who you were meeting. All Shayla had to do was tell me you were with a blonde bimbo and I knew exactly who you were with. What about Lila?"

"What about her?"

"You've got to be fucking kidding me. What about her? How about you being in love with her, first of all. Then staying by her bedside after she was shot, only to turn around and ignore her, and now this, with Candi. How could you cheat on Lila?"

"Cheat on her? Hmmm. I did not know we were in a relationship," Drake said, getting defensive.

"Jesus, Drake. What the fuck is wrong with you? Clearly you two are in a relationship, whatever kind it is. Don't try to deny it. How can you sleep with Candi? Why do you keep hurting Lila?"

"I did not sleep with Candi. We just met for lunch."

"Yeah, right. When have you and Candi ever had lunch? When have you not slept with Candi when she strolls through town?"

"Today."

"You're not very convincing."

"I don't have to check in with you every time I see someone."

"No, you're right, you don't," Drew said angrily. "You are going to fuck this up. You're going to lose Lila and I highly suggest you get your shit together before it is too late. Don't fuck this up so bad that she leaves us. You may lose her, but the company needs her."

Drew stormed off, grabbed his keys, and headed home. Now he was fuming. He did not know what his brother's problem was. Drake has never acted like this before. Sure, he never did the relationship thing, the women he was with always knew the deal, but it was different with Lila. Drew knew it, so did Drake. This was why Drew was so perplexed with Drake's actions. He admitted he loved Lila, was going to tell her, and suddenly changed direction.

Drew understood he was in a hard position. Drake was his brother and also his business partner. He loved him and would always be there for him. On the other hand, he also loved Lila. She had become such a good friend as well as a fantastic employee. Drew wanted to support her as well. What a dilemma. What a mess.

Drew arrived home fifteen minutes later. Shayla was in the

kitchen starting to prepare dinner. He walked over, hugged and kissed her.

"Where's Lila?"

"Still upstairs. She has not come down yet."

"Jesus. You think she is okay?"

"I don't know, Drew. You could tell she was trying so hard to be strong, but the hurt was written all over her face. When I went up to change, I heard her crying. If it was me, I wouldn't be alright. That plastic doll was looking down at her, like she was inferior. It was so obvious." Laughing a little, she said, "What was funny though is that Candi was so oblivious to the few little jabs Lila got in."

"Good for her. I saw Drake before I left."

"You did?"

"Yep, and I laid into him. Told him how he was fucking this up."

"Good for you. He needs a good butt kicking."

Chuckling at his sweet wife because she never cursed, Drew said, "Well, he's too strong for me to kick his *butt*. I just hope my words make an impact."

"If he will listen to anyone, it will be you."

"I hope so."

Shayla and Drew both turned their heads as they heard Lila coming down the stairs. Walking into the kitchen, a big yawn escaped.

"Hey, guys. What's up?"

"Just getting everything ready for dinner. You have a good nap?"

"Yep. Slept longer than I expected. So what's for dinner? Can I help?"

"Stir fry. I've got everything chopped. You can help when we are ready to cook."

"Sounds good."

"Lila," Drew said, looking at her.

Lila picked up on where Drew was going. "Stop. Don't even say anything."

"We just want to make sure you are okay," Drew said.

"He's right, Lila. We love you."

"I love you both as well. Am I upset? Yes, but I am going to be fine. I have been through hardship before. I will get through it this time, too. If you could just not talk about it tonight, I would really appreciate it. I know you both are here for me, and I promise I will reach out if I need to talk, advice, whatever. I just want to get back to work and move forward."

Drew walked over to Lila and pulled her in for a hug. "Okay, I understand and can respect that. Now, let's get dinner cooking. I'm starving."

Lila squeezed him then gave him a kiss on the cheek. She went over to help Shayla finish dinner. They ate out on the deck as usual. The three of them enjoyed a nice dinner and watched a movie together. Lila knew everything would work out as long as she had these two wonderful people in her life.

18

Lila woke up early and decided to head into the office on her own. Leaving a note on the counter for Drew and Shayla, Lila drove to the office. She was the first one to arrive as it was only 7 o'clock in the morning. The quiet would be good in order for her to catch up on some work before the others started to arrive. She checked any emails that came in after they left yesterday, went over all lingering items she normally handled, then started to review the client and transaction list seized from Perez' compound. Dallas had forwarded her the information yesterday afternoon. There were a lot of names on the list, many of which were listed multiple times. It was very disturbing to know so many women had been taken and sold. Lila decided to convert the list into a spreadsheet in order to be able to manipulate the information.

She sorted the list by the buyer since the women's names were only first names, then date of purchase, followed by the remaining information including purchase price, woman sold, etc. Lila felt it would be best to focus on one buyer at a time. The first name on the list had four entries. His name was Samuel Adams, like the founding father and beer. Lila read the second name, John Charles. Another generic name. Interesting. Scanning the rest of the list, each and every name listed was a common, generic American name; nothing unique, no indication of ethnicity, no name that would stand out. What was it about the list that was bugging her? There was something there that she just could not pinpoint. Suddenly, like a lightning bolt, it hit her just as Dallas came around the corner, a pattern.

"Hey there, darlin'. You are in early," Dallas said as he walked up to her desk.

"Hi, Dallas."

"What you working on?"

"Going over the client list. I think I found something, a pattern."

"Really? I started reviewing the information yesterday. Drew wanted me to see if I could find anything. Give me a second. Let me grab a chair so you can show me what you have found."

Dallas headed to the conference room to grab a chair. Just as he was bringing it behind Lila's desk, Drake approached them. He saw Lila and stiffened slightly.

"Hey Drake."

"Dallas," Drake responded.

"Lila. Do you have a minute? I need to speak with you."

"Actually, no, I do not Mr. Donovan, unless of course it is an emergency. I am in the middle of reviewing the Perez documents and believe I have located a pattern."

Lila referring to Drake as Mr. Donovan did not go unnoticed by Drake or Dallas.

"It can wait. I don't want to interrupt. Is it something we should have a briefing on?"

"Probably, but not yet. Dallas and I need to do a bit more work to support my theory."

"I understand. Just let me know when you want the team to meet."

"We will reach out, sir, if my theory appears promising."

Nodding at Lila, Drake walked back toward his office.

"Whoa, girl. What was that all about?"

"What?"

"Mr. Donovan?"

"Just keeping it professional. He wants to act like a jerk on a personal level, I will only deal with him professionally. So, ready?"

"Sure, darlin'. Show me what you found."

"So, I converted all the data into a spreadsheet to make it easier for me to review. I arranged it by each buyer. I wanted to see how many women each of them purchased, when they purchased them, etc. Figured it would be easier to work one scum bag at a time. After looking at the list, something stood out and appears to be a pattern."

"What did you see?"

"Look at the names. They are all typical American names, but very plain, very generic, common names. There are no ethnic names on the list, nothing that will identify the nationality. These are code names for his buyers. I kept looking to try and figure out how we could identify who the buyers are by the code names. I'll bet you a million dollars the first initials of each name are the buyers' real initials. If my theory is correct, we just need to figure out who they really are. See, the first person is Samuel Adams. I think the buyer's first name starts with an "S" and the last name starts with an "A.""

Dallas looked over the list, turning to Lila shaking his head.

"What?" she asked.

"Unbelievable. Damn, you're smart. I think you are right. No one picked up on this and you did, what, in an hour? So was Perez, smart trying to protect his clients. Since we cannot identify them by the false name, do you have any ideas?"

Tapping a pencil on her chin, Lila scanned all the information for a few minutes. Then her face lit up. "If we, or the FBI, can trace where the payments originated from, even if the account is not fully identifiable, we may be able to narrow down suspects based on geographic location. See, I'm thinking if we determine a location, let's say Paris, there will only be so many people in France that could afford to or would purchase these women. At least I hope so. We can use their initials to try to significantly narrow down the suspect list. Hopefully there is not a large number of extraordinarily wealthy people with particular initials, in a particular region, who would fit the profile of participating in sex trafficking."

"Darlin', first Perez and his cronies and now figuring out how to track down the buyers; amazing, you are just amazing. I think we need to have a briefing, and stat," Dallas said.

"Let me call Drew, and then we can get everyone here."

"Drake's already here." Lila gave Dallas a look. "Fine, call Drew."

Lila called Drew. He and Shayla had just pulled into the parking lot. She told him she and Dallas had a lead. Drew instructed her to message everyone to meet in 30 minutes in the conference room. Lila sent out a group message, and she and Dallas made copies of the spreadsheet to hand out to everyone. Drew and Shayla arrived and walked into the copy room.

"Hi, guys."

"Hi," Lila and Dallas said.

"Lila, should I get Agent Harris to call in?" Drew asked.

"I think that would be good. We probably will need his input and help anyway."

"Okay, Shayla—"

"On it," Shayla said, walking away.

"Alright, I am going to check messages and will see you at 0900."

The team started to arrive. Rocco, as usual, brought donuts to share, and everyone gathered into the conference room. Shayla got Agent Harris on the line while Lila pulled the spreadsheet up on the large television monitor in the room. As everyone arrived, Dallas handed out a hard copy of the list. Everyone settled down, ready to hear what they had to say.

"Lila, please proceed," Drew said.

"This morning, Dallas and I were reviewing the client and transactional list retrieved from Perez's compound. Putting the information into a spreadsheet and sorting by name, we noticed a pattern. Look at the names. Does anything stand out?" Lila asked.

The team looked at their copies.

"I just see a bunch of names of dudes," Jax said.

"Look closely. All of the names are typical American male names.

"You're right," Garrett said.

"But what stood out more to me is that it was done on purpose, to protect his clients."

Lila went on to explain her theory on how they used the names and it was really just the client's initials.

"I think you are on to something," Drew said.

"Oh, there's more. Lila, please finish," Dallas said.

"I believe if we can track the money transfers, narrow down the location of the funding source, we may be able to narrow down a list of suspects. There can only be so many individuals who are wealthy enough who will fit the profile and also have the same initials. Maybe Agent Harris' team has more information on the money trail."

"The team has been working on tracking the source of the financial transactions. We can send you what we have so far, or you can meet with our team to discuss. I think you are on the right path."

"Yes, I agree. Great job, Lila and Dallas," Drew said proudly, others agreeing with him.

"Don't thank me. Lila figured all this out this morning. I just reviewed the documents and agreed with her theory."

"Well, excellent work, Lila. We've looked over the material, so has the FBI for a few weeks now, and you figured it out in a few hours. It is unbelievable and commendable. You are such an asset, Lila. I want you and Dallas to keep working on this. Coordinate with Agent Harris and his team, and see what you can find with the financial records."

"Will do."

"I want the rest of you to start gathering Intel on individuals who may fit the profile of potential sex trafficking clients so we can compare with what Lila and Dallas come up with."

"Roger," several of the guys responded.

"Good, we need to wrap this meeting up. Drake and I have a meeting with another high-profile client. Any pending questions we have not already addressed?" Everyone shook their heads no. "Alright, good work. Let's find these assholes."

At that, the room dispersed. Lila and Dallas stayed back to talk with Agent Harris to arrange a meeting with the FBI's technical team on the financials. They scheduled to meet with them after lunch in their Dallas office. The team got to work, everyone splitting off to see what they could find. Lila and Dallas kept looking for any other patterns on the client list and started cataloging the initials on another spreadsheet where they could coordinate all potential suspects for each client. Lila wanted to be prepared when any additional information came in. At about eleven, Dallas and Lila were getting ready to leave when Drake approached.

"Lila, do you have a minute?" he asked.

"Unfortunately, no. Dallas and I are heading out. We are grabbing lunch before we meet with the FBI."

"Fine, but we need to talk when you get back."

"I have a feeling we will be there the remainder of the day. Sorry. Maybe I'll have some time later this week," she said as she grabbed her stuff and went toward the exit, Dallas trailing behind.

"Slow down there, sunshine. You act like you are running away from the Big Bad Wolf."

"I'm not running away from him. I just don't care to hear what he has to say."

"I never mentioned Drake."

"Yes, you . . . well, whatever. Let's get some lunch. I'm hungry."

Chuckling at Lila, Dallas opened up his truck door for her. "Madam," he said gesturing with a bow for her to enter. "Let's get some grub."

ONCE AGAIN, Drake was left standing there, shot down by Lila. All he wanted to do was talk to her about Candi and what she thought she saw. To explain to her all he was doing was having lunch, nothing more. He only met with Candi to break things off. To tell her they could no longer see each other when she rolled through town.

It was not like he and Candi were ever committed in the first place. They knew their relationship was strictly sex. It worked for them because they both were part of the same lifestyle and did not want commitment.

Well, he used to feel that way. Drake knew Candi had men she hooked up with all over the world. She knew he was with other women; a mutual understanding that worked, up until Lila. She had fully disrupted his life. Nothing was or would ever be the same. Now she barely spoke to him; calling him Mr. Donovan. What was up with that? They were clearly past formalities.

Footsteps approached, but Drake's eyes were still glazed over, still stunned by Lila's dismissal.

"What's wrong with you? You look like you just got sucker

punched," he heard Drew say. The words brought him out of his trance.

"Lila."

"What do you mean, Lila?"

"I have tried to talk to her twice today and both times she blew me off. Women can be so difficult. She also called me Mr. Donovan instead of Drake."

"Can you blame her? You haven't been very kind to her since she woke up after being shot. How do you expect her to act? I told you that you were going to blow it."

"Yeah, I know, but I don't know how to fix it."

"First bit of advice, if you want it, is to understand she is probably angry, upset, hurt, and who knows what other feelings she is dealing with right now. Respect that her feelings will not change overnight. You may need to eat some humble pie as well."

"I can deal with that. But if she won't talk to me, won't let me explain, how am I supposed to make amends? I know I fucked up."

"Yes, you did."

"God, man, what am I going to do? I can't lose her. I sure did mess everything up, but I have never loved someone before, never wanted a forever with someone. I really don't know how to act, how to handle it all. Fuck. I feel like a teenager with his first crush instead of a man in his thirties."

"You did not handle it well, that's for sure. The only thing I can say is be honest with Lila. Tell her how you feel, don't hide behind your macho facade. I know it can be scary. I've been there."

"I just hope she gives me a chance to do so. So far it's not looking too good."

"Me, too. I love Lila and she's good for you."

"She sure is."

DALLAS AND LILA never returned to the office. They spent the entire afternoon at the FBI's Dallas office going over the financial transactions. Since Dallas drove, he just took her directly to Drew and Shayla's house. Lila could catch a ride with them to the office in the morning. When they arrived back at the house, Shayla was in the kitchen making a salad, and Drew was on the deck at the grill. Walking in, they said their hellos.

"Mmm, what's for dinner? I'm hungry," Lila said.

"Steak, salad, and potatoes."

"Yum. Can I help?"

"Nope. I'm almost done, and Drew already has the potatoes on the grill. You want to stay for supper, Dallas?"

"Hell yeah. You know I won't pass up a steak dinner," Dallas said.

Shayla and Lila just laughed at him.

"At least let me set the table."

"Sure, make sure you grab five plates. Drake's coming."

Lila stopped in her tracks and stared at Shayla. She could not believe they would invite him over after what he did. She thought they were her friends. Then reality struck. Pushing aside her negative thoughts, she understood. Drake was Drew's brother, Shayla's brother-in-law. She couldn't expect them to never socialize with him just because of her.

"I'm sorry, Lila. I told Drew we should give it a little more time, allow you to deal with what has happened. But Drew felt bad for Drake. He said he looked so lost today and he needed to be around family. How could I tell him no?"

"You're right, Shayla. He is your family, and I would never want to cause issues in your relationship. I'm an adult. I will deal with it. You better stay Dallas . . . for moral support."

"I wouldn't miss this for a million dollars. Tonight's going to be entertaining," Dallas said.

Lila punched him on the shoulder. "For that comment, help me set the table. Want to eat on the deck?" Lila asked Shayla.

"Yes, thanks. Lovin' the weather we are having. I will eat outside whenever I can."

Lila and Dallas set the table, then Dallas grabbed a beer and headed back out onto the deck to talk to Drew. Lila decided to head upstairs to change. Sitting on her bed, she took a moment to calm her nerves and gather her thoughts. She had experienced heartache before and moved forward, but this was Drake. Before him Lila believed she had been in love, but she was wrong. She loved Drake, and that didn't stop just because he was being an ass.

Lila wondered if Drake would try to talk to her tonight. He tried twice earlier in the day, but she purposely brushed him off. Even if he came to her feet groveling for forgiveness, she was not going to make it easy on him. He had been so mean, so hurtful, she was not going to let him off the hook without him working for her forgiveness. This was, of course, if he really still cared about her. He may want to talk to her to tell her he doesn't want a relationship and basically everything was just for the operation. That is what scared Lila the most, Drake not wanting her. She knew he was the one, and she would be devastated by his rejection.

Closing her eyes, Lila took a long, slow breath, opened her eyes, and got up to change into a pair of shorts and a tank top. She put her hair up on the top of her head, and then headed downstairs to the kitchen. Shayla was still in the kitchen, but as soon as she glanced toward the deck she saw Drake. He must have arrived when she was upstairs changing. Giving herself a little pep talk, she told herself she could do this.

"You okay?" Shayla asked.

"I'm fine. I will be fine."

"Are you sure?"

"Yes. I have to deal with him eventually. Guess there's no time like the present."

"True. No matter the outcome, sometimes it is just better to tackle our problems head on. Allows us to move forward."

"Yes, it does. Doesn't make it any easier, but it does."

Drake spotted her through the window. Beautiful. He thought Lila was beautiful no matter what she was wearing, if she did or did not have her hair and makeup done. He actually preferred her more natural. Lila did not need anything to enhance her beauty. Drake just stared at her, longing etched on his face. Dallas and Drew looked at each other, feeling sorry for Drake. Sure he fucked up, but was it truly his fault? The guy was a warrior at heart. It had been ingrained in him for so long to be tough, not to allow emotions in as it would interfere with the mission. Seal training just does not go away once you are out, especially given the type of work he did now. Then Lila arrived and disrupted his entire world. Drake really did not know how to handle loving someone, wanting to always have someone by his side, day and night, for eternity.

This was a new life, a life he never thought he would want. Now he had to learn how to open up, let someone in. He knew he loved Lila. Wanted to take care of her, cherish her, but would she forgive him? Would she give him the opportunity to learn how to love, to prove to her he wanted her in his life, always? Drake would heed Drew's advice. He would apologize, tell her how he felt, and give her the time she needed. He was the one that messed up, now he had to deal with the consequences. As long as the final outcome was Lila's forgiveness, he would do whatever it took.

The ladies came out on to the deck and broke his train of thought. Shayla had a tray with the steaks, Lila following behind her with two beers in her hand, a guarded look on her face. She headed over and stood next to Dallas and handed Shayla a beer once she gave Drew the tray.

"Hey, Drake. You snuck in," Shayla said.

"Hey, Shayla, Lila,"

"Hi," Lila softly responded.

Everyone was quiet for just a moment, feeling the thickness building in the air. Dallas came to the rescue, breaking the tension between Lila and Drake.

"We had a good visit with the FBI today. I think we have something to really work with. To start figuring out who these assholes are who were purchasing these women and girls."

"That's great," Drew said. "So Harris' team has made some progress?"

"Yes, they have. Lila filled them in more on her theory. A few of the techs and analysts are going to work tonight and send us what they can in the morning so we can start piecing locations to suspects."

"Perfect," Drew said.

"You all did some good work. You have really been instrumental in this case, Lila," Drake said.

"Thank you, Drake. I appreciate the kind words," Lila said nervously, but hopeful. Drake was not one to hand out compliments easily, but it did seem genuine. Lila looked at him a little more closely after his comment. She then saw what Shayla told her Drew said. Drake did look lost, a sadness on his face that she had never seen before. A total contrast to yesterday when she and Shayla unexpectedly came face to face with him and that bimbo.

"He is right, Lila. If it was not for you, I do not know where we would be on the case at this time," Drew added.

"So true. Every pivotal turn in this case was because of you, what you sacrificed, let alone how smart you are. That's my girl," Dallas said putting his arm around her.

Drake stiffened. All his thoughts went to Dallas calling Lila 'his girl.' She was his, not Dallas', and now he had his hands on her. Who the fuck does he think he is manhandling his woman, he thought. He allowed Dallas to participate at the club because he trusted him, now he was making moves on his woman. He had better get his hands off of Lila before he broke them.

Lila sensed the tension in Drake. What was up with that? Why did he seem pissed? She then realized Dallas had his arm around her. Hmm. Is he jealous?

This could be a good thing. She could use it to her advantage just to get back at him a little. Lila was not a vindictive person, but Drake needed to be brought down a notch or two. This may be the perfect opportunity.

Dallas was a friend, only a friend, and she knew Dallas did not have any intentions other than friendship. Lila wondered if Dallas would go along with her, give Drake a little bit of his own medicine. She would ask him later as a little plan started creeping into her mind.

"Oh, Dallas, stop. Yes, I was a part of this operation, but it took each and every one of us on the team to get where we are. That is what it is all about, working as a team to get the job done. No lone cowboys."

"I think she is right," Shayla said. "It takes all of you to get a job done."

"Exactly," Lila said rubbing Dallas' arm. "So when are the steaks going to be ready? I'm hungry and they smell so good."

"Should not be much longer," Drew replied.

"Perfect. I will go in and get the salad and dressing so everything is out when the steaks are done. Can you hand me the tray? I will wash it while I am in the kitchen."

"I'll come help," Dallas said, following Lila back into the house.

"Is there something going on between those two?" Drake asked.

"Who, Dallas and Lila?" Shayla asked.

"Yes."

She laughed, "You are kidding right? No, I highly doubt that. Lila would have told me. They are friends. Why does it matter to you anyway, Drake? You have Candi don't you?" Shayla said with a slight smirk on her face. Drew noticed and tried to contain his laughter. Drake was oblivious.

"There is nothing between me and Candi. I already told Drew. Yes, I used to see her when she would come into town occasionally, but I told her yesterday that could not continue."

"Really? It did not look that way when I saw you two yesterday. Why break it off with her, it's not like there is any reason to, is there?"

"Why are you giving me a hard time? You know why."

"Enlighten me."

"Lila, that's why and you know it."

"If it is because of Lila, you surely have not been very convincing. To me, it seems like you have been ignoring her and doing everything you can to push her away. I thought something was building between you two."

"Shayla, you know it was, is. Why are you being so hard on me? I have never loved someone before and—"

"Ah, so you love her, do you?"

"Yes, fuck, you obviously know I do."

"Yes, I do," she said smiling.

"Then why are you harassing me?"

"I'm not harassing you. I am just trying to make sure you realize what you have done, and if you do not do something about it, and soon, she may not forgive you. She has been through enough crap in her life; she deserves to be treated like a queen, not pushed aside until someone decides she is worth it."

"You are right. I know I fucked it up. I do not know why I stepped back. It just seemed like every time I tried to talk to her after she woke up, someone else was in there. We never got a minute alone. Then I got scared. Shayla, I have never been scared before, but I was with Lila. I don't know what to do," Drake said, distress in his voice.

Shayla softened. She felt sorry for Drake; he was her brother and she loved him and realized that he truly had no clue how to love and how to handle his emotions. She must help him. Help him get Lila back. Shayla knew Lila still loved him, but it was just going to take a little bit of work.

"Drake, I will try to help. I cannot do it for you, you will have to handle this yourself, but I can give you some suggestions from a woman's perspective."

"You will?"

"Yes, but we will have to talk later, they are coming back. One thing I can tell you now is be patient. You need to give her time and prove you are serious, and stop getting jealous of Dallas."

"I will be patient, and I am serious. I am also not jealous of Dallas."

"Really? I saw you with my own eyes when he put his arm around her. You don't fool me big guy."

Drake knew she saw right through him, so there was no sense in denying he was getting jealous. Shayla always could and always did tell him like it is. She was never someone to interfere, but she would not hesitate to give her opinion when necessary.

LILA AND DALLAS were getting the salad and condiments and cleaning the tray when Lila spoke quietly to Dallas. "Did you see how Drake reacted when you put your arm around me?"

"Yes, the man was pissed. You know he still has feelings for you. I am guessing you do as well. Both of you are so obvious. I do not know why y'all don't just make up, get married, and have a bunch of babies."

"I think you are getting a little ahead of yourself, Dallas;

but yes, I do love him. Even though he has been distant and even after the lunch incident yesterday, I still do want to be with Drake, but I need your help."

"I heard about the lunch. How can I help?"

"Well, you saw how he reacted when you put your arm around me. His irritation got worse when I rubbed your arm. I think I want him to work for it a little bit. Drake needs to understand he can never treat me like that again, that I will not tolerate it. Maybe the best way to do that is by making him jealous."

"What's your plan?"

"Just keep flirting with me. They all know you are a flirt. I will express some interest. That will get to him. I will still keep myself slightly distant as well, professional. Make him grovel a little. Oh, I have it! Let's pretend you want me to be your roommate. Your place is a little big, isn't it?"

"Yes."

"Everyone knows I was going to get my own place once the operation was over. We can pretend you are asking me to move in and be your roommate. You know, you have plenty of room, are gone for periods of time for ops, and it does not make sense for either of us to have a lot of extra expenses. I think Drake would flip out if he believed I was moving in with you."

"You think this is a good idea? You have seen him, haven't you? He will kick my ass. Drake can be very cold and calculated if the circumstances warrant, and this may just be one of them. You have not seen him turn everything off and turn into a Seal. I have, and I would like to live, or at least not have this pretty face messed up."

"Oh, Dallas. I would never let it get that far. Just enough to get a rise out of him and put him in his place."

"This is not like you, my little sunshine."

"I know, but he hurt me. More than I have been hurt before. He deserves to be taught a little lesson."

"You owe me, little one, especially if he comes after me."

"Yes, I will owe you one and don't worry, if I am right, he will be coming after me, not you."

"You better be right.

LILA AND DALLAS returned with the salad, dressing, fixings for the potatoes, and the clean tray just as Drew was ready to take the steaks off the grill. Lila handed him the tray then started serving salad into each bowl. S

hayla had gone in to get drinks for everyone while Drew took the steak and potatoes off the grill. Everyone took a seat, Lila making sure she was next to Dallas and on the opposite side of the table from Drake.

They passed around the tray, and everyone started to dig into the meal. The food was excellent, as usual. Drew was fantastic at grilling, and his steaks were always perfect. Actually, Drake was just as good, as Lila has had the pleasure to experience. He had served Lila steak when she was staying with him preparing for the op. The conversation was light and easy going. They talked about all kinds of things. Shayla mentioned wanting to go to the beach since she had not been for some time. Lila was in agreement.

"I would love to go to the beach. I have never been to a Texas beach before."

"You will love it. With everything you have been through, I think you deserve a vacation," Shayla said.

"I wouldn't mind one, but not until we make some progress on the buyers. I really want to get this pieced together and start seeing these bastards arrested. Maybe in a little bit we can go." Then she turned to Dallas and said, "You should go with us. We would have a blast."

Dallas knew what she was up to and saw Drake's facial expression change. Playing along, Dallas agreed.

"I'd love to go to the beach. The last time I was at the beach it was in South America on an op, and it was plainly not a vacation. Of course, being able to look at you sexy ladies in bikinis will only tempt me more."

Bingo. That did the trick. Dallas could tell Drake was fuming. He was doing everything he could not to explode right then and there. The color in his face started to redden, his jaw clenched, and his body was tight, almost like he was standing at attention. Dallas could tell it was taking every ounce of control for Drake not to respond to Lila's invitation. Not one of them invited him to tag along. Dallas just hoped that he made it out alive through Lila's little plan for Drake. He already committed, so Dallas kept laying it on thick, encouraging a little beach excursion, even if Drew and Shayla could not get away.

If Drake found out they were playing him, Dallas would be dead, even though he agreed Drake deserved a little payback after how he had been treating Lila. Everyone knew they loved each other and could not understand why Drake was acting this way, thus Dallas played his part. He just hoped Lila knew what she was doing. She had not witnessed Drake click into a warrior before, and if it was unleashed, Dallas was not sure how Lila would respond. He only hoped if Drake did click, it was only to make sure Lila became his and it would not backfire on her.

19

The evening progressed, but the tension flowing through Drake never ceased, even though he tried to participate in the group's conversation. They all could tell he was trying to keep things light but was struggling. Dallas and Lila continued their flirtatious behavior without taking it too far. The unspoken words between them kept Drake on his toes, ever so slightly. A little touch here, a tease there, subtle actions to keep Drake wondering if there was a budding relationship between Lila and Dallas.

What made the evening even more entertaining was that they realized Drew and Shayla had picked up on what they were doing and added their own spin. Shayla encouraged Lila to continue on with her apartment search, that she needed to be able to get back on her feet, have the independence she deserved. Not that Shayla or Drew were kicking her out, just that they knew how important it was to Lila. Also, Shayla kept reiterating when things settled enough on the investigative end of the operation, for Lila to take a long-deserved vacation, even if she and Drew could not join Lila and Dallas. Drew was in agreement with whatever any of them said and would glance periodically at his brother to see his reaction; doing everything he could to contain his smirk when he saw agitation on Drake's face.

What made this all so interesting to both Drew and Dallas was that they knew how focused, attentive, smart, and strikingly sharp Drake was. Those attributes were what made him an exceptional Navy Seal and now an excellent Operations Director of the firm. This was the first time in over a decade they had ever seen Drake rattled, all because of a spit fire little blonde.

A few hours passed, and Dallas was getting ready to say his goodbyes. Lila said she would walk him out, just one more little poke at Drake before the evening was over. In her peripheral vision, Lila noticed Drake followed her. She could see his shadow through the glass on the sides of the front door. She took her time before she came back into the house and practically ran into Drake in the foyer. It was obvious he was waiting for her.

"Oh, Drake, you scared me. You heading out as well?"

"Yes, but I would like to speak to you first."

Lila knew there was no way she would be able to blow him off this time. What excuse would she have?

"Okay."

"I want to talk to you about several things, but first I want to explain about yesterday. What you think you saw at the Bistro."

"Look, Drake, technically you do not owe me any explanations. What you do on your personal time is none of my business. What was between us was just for the op, right? That has been made very clear. You are free to see whomever you want, even if it is Bimbo Barbie."

"You are wrong, Lila, on so many levels. I do owe you an explanation, actually many. This is just hard for me. I am new to all of this, and my words may not come out as I intend."

Lila started to get nervous. She thought Drake still had feelings for her, but buried deep within were insecurities which never fully seemed to dissipate. They were always with her, like one remaining leech you cannot get unattached, leaving her with the uncertainty they would have any type of future together. Patiently, without saying a word, Lila waited for Drake to speak.

"See, Candi and I were just having lunch. She is someone I would see on and off whenever she was in town. We met at *The Manor* several years ago. She is a flight attendant, as I believe you already know, and does a lot of international flights. She is only in the Dallas area every three to four months. We would meet up when she was in town. Neither of us wanted any kind of relationship, just have a little fun, thus it worked. I know Candi is very self-centered, but it works for her, and I really did not care as I was not looking for a relationship. We would just meet and have a good time."

"Drake, I really do not want to hear about your sexual escapades with that bimbo. Do you have a point here?"

Dropping his head, realizing he is not going about this very well, Drake looked up and spoke again.

"Sorry. I told you my words may not come out the way I wanted. What I am trying to say is when Candi called me, telling me she was back in town and wanted to see me, I asked her to meet for lunch, something we have never done. She knew something was up. The reason I wanted to meet her was to tell her that we could no longer see each other. I figured I owed her that much. The reason I could not see her anymore was because of you, Lila."

"Me? Why?"

"Because I care about you. Sure this all started out because of an operation, but there was something about you from the first day I met you. I know I was a jerk then, and have also been a jerk lately, but something was there, wanting to be explored. I felt you were mine from the start. That is why I would not allow anyone else to be your Dom for the op. Everything I did was calculated because I wanted you, wanted to be with you. When we started the training, and especially when you stayed with me, I knew how I felt. I want to be with you Lila. I want you to be mine."

Lila was stunned silent. He was saying a lot of things she wanted to hear, but not everything. He wants her to be his, but for how long? A week? A month? Is this just so no one else can have her, but he is not willing to give her what she needs, what she deserves? Lila was still guarded, rightfully so.

"If you want me to be yours, then why have you basically ignored me since I woke up from the shooting?" she asked quietly.

"Lila, I have no good explanation for that except I was scared."

"What were you scared of?"

"You, having a relationship, not knowing how to do this . . . a lot of things. You already know I have never been in a relationship. I really do not know how to be in one, and know I say the wrong things. I am sure I will continue to do or say something you do not like, but I do know I want you. I hope you can forgive me for being an ass since you got shot and give me another chance."

"Drake, I don't know," Lila said, then noticed Drake starting to get worked up, ready to speak. Lifting her hand to stop him, Lila said, "Let me finish. You hurt me, a lot. You had to know I had feelings for you before everything happened, but when you were not there for me after waking up, then seeing you with that, that . . . bimbo, it took my feelings to a new level. I was hurt, angry, upset, everything in between. The only reason I did not crumble was because of Shayla, Drew, and Dallas. They have been there for me, and Dallas has treated me how a lady should be treated. He has shown me my worth and that I should not accept being treated as anything less than an equal and with respect. I just don't know if you can do that."

Lila knew she hit a nerve with that comment. She added the part about Dallas just to spite him. Yes, he was expressing his feelings, but the hell with it. She was done with being hurt by men and not standing up for herself.

"Lila, I understand I was wrong and did not go about this the right way. How am I supposed to learn to be better if I never get the chance? You know I am a dominant and tend to control situations, kind of goes with the territory. I am sure that does not help, but I promise I will try to learn, to change."

"You see, Drake, I know you are a Dom, and in actuality, I love that part of you. I realized I can be submissive but also a strong, independent woman at the same time. I want that in my life, the dominance, but I also want to be respected, treated as an equal, cherished. It's a balance. At times you will be the strong one, and other times I will step into that role. I know it sounds weird being treated as an equal in this type of relationship, but respect and being an equal partner is necessary for a healthy relationship."

"You are so right. I do respect you, Lila, and I do think you are my equal, actually you're much more. I promise I will cherish you forever if you just give me a chance."

"Drake, you are just going to have to give me some time. A lot has happened over the last few weeks, and I need to make sure I am not setting myself up to be hurt again. I already had some bad relationships, and I do not need another one. Also, I do not want to just be a 'right now' with you. With everything that I have been through in the past and recently, I want to be with someone who is looking toward the future."

"I am."

"You say that now, but I also think you need time to be sure. I want it all Drake. I want my life partner to love me unconditionally, take care of me, treasure me, all of it, and I will do the same for my partner. Can you be that person? Do you know if you even have it in you?" Again, Drake started to talk. "Please don't. I want you to think about what I have said. I also need to think. Please give me the time I need, but if you realize in the interim what I want, what I need, is not something you can give me, please tell me. Will you do that?"

"Yes."

"Thank you."

"How long do you think you need?"

"I don't know. You will just need to be patient. Will you please do that for me?"

"I will try."

"Good. Alright. I better go help clean up, and then I want to get to bed. Today was a little taxing and I am tired. Have a good night, Drake. I will see you in the office tomorrow," Lila said as she opened the front door for Drake to leave.

Drake did not argue and left without complaint. He would be patient, give her the time she needed to think about everything. He wanted her, needed her in his life, forever.

Immediately after he left, Drake realized that he never told Lila he loved her. What an idiot. Why didn't he get it all out? He wanted the forever with Lila, and he did not tell her. Fuck, he sucked at expressing his feelings.

The right time would prevail, and he would unload his heart. The thought scared him, but he was excited about a future with Lila. Unfortunately, patience was not one of his strongest traits. Fighting his propensity to move forward with gusto would be a challenge.

Lila strode back into the kitchen and noticed Shayla and Drew had already brought everything in from outside. Shayla was putting the remaining food away in the refrigerator, so Lila walked over and started cleaning the dishes.

"You don't have to do that."

"Yes, I do. You two cooked, the least I can do is clean. It's not like it will take long anyway. We don't have any pots and pans to clean."

"So, I noticed Drake walked to the front door after you walked Dallas out. Did he try to talk to you?"

"Yes, he did."

"You can tell me it is none of my business, my feelings will not be hurt, but I am curious as to what he had to say."

"Shayla, I tell you everything, and you are fully aware of this entire situation, so I am not going to withhold anything from you. Actually, you should be the one telling me to keep it to myself as he is your brother-in-law and I am your friend. You should not be put in the middle of this."

"As always, thinking about someone else's feelings. That is just one of the reasons I love you so much," Shayla said whole-heartedly. "But of course, you know I am nosey. Give me all the dirt."

"Thanks. I love you, too. Basically to sum up our conversation, Drake said he has feelings for me, wants me to be *his*. He explained he only met with Candi to break it off with her, to tell her he could no longer see her because of me. Drake explained their relationship was very casual and he only saw her a few times a year. Also, he acknowledged he has been an ass since I woke up in the hospital, and he could not explain and did not understand why. Only thing he said was that he was new to this, has never had a relationship before, and did not know how to handle the situation. He knew he handled everything wrong and wants me to forgive him. To give him a chance."

"What did you say?"

"I told him I needed to think about everything, that I just did not want to be his right now. I wanted to be loved, cherished, and taken care of, an equal partner in a relationship. I asked him to think things through as well. To make sure he was going to be able to give that to me, and if he could not, he needed to tell me, to break it off. I reiterated I already had some bad experiences and would not put up with being treated poorly again. I only wanted to be with someone who wanted the same. Maybe not those exact words, but you get the point."

"Did Drake agree to give you time?"

"He said he would, but who knows with Drake." Lila smiled. "I did get one little dig at him. I told him how you, Drew, and Dallas have been my rocks and Dallas has shown me how a lady should be treated. I could tell that little bit of information got to him."

"Oh, you little devil," Shayla said, snickering. "So, are you going to give him a second chance? You know, Lila, if you do, you will need to be patient with him as well. He will make mistakes. This is a first for him."

"Yes, of course I want to give him a second chance, and I don't expect him to be perfect. I am not perfect. I know it is a little cruel, but making him wait is serving dual purposes. He needs to experience a little taste of his own medicine, wait at least a little bit like I had to. Also, I want him to be 100% positive he wants this relationship; make sure he does love me. He did not say those words, but I must know it is true before I allow myself to completely forgive and let it all go. I want to go into this relationship knowing I can tell my insecurities to fuck off and fully give him my heart."

"Very wise, and a good decision. I know Drake loves you. I think you did the right thing, though; make him think about everything, make sure this is truly what he wants. You both deserve happiness. I just hope that happiness is you two together. You know, I do have a vested interest; my best friend with my brother-in-law, what could be better?"

Lila hoped she did the right thing by not forgiving Drake right then and there. Her insecurities started rising to the surface once again. She was so tired of feeling inadequate.

Several of her past relationships left her feeling this way, especially the last one after the physical trauma that ensued. Drake's actions also did not help, nor how that Candi woman looked down on her. She knew she was a good person, smart, and would make someone a great partner. She just hoped Drake would be that person.

She missed him, missed being in his arms, missed their talks, just being together. Her body ached any time she was close to Drake. She wanted to rip his clothes off and devour him, have him devour her body as well. They were magnetic in the bedroom. A kind of electricity she never experienced. It felt right, like two people who were the perfect match in every way. Well, at least that is how she felt. It was not like Lila had slept with a lot of people. Sure, she had been with a few men, but Drake . . . did he even know how many women he has been with? Lila knew it was a lot, and he would also partake in multiple partners at once, even shared women. Did she satisfy him? Could she? Was she enough? Did he compare her to others when they were intimate? Could Drake be with only one woman for the rest of his life? Lila would never be able to share her man with anyone. All these thoughts confused her. She worried if he would be able to give all that up for her.

Lila would never ask Drake to give up the alternative lifestyle. In actuality, she enjoyed him dominating her, being his submissive. Surprisingly, she even liked going to *The Manor* with him. It opened her eyes to so many new experiences she never thought she would enjoy. Lila did not want this part of him to end if they pursued this relationship. She worried he would become bored and leave her. Once again, those stupid insecurities peeked out to see if they could control her.

Enough of this crap. Lila was not going to allow doubts to infiltrate her thoughts. No matter what happened, if Drake decided he did not want a lifelong commitment with her, Lila was strong, smart, and had a great career. She'd found a new purpose and wanted to explore all the possibilities.

While she loved the law, her first career, she found being on a team, investigating, and now being part of an operation exhilarating. She wanted to continue training, become an agent, and be a regular team member on operations. She proved she could do it, had the strength and wherewithal to pursue this new career. Lila would not let anyone stand in her way. If Drake did want a relationship, he would have to accept this part of her as well. If he didn't, at least she would be doing something that felt like she was making an impact in someone's life or for the security of her country.

20

The next morning, Lila and Dallas started reviewing the updated transaction reports from the FBI. They forwarded a copy very early that morning so they could start comparing and analyzing the information. Lila and Dallas were in the tech room so they could spread out on the table in the middle while also having the accessibility of the computers. The report from the FBI allowed them to narrow down the originating location of 17 of the buyers. On the existing spreadsheet, Lila then matched the locations to the buyer and their initials. This enabled them to focus on the locations and the initials. Dallas was reviewing any potential suspects the team was able to provide. Sad to say, but the team came up with quite a list of people who were wealthy enough to make this type of purchase and prioritize them by potential, meaning who would be more likely to participate in this type of illegal activity.

For the first buyer named Samuel Adams, or the initials SA, the FBI was able to narrow it down to Dubai. Lila and Dallas were able to narrow it down even further to eight potential suspects with those initials who were located in the Dubai region. They continued this process for as many of the buyers they could. Then Lila came across the initials for the buyer intending to purchase Caroline. The FBI found documentation alluding to the man who had seen video and pictures of Caroline and wanted to purchase her even though she was not compliant. The communication indicated he would enjoy the process of 'taming the whore.' The thought of this man wanting to hurt Caroline made Lila sick.

The FBI traced the payment back to Russia. It went through many locations, but they were confident the source was Russian, especially since some of the words used in their communications were indicative of broken English spoken by a Russian. Perez' list had the name as Mike Price, thus the initials were MP. There were a lot of suspects from Russia whose last name started with "P", but only a few whose first name started with an "M." Lila listed the names on the spreadsheet. Dallas looked at her list and was taken aback when he read the three names that matched the initials. One name in particular: Magar Petrov.

"Jesus. My fucking God," Dallas said rubbing his hands over his face.

"What is it?" Lila asked, concern echoing in her voice.

"One of the names on the list, Magar Petrov. If he is the man who wanted to purchase Caroline, which I highly suspect he is, we have a problem."

"What is the problem? You obviously know about him. Fill me in."

"Petrov is part of the Russian Mafia. Actually, very high up; one of their main leaders. He is ruthless, brutal. If it is him, and based on the communications, Caroline, or any woman who ended up in his hands would suffer horribly."

"We need to update everyone, stat, on what we have, especially the senator and Trent. They need to know about the suspects who wanted to purchase Caroline, especially if it was

Petrov. If he knows or finds out she is a United States senator's daughter, would he just let it all go, or would Caroline still be at risk?"

"I see where you are going with this, Lila, and I agree. If it is Petrov, I do not think he would stop trying to get Caroline just because Perez was busted, especially if he knows who her father is. His hand stretches all over the world, unfortunately."

"That is what I was afraid of. We don't want to take any chances. Trent will need to be vigilant, and we need to make sure he has the most updated Intel. They need to know where they stand, deal with any extra security needs if necessary."

Dallas noticed Drake standing in the doorway. Lila's back was toward the door, she was fully engrossed in analyzing the data. She did not realize he was there. Dallas thought this was the perfect time to help Lila with her plan in tormenting Drake.

"So Lila, have you thought about my offer to be roommates?"

"What?" she said looking up.

"Being my roommate, moving into my place. Like I said the other day, you are looking to get your own place, I have plenty of room, and I am always in and out, so it would be nice to have someone there."

"Oh, oh," she said, finally catching on. Drake must be listening, so Lila decided to play along, taking Dallas' lead.

"I have thought about it, and I believe you are right. It does not make sense to get my own place. I will have plenty of room at your condo, and it will save both of us a lot of money. Shayla and Drew are not pushing me to leave, but I am sure they would like their house back. I don't want to continue intruding on their private time."

"Nothing worse than a cock blocker."

"Goodness, Dallas, always crude. So when should I move in?"

"Anytime. We can move you in this weekend if you would like. This will be perfect. We get along tremendously, and what could be better than waking up to your face every morning."

Those words did the trick. Drake clicked and his face immediately reddened as he exploded into the room. Coming toward Dallas, he grabbed him by his shirt and put him up against the wall. Dallas just let him, did not fight back as he knew Drake. He would not do anything to him if he was not fighting back, especially one of his best friends.

"Who the fuck do you think you are moving in on what's mine. I let you help with the fucking op, and now you think you can slide in, try to steal her. Fuck you, Dallas. I thought I could trust you, thought you were my friend," explosion and anger colored his voice.

"Sorry Drake. I did not know you were together, officially. Figured why not, Lila and I are friends, she's beautiful, who would be a more perfect roommate. Also, you never claimed her."

"The fuck I didn't. I claimed her before the op started, right after her proposal."

Dallas didn't need to think. He knew Drake claimed her the moment he said only he would act as her Dom during the op.

"Oh, yeah, you may have said something. But you sure have not acted like her Dom, so I thought it was all over. She was available," Dallas added, digging a little bit deeper.

Drake jacked him up higher on the wall, pressing hard into his body. That is when he felt a blow to the back of his knees; Lila.

"Get off him," she screamed. "Are you crazy? Put him down right now."

Drake let go of Dallas, and Lila got in between them. Others started trickling into the room after hearing the altercation.

"What the fuck is wrong with you, Drake? You have no right."

"You are mine!"

"Yours? Oh, so I guess you forgot all about our conversation last night, you know, about being patient."

"Well that was before I knew Dallas was moving in on what is mine and now you want to be his roommate? That is not happening."

"You think you can tell me what I can and cannot do? Where I can live, who I can be around? I don't think so," Lila's words echoed loudly throughout the room.

"Yes, I can. I'm your Dom, you're my Sub. It's about time we started acting like it. I've had enough of this shit."

Just as those words escaped his lips, Drake grabbed Lila and tossed her over his shoulder, turned, and started to leave the room. Lila was punching his back to no avail, screaming for him to put her down. Jax, Jace and Garrett were already in the room and just moved aside, grinning from ear to ear at what was happening. Drew, Shayla, and Rocco were heading down the hall in the direction of the raised voices when Drake barreled out of the door, Lila still over his shoulder. Shayla was getting ready to say something when Drew grabbed her arm, stopping her. Drew shook his head no and mouthed, "Let them go."

Drake continued through the lobby, out the front door, heading toward his truck. Lila was still screaming at him to put her down, a plethora of expletives coming out of her mouth. Once he reached his truck, he put her down but still held onto her arm. Opening the door, Drake gestured for her to get in.

"No."

"Get in Lila, or I will put you in myself."

Lila scowled at Drake but got up in the truck, arms crossed, very pissed. Drake went around the truck to get in the driver's side, keeping his eyes on her the entire time to ensure she would not bolt. Once he got in and buckled up, Lila laid on the verbal assault.

"Who do you think you are? Doing what you want, putting me over your shoulder like a sack of potatoes. You have no right. You think you are a fucking caveman? You just blew it Mister, you went too far."

"Lila, enough," the firm dominant voice filled the truck.

His demand confused her even more. Goosebumps quickly spreading, her body responded to his demand. Fuck this crap. Why was her body betraying her when she was so mad at Drake? This had happened before. Her body responding one way when her mind was somewhere else. Only Drake did that to her, making her so angry, but desiring him simultaneously. Lila was so embarrassed, wondering what all the guys thought of her? Ass in the air for everyone to see.

No one stopped him or even said a thing. Not even Shayla. Well, Lila did see Drew pull her back when she glanced her way. Lila guessed no one was stupid enough to stop Drake when he was angry. Mad at the entire situation, Lila just turned away from him and looked out the window, not really seeing anything as they sped down the road. She realized he was taking her to his house when he slowed to enter the gated community. For a brief moment, Lila wondered if she could jump out of the truck when they passed Drew and Shayla's house. Knowing that was not a good idea, she remained still.

Drake turned into his driveway, pulling his truck into the garage. Coming around to the passenger side, he opened the door for Lila. She refused to move.

"Lila, we can do this the hard way or the easy way. Please get out."

Huffing, Lila exited the truck, and Drake led her into his house.

"Upstairs."

"No."

"Yes, and no arguments," Drake said as he nudged her further inside. Drake guided her to the master bedroom. Lila just stood in the center of the room, arms still crossed over her chest, not moving. Drake went into a drawer inside the closet and came out with handcuffs.

"Sit and give me your arm."

"No way. I'm still angry with you."

"Lila, do it, now."

Once again, his dominance overtook her. She complied, sitting and holding out her left arm. Lila knew Drake would never hurt her. He may be a seal, a warrior, someone who has killed, but never, ever did she think he would lay an unwanted hand on her or cause her physical harm. Mentally was another question.

"This is not the way I wanted to go about this, but you left me no choice."

"No choice? You're crazy."

"Yes, no choice. I was going to do what you wanted, give you time no matter how difficult it was, be patient, but as soon as I overheard you and Dallas talking about you moving in with him, my patience was out the door. This is the only way I could guarantee you would listen to what I have to say. Many things were left unsaid last night. You will not be moving in with Dallas."

"I do not believe you get to make that decision."

"You see, as your Dom, I do."

"Who says you are my Dom? I do not think I made any final decisions."

"You already did. I saw your body respond to me, Lila. You stopped arguing. A Sub will always listen to her Dom, even if she is upset at him."

Fucker. She knew Drake was observant. She should have known he would not miss her body's response to him. Lila could not deny it. She always responded to Drake, another reason his earlier rejections hurt so much.

"Lila, I would like you to listen to me. Truly hear what I have to say to you. I need to tell you what I didn't last night. After you hear me out and think about what I say, if you still want to leave you can. Can you do that?"

Nodding her head yes, Drake took a deep breath preparing to let it all out. Lila noticed his facial expression change, a look of uncertainty spreading. Drake was never uncertain, about anything.

"Lila, you cannot move in with Dallas. You need to move back in here, with me."

Lila started to speak, but Drake stopped her.

"If you could please just let me finish. I need to get this out. You can ask or say anything you want when I am done."

Lila nodded in agreement.

"Like I said, I want you to move back in with me. You belong here, with me. Maybe this between us all started in an unorthodox way, but as I said, I knew the first time I saw you that you were different. You are a Dom's dream, my dream. You're adventurous, even while cautious, trusting me to give you what you need, to please you. I want to keep doing so. I want only you, Lila, no one else. Knowing how you overthink things sometimes, you probably have wondered how could I be with only one person. Will you be enough? The answer is yes. I never thought I would want only one woman, or have a permanent relationship, but Drew warned me. He said when the right woman came into my life, it would hit me like a ton of bricks. God, I never imagined how right he was.

"Lila, I want to be your Dom, but more so, I want to be your partner. It is not all about sex or our lifestyle, it is about love. I did not say it last night, and I could have kicked myself. I love you Lila, deeply and truly love you. I think I fell in love with you even before we started preparing for the operation, when you put me on my ass by your words. You are perfect for me. You're beautiful, smart, loving, and tough, just perfect. You won't put up with my shit and will put me in my place when it's needed. You also melt into submission so beautifully, by your choice alone. Everything I ever dreamt about.

"You see, I still want to spoil you, cherish you, and take care of you, but also want you to know we are equals. We balance each other so well. Where I am weak, you are strong. When I am being unreasonable, you bring me back to reality. You are my everything. I want it all with you, Lila. I want forever. Please, please, will you come back to me? Will you marry me?"

Tears streamed down Lila's cheeks. He loved her, wanted to marry her. Drake said everything she wanted to hear. Assured her she was the only one, and she believed him. The sincerity of his words mirrored on his face. Lila did not doubt him. She knew he had never said those words to any woman. She was the first and would be the only woman to ever hear 'I love you' from Drake Donovan. This realization made her cry even more. Lila was quiet, her emotions overpowering her. Her silence made Drake unsettled.

"Say something, please Lila. I know I'm not perfect. I will make mistakes, probably many, but if you love me, if you will give me a chance, I will do everything in my power to make you happy. I would rather die than ever hurt you again."

"I love you, too . . . and, yes."

"You do? Thank God." Drake paused, then his eyes widened. "Wait, when you said 'yes,' does that mean . . . ?"

"Yes, Drake, I will marry you. I love you so much."

Drake pounced on Lila, hugging and kissing her. He had never felt such an overwhelming rush of happiness until this moment. This must be what Drew was talking about. When you find the one, your soul mate, life partner, it creates an over-whelming explosion of emotions, which he was experiencing at this moment. Lila pulled away for a second, lifting up the elbow of her handcuffed arm, bringing Drake back to the present.

"Would you mind?"

"Oh shit, sorry."

Drake quickly removed the handcuff.

"One last thing," Lila said, her words stopping Drake dead in his tracks. "I don't want to only be the Executive Assistant. I also want to expand my role and be an agent with the firm, participate in future operations. After this experience with Caroline, I know this is something I was meant to do. Do you have an issue with that?"

"Lila, I don't want you to get hurt again. Seeing you get shot just about killed me."

"Drake, I could get hurt driving my car. You cannot prevent everything."

"But in this line of work our chances increase, significantly."

"I understand, but it is important to me. How about this, I continue training, we all, as a group first, and then us as a couple, agree if I am ready for the particular operation or event before I am put in a situation. Could you work with that?"

"Yes, I think I can work with that. I may not always like it, because I love you and want you safe, but I can see this is important to you. So, yes, I can agree to those terms."

"Thank you. You know, I worry about you too, but would never ask you to change or stop for me. Thank you for understanding and agreeing. It means a lot."

"Well, at least until we have kids; we may have to renegotiate then."

"You want kids?"

"Don't you?"

"Of course."

"Good. I never thought I would, but finding you changed my perspective on life. I want it all, the entire deal, only with you Lila. We have plenty of time, but yes, nothing would make me happier than to see you pregnant with my child."

Lila put her arms around his neck and kissed Drake deeply.

"So, do you think we can start practicing?" Lila asked. "I have really missed you."

"I have missed you too Lila, so much."

Drake put his arms around Lila.

He gently laid her down on the bed, softly kissing her lips. Lifting up ever so slightly, he just looked at her, brushing her hair away from her face, telling her how beautiful she was. Closing the space, Drake touched his lips to Lila's, coaxing her mouth open to receive his tongue. Lila complied without hesitation, their tongues tangling like their lives depended on this kiss.

Hands touched and rubbed all over each other's bodies. The heat built between them, urgency evident in their kiss. Lila pressed her hips up against Drake, grinding into him, seeking pleasure. She felt the instant hardening of his shaft as she rocked her hips against him. He desired her as much as she desired him. The feel of his manhood sent moisture flooding. Lila needed him, desperately needed to feel him inside her.

"Drake, please make love to me. Please."

She did not have to ask him twice. Drake slowly rose onto his elbows kissing Lila all over her face, forehead, temples, cheeks, nose, and then back to her lips. His right hand slid to the front of her sundress and slowly started working the buttons loose. The entire front of her dress was a long line of buttons from her décolleté to her hem. Drake's kisses traveled to her collar bones, moving to the swells of her breasts while his hands inched lower, one button at a time. He opened her dress enough to expose her breasts. She wasn't wearing a bra; firm light pink peaks stared up at Drake, coaxing him.

Bringing himself to her, Drake took one firm nipple into his mouth, sucking, licking, caressing. Groans escaped Lila as her arms reached around Drake's back, holding him firmly against her. Drake released her nipple and slid his tongue over to her other breast, repeating the devouring. Pleasure rose higher and higher, straight to her core. Lila felt an orgasm creep up quickly just from the exquisite pleasure his mouth rained on her breasts.

"Drake, please."

"Not too fast, Lila."

Quickly breaking away from his feast, Drake unbuttoned the rest of the dress, opening it and taking it off Lila. Cool air swept across Lila's nipples, hardening them even more. He gazed over her body for a few moments. She was beautiful, perfect, and desirable. Reaching toward her hips, slowly he pulled off the little white lace panties, feeling Lila's moisture.

She was so ready, desperate to be taken, but Drake could not resist tasting her first. Resting himself between Lila's thighs, his fingers traced up and down each side circling her opening, then her bud. Squirming, Lila rose up and tried to coax Drake into giving her what she desired. Replacing his fingers with his tongue, Drake licked and sucked everywhere except where Lila was the most sensitive.

Lila was going crazy; her need for relief overwhelming. She was not going to be able to withstand the torment much longer. Sensing her urgency, Drake latched onto her bud. Immediately Lila spiraled out of control. Glorious sensations surged throughout her entire body.

Drake was relentless.

His tongue swirled, licked, and sucked. Her sweet honey saturated his face, opening the flood gates of desire. Lila was close, so close. Drake reached up and lightly twisted her nipples, sending Lila over the edge. Screaming out his name, she grabbed his head, pushing herself into his face.

Drake continued without hesitation. He wanted to give Lila every ounce of pleasure possible, not surrendering until she was ready to come down. Drake felt the tightness of her body slowly start to subside as she came down from her orgasm. He continued to slowly taste her, extending her pleasure, ending with soft kisses to her inner thighs.

"I need to be inside you," Drake said as he pulled himself up, quickly divesting himself of his clothing.

His arousal was evident. His long, thick shaft stood at full attention, desperately seeking the contentment only Lila could provide. She was already reaching for him, her need for the connection just as urgent. Moving on top of her, Drake entered Lila in one quick stroke. She screamed out, such pleasure only possible with Drake. Drake held still for a moment, not wanting to empty himself too soon. It felt like home. A strange thought, given the circumstances, but he knew he was where he belonged.

Starting to move, Drake bent down and kissed Lila. The deepening of their kisses mimicked each stroke of his flesh inside her. Lila was so tight, her walls squeezing and pulsing against him.

Wrapping her legs around Drake's waist, Lila tilted her hips, allowing Drake to fully fill her, burrowing deep. Holding her closely, Drake kissed Lila as he made love to her. Lila matched his strokes, lifting her hips, closing the gap.

This lovemaking was different. They both felt a closeness with each other never experienced before. Maybe it was because they finally confessed their love or they both finally fully opened their hearts to another person. Their love was truly being expressed through their bodies.

Drake quickened his pace and Lila gripped his shaft even tighter, both of them seeking the ultimate pleasure. Their kisses ceased as their breaths increased, their bodies building toward the peak. Looking into each other's eyes, Drake prayed he could hold on until Lila was ready. He felt her body stiffen, her breath coming out in small pants. Drake knew she was very close, as was he.

"Come for me, Lila. Now!"

His demand was all she needed to let go, screaming out in pleasure but never breaking eye contact. Drake followed shortly thereafter, spilling his seed inside her. The deep love for one another communicated through their gaze. Drake and Lila laid there, in each other's arms, for what seemed like an eternity, still joined intimately. Their lovemaking cemented their connection, their love for each other, and the future they got to look forward to. Today was a new beginning, the start of their forever. They stayed in bed the rest of the afternoon, making love several more times.

21

Evening rolled around, and Drake and Lila realized they'd skipped lunch and were quite hungry. Lila suggested take out, but she needed to talk to Shayla. She knew Shayla would be worried, especially after how she left the office. Lila also needed to get some clothes since she would never spend another night away from Drake. They had been apart long enough. Over the weekend they could officially move her back in, but she needed a few things to tide her over. Lila sent Shayla a text to make sure she was home and told her they would be over shortly.

Lila and Drake took a quick shower to freshen up after their day of lovemaking. It took everything in their power to keep their hands off each other. They felt like teenagers, could not get enough of each other. After dressing, Drake pulled Lila into a hug.

"You ready to face them?"

"Of course, why wouldn't I be?"

"You know they are going to have questions."

"I figured as much. We'll just tell them the truth. I will

leave out some of the details," Lila said with a smile, "but I do not hide anything from Shayla."

"I know. I'm glad you two are so close; soon you will be related."

"Wow, you're right. My best friend will be my sister-in-law. How lucky am I?"

"I'm the lucky one. Let's get going, or we will never get out of here."

Chuckling at Drake, the two went downstairs to Drake's truck and headed down the street. Pulling into Drew and Shayla's driveway, the front door swung open before they were even out of the truck, Shayla waited for them at the front door. As soon as Lila got to the door, Shayla pulled her into a hug.

"I was worried about you. It's not every day you see a woman being carried away without her consent," Shayla said, cutting her eyes to Drake.

"I'm fine, Shayla. Drake would never hurt me. Let us come in, and we will explain."

They went inside and to the family room off the kitchen where Drew was kicked back in a recliner, hands behind his head, a large grin across his face.

"Look what the cat dragged in," Drew said. "So, do you hate him Lila, or did you two make up?"

Sitting down next to each other on the sectional, Drake grabbed Lila's hand and said, "What do you think?"

"I think you two kissed and made up, are going to get married, and have lots of babies," Shayla said teasingly.

"Well, you are right. Not sure on how many babies, though," Drake said.

"Wait? What? Oh my God! Is what he is saying true Lila?" Shayla asked, excited.

"Yes. While I do not think Drake's approach to get me alone to talk was ideal, we did talk. Finally said all the things that were left unsaid last night, got it all out. We made up, he asked me to marry him, and I said yes."

Bursting from her spot on the sectional, Shayla jumped on top of Lila, hugging her, then turned her attention to Drake and hugged him.

"It's about time. My God, I am so happy," she said, then punched Drake in the arm.

"Hey, what was that for?"

"For being an ass and taking too long to tell Lila how you felt. Everyone knew you two loved each other and was wondering what you were waiting for. You know you were making us all miserable."

"Well, I have Dallas to thank, uhm, well, maybe not. He was trying to move in on what was mine."

"Ah, Drake, there is a little something that you should know. Please do not kill me or Dallas."

His blood pressure started to build. Drake worried they already hooked up because of his being such a jerk.

"You two didn't . . . ?"

"Oh, God, no! We did kind of trick you. You see, I wanted to torment you a little, get back at you for being so cold with me. Dallas and I are friends, good friends. I love him like a brother. Last night we purposely flirted and talked about a vacation together. Also, we were never going to be roommates. Dallas saw an opening and took it. He is a brave man, actually. You looked like you were going to kill him. I asked him to help me, and I think he knew all along it would get to you, and you would either run or come back to me. Guess it worked out well."

"You sneaky little girl. I should put you over my knee right now," he said, tickling her.

"You know, I may like that."

"God save me from this heathen," Drake said, looking up.

They all laughed at his reaction.

"Wait a minute. You two were talking about the vacation last night. Were you in on it as well?"

"Kinda. We picked up on what they were doing, so Drew and I just added our two cents," Shayla added.

"All of you are on my shit list."

"So when is the wedding?" Drew asked.

"I am not sure. We have time," Lila said.

"Fuck that, I want to get married as soon as possible."

"Well, Drake, you did fail at one thing. Where is the ring?" Shayla added.

"Oh, I will take care of that. I had to make my move before I lost this beauty. We will get one tomorrow. Lila can pick out whatever she wants."

"I want you to pick it out for me. Surprise me. It would mean a lot if you chose the ring for me."

"Really?"

"Yes, really."

"I may need some help . . . Shayla, if Lila wouldn't mind, would you come with me? I will pick it out, but I want to make sure she will like it. Would you mind if she helped?"

"Of course not."

"Wait, wait!" Shayla said

"What is it?" Lila asked.

"If y'all are getting married, that will make you my sister-in-law. Oh, wow. This is great. Not only are you my best friend, you will now be my sister. How wonderful is this?"

"It is wonderful."

"Yeah, Lila already basically said the same thing to me."

"So, I am guessing you will be moving out soon," Drew said.

"You guessed right. I needed to come get some things. I think Drake and I will move the rest of my things this week-end. Guess I will have to disappoint Dallas," Lila said, teasing Drake.

"Oh, you will be put over my knee as soon as we get home."

"Drew, Shayla, I do want to talk to you two about work." Getting serious, Lila turned to face Drew and Shayla. "Drake and I already discussed this, and he agreed because it is important to me. While I like being the Executive Assistant and I am not trying to stop handling those responsibilities, I would like to expand my role and continue to train and work on future operations, be an agent as well."

She paused and held her hand up. "Before you say anything, I gave this a lot of thought. This is very important to me and Drake understands, even if he may worry about my getting hurt again. Being a part of this operation and even the follow-up investigation aspect of the process called to me. I believe I am meant to do this, to help others. I know I need a lot more training, but the team is exceptional. I know I will be trained by the best, especially with Rocco helping me. I told Drake that it would be a group decision if and when I am ready for certain types of ops. The entire team will decide, and then Drake and I will discuss to make final decisions. Do you two think you can agree with this? I don't need an answer right away, just please consider it."

"Well, it may put some extra work back on Shayla and, if necessary, we could hire someone part-time, but you have already proven yourself Lila. I agree you need more training, but you learned so fast for this operation, I think you would be a good agent. We can make sure an assignment is the right fit for you. We handle so many things and having a female on the team would be good, no offense to you, Shayla."

"None taken."

"Shayla, are you okay with this?" Lila asked.

"Yes, I understand and had a feeling you would not be satisfied going back to being just an Executive Assistant. I just don't want you hurt again."

"I know. Drake feels the same way, but I could get hurt driving my car down the street. You never know what life will bring, and I do not want to regret not doing something meaningful."

"What about when you two have kids?"

"We have already discussed that and agreed that we would reevaluate when we get to that point. I know changes will be necessary, but in the meantime, I want to expand my role."

"It's settled then. You will just be our Jill of all trades," Drew replied.

"Thank you, all of you. I finally feel at peace, at home where I belong."

The next morning Lila and Drake went into the office a little later than normal. They were a little tied up that morning; literally she was tied up. Drew had called a team meeting, and Drake and Lila were the last to arrive. When they sat down, everyone's eyes were on them, especially after the 'incident' yesterday. Drew said he called the meeting because some decisions were made yesterday, and Lila would continue her training to work on operations eventually as a full-fledged agent. The group clapped and was pleased, adding they knew she would be perfect. Then Drew turned the floor over to Drake, stating that Drake had some additional news to share with the team.

"Yesterday, you all got to see me behave in a not-so-professional way, taking Lila out of here over my shoulder, but I can say it was the best thing I ever did. I also need to thank you, Dallas."

"Me, why?"

"Because if you did not go along with Lila's plan to fuck with me, who knows how long it would have taken me to get off my ass and get back what was mine. We want everyone to know that yes, I realized I was acting like a fool. Lila forgave me, and to top it all off, agreed to be my wife."

The room exploded in hoots and hollers. Congratulations came from every angle. Rocco came forward and hugged and kissed his girl, then turned to Drake and told him it was about time. Drake grabbed and hugged Dallas, thanking him again. It was a wonderful day. Lila had never felt this happy. She loved her job, loved her friends, and found her soulmate all because she decided to take a chance in Texas.

EPILOGUE

Magar Petrov was sitting at a large, ornate, wooden desk at his fortress somewhere on the outskirts of Moscow, papers in one hand, a glass of vodka in the other. His patience was wearing thin as he waited to hear back from his men about his purchase. He has tried to reach Perez numerous times without success, getting angrier as time passes. Perez will pay if he does not deliver. He paid a hefty price for the merchandise and does not like being made a fool of. Perez may have some power, but not even close to the reach of Petrov.

"Sir."

"Yes? What did you find?"

"The seller's compound in Texas has been raided. The government has him in custody. The girl is gone."

"Gone? Gone?" explosive anger radiated throughout him. "I have already paid for the whore. Where is she? Are you here just to tell me this, or do you have any information on her whereabouts? I want my property, or I will make sure Perez is dead!"

"Sir, we did find out some information about the girl."

"Well, don't make me wait. What did you find out?"

"Her name is Caroline Henderson. She is the daughter of United States Senator Stuart Henderson."

Anger subsiding, a smile broadens his face. "Even better. Now find her; go get what belongs to me."

ABOUT THE AUTHOR

L.M. Sutton's love of writing started as a young adult. After many years as a legal and business professional, she decided to transition from writing for pleasure to sharing her work with others. Sutton has always been drawn to novels that are a blend of romance, erotica, and action. This has led her to the launch of her premier novel *The Trade*, her first book in the Donovan Security Series. When she is not writing, she enjoys a quiet afternoon curled up with one of her favorite authors, spending time with family, and the outdoors. She lives in Maryland with her husband and four-legged children as her two-legged children have already left the nest.

LMSuttonAuthor.com
Facebook.com/LMSuttonAuthor1

Made in the USA
Middletown, DE
30 September 2020

20878979R00157